"[Dunn has] a superlative talent for three-dimensional characterization, gripping dialogue, and plots that featured gasp-inducing twists and betrayals."

—TheExaminer.com

"The general is a terrific villain—strong, sly, scheming, sick, smart, and really, really evil. And as Dunn spins out the story, the whole scenario seems to become more and more believable. The adventurous episodes and personal battles between Cochrane and the general are extremely involving. While reading them, the reader starts thinking, 'I wonder if Dunn actually was involved in a battle just like this.' I'll bet he was. And on top of all that, there is a fascinating shocker at the climax."

—*National Book Examiner*

"Great talent, great imagination, and real been-there done-that authenticity make this one of the year's best. . . . Highly recommended."

—Lee Child, author of *Night School*

"You can thrill to the high-pressure intrigue as CIA and MI6 agents bumble into each other, unfortunately rubbing out the wrong principles in their haste to save their ideals. . . . *Sentinel*'s characters are thoroughly and irresistibly believable."

—TheExaminer.com

"*Spycatcher* makes a strong argument that it takes a real spy to write a truly authentic espionage novel. . . . [The story] practically bursts at the seams with boots-on-the-ground insight and realism. But there's another key ingredient that likely will make the ruthless yet noble protagonist, Will Cochrane, a popular series character for many years to come: Dunn is a gifted storyteller."

—*Fort Worth Star-Telegram*

"Dunn, a former MI6 field officer, skillfully handles the usual spy business—uncovering high-placed traitors, blowing the other guy up, fighting one-on-one, and crossing and double-crossing each other.".

—*Publishers Weekly*

"A real spy proves he is a real writer—and a truly deft and inventive one. This is a stunning debut."

—Ted Bell, author of *Patriot*

"Like le Carré and Fleming before him, [Dunn] is the real thing, a former member of SIS turned fictional chronicler of the secret world. His [hero], though, is a more muscular creation than Smiley, or even Bond. Meet Will Cochrane, a one-man weapon of mass destruction; 007 is a cocktail-sipping lush compared with Cochrane."

—*Daily Telegraph* (UK)

"Not since Fleming charged Bond with the safety of the world has the international secret agent mystique been so anchored with an insider's reality."

—Noah Boyd, author of *The Bricklayer*

"The cat-and-mouse game [is] a real surprise. An icy-edged psychological thriller."

—*Library Journal*

"A terrific thriller with a superb new hero. . . . Written with confidence by a man with the credentials to back him up . . . Bond and Bourne can take a back seat."
—Matt Hilton, author of *Judgment and Wrath*

"A spellbinding, realistic novel. . . . *Sentinel* is a fast paced and riveting book with pure action and intrigue. The many twists and turns makes for a very interesting and captivating book."
—Blackfive.net

"An exciting novel that will keep you in suspense right up to the end."
—Yahoo Voices

"Once in a while an espionage novelist comes along who has the smack of utter authenticity. Few are as daring as Matthew Dunn, fewer still as up-to-date. . . . Is there anyone writing today who knows more about the day-to-day operations of intelligence agencies in the field than Matthew Dunn?"
—John Lawton, author of *Then We Take Berlin*

By Matthew Dunn

ACT OF BETRAYAL

A SOLDIER'S REVENGE

THE SPY HOUSE

DARK SPIES

SLINGSHOT

SENTINEL

SPYCATCHER

Novellas

SPY TRADE

COUNTERSPY

ATTENTION: ORGANIZATIONS AND CORPORATIONS
HarperCollins books may be purchased for educational, business, or sales promotional use. For information, please e-mail the Special Markets Department at SPsales@harpercollins.com.

MATTHEW DUNN

ACT OF BETRAYAL

A WILL COCHRANE NOVEL

WILLIAM MORROW

An Imprint of HarperCollinsPublishers

This is a work of fiction. Names, characters, places, and incidents are products of the author's imagination or are used fictitiously and are not to be construed as real. Any resemblance to actual events, locales, organizations, or persons, living or dead, is entirely coincidental.

ACT OF BETRAYAL. Copyright © 2017 by Matthew Dunn. All rights reserved. Printed in the United States of America. No part of this book may be used or reproduced in any manner whatsoever without written permission except in the case of brief quotations embodied in critical articles and reviews. For information, address HarperCollins Publishers, 195 Broadway, New York, NY 10007.

First William Morrow premium printing: July 2018
First William Morrow hardcover printing: October 2017

Print Edition ISBN: 978-0-06-242723-6
Digital Edition ISBN: 978-0-06-242724-3

Cover design by Richard Yoo
Cover photographs by ©kropic1/Shutterstock (White House);
©serpetko/Shutterstock(traffic)
Title page photograph courtesy of Shutterstock, Mishela

William Morrow and HarperCollins are registered trademarks of HarperCollins Publishers in the United States of America and other countries.

18 19 20 21   QGM   10 9 8 7 6 5 4 3 2 1

If you purchased this book without a cover, you should be aware that this book is stolen property. It was reported as "unsold and destroyed" to the publisher, and neither the author nor the publisher has received any payment for this "stripped book."

To my father—a sailor, a fearless
adventurer within exotic climes,
an intellectual, a photographer of life,
a historian, and a compassionate savior of
muddled lives. Ultimately, a true man.

Be sober, be vigilant; because your adversary the devil walks about like a roaring lion, seeking whom he may devour.

—1 PETER 5:8

ACT OF BETRAYAL

PROLOGUE

Berlin
Three Years Earlier

Will Cochrane assembled his customized Barrett .50 sniper rifle and lay prone on the grass, waiting to execute a terrorist.

Ahead of him was a deserted country road, seven miles beyond the outskirts of the German capital. The spy and former special forces soldier was motionless. He had to strike a man's head while he was driving at speed. The wind was fast; humidity was high; Will was elevated from the road; and the distance from him to target was 520 yards. All of these factors made the task nearly impossible. Plus, his powerful projectile had to punch through glass that could be reinforced to protect its driver. The Barrett's power was such that it would penetrate bulletproof glass. The problem was the bullet could be misdirected on impact with the car's window.

If he missed, the chance of a second attempt would be unavailable. The terrorist would have escaped.

There were probably only a handful of men in the world who could make this shot. But among those men, Will had an extra quality: he could make the shot and get out of Germany without anyone knowing he'd been here.

He had one opportunity. One bullet.

The man Will was waiting to kill was Otto Raeder, a highly elusive German financier of terror cells. Will had never met him and didn't know what he looked like. Will's friend Unwin Fox, of the CIA, had recently established that Raeder was in Berlin. He was a high-priority target. Fox's intelligence said that Raeder was shortly due to courier $5 million to a terror cell in Munich. That couldn't happen. But Fox couldn't tell his CIA masters about his intel on Raeder. If he did, they'd be duty bound to pass the information to the Germans, who would attempt to arrest Raeder. Possibly, he would be acquitted in a court of law due to lack of evidence against him.

Raeder needed to be wiped off the planet. This had to be off the books.

A black op without U.S. state sanction.

When Fox had brought his best assassin in for the job, he'd said to Will, "There are many details I'm not going to give you. Do you understand why?"

Will had replied, "You are breaking the law.

You don't want me to know the scale of this. Otherwise I'm implicated."

"Yes."

"Who else is involved?"

Fox responded, "Three others. There is no point in me giving you the identity of two of them. But I have to tell you who the other person is. His name is Colonel Haden. He's been watching Raeder for days, tailing him in Berlin and elsewhere, watching for patterns of behavior. On the day of the hit, Haden will be following Raeder. His job is to communicate with you. Haden will give you proof of ID. He will call the shot."

"Who's Colonel Haden?"

"He's ex–Delta Force, now works in the Pentagon. I couldn't take this to the CIA. But I knew Haden would help me on this."

Will had asked, "You trust Haden?"

"He's a psychopath. But he'll get the job done."

Now, outside Berlin, Will waited. He'd never met Haden, though an ear-and-throat mic gave him direct comms with the colonel.

On the deserted country road, two cars came into view. The first was a red sedan, the second a blue pickup truck. They were approximately one hundred yards apart.

Fox had given him the license plate of Raeder's vehicle. It was the blue truck. Clever. Haden was following Raeder from the front. That was a rare skill, but special operatives excelled at that tactic.

Will focused his gun's sights on Raeder. He was in a hoodie and sunglasses. Will looked at Haden. He too wore apparel to cover his features.

This was normal for surveillance officers and terrorists who didn't want to be photographed.

Haden said into his throat mic, "You got him?"

Will responded, "Yes."

"Don't screw it up. Green light to shoot when you're ready."

Will retrained his gun on Raeder. Adjustments to line of sight were made. He breathed in deeply and half exhaled before holding his breath. He pulled the trigger.

His projectile ripped Raeder's head off.

Unwin Fox was with Howard Kane and Charlie Sapper in a Pentagon office.

Kane was Haden's deputy. He was a Harvard-educated civilian, midthirties, ruthless in his ambition to rise up through the ranks of the Pentagon and ultimately make it to the top on Capitol Hill, and he loathed having his career eclipsed by Haden's shadow. But he respected the colonel. Together, he and Haden were responsible for liaising with the United States' special forces community. Their job was one of the most influential tasks in the Pentagon.

Kane was on the phone with his boss. He snapped his cell shut and said to Fox and Sapper, "The colonel has examined Raeder's vehicle. Raeder's dead. But there's no cash in the vehicle. Your intel was wrong. This wasn't a cash-run."

"Jesus!" Fox slammed his hand onto the table. "Doesn't matter, though. We didn't need evidence. I know for a fact the bastard made cash-runs in the past."

"It doesn't matter providing what we did doesn't get out!" Sapper was a senator. Tall, ambitious, and smart, Sapper looked like Marlene Dietrich, and she deliberately dressed to mimic the actress's elegant yet cold persona. "I'm fully aware that the only reason you brought me in on this was because you needed political backing if things went wrong."

"We're grateful for your involvement, Senator," Kane said. He called Haden again. There was no reply. Frowning, Kane said to the others, "The drill was clear. Haden calls the shot, Cochrane shoots, Haden checks proof of death and collects the cash, and my assets get rid of Raeder's body. But throughout, Haden has to maintain contact with me. Why's he not answering?"

"And why's there no cash?" Sapper was pacing. "Could be Haden's just got no cell signal right now. What about Cochrane?"

"He has different protocols. He had to make the kill from distance, vanish, and not communicate with us until he's back in the States. Right now, he won't be anywhere near the kill zone."

"So where the hell is Haden? Why is he not answering his cell? And where's Raeder's cash? If the Germans or anyone else gets wind of what we've done, we're screwed unless we can prove that Raeder was about to fund a terror cell." Sapper stormed out of the room while saying, "I was prepared to cover for you guys—still am—but you better fix this or my career is ruined."

After she was gone, Fox looked at Kane. "Something's not right."

"I know." Kane looked frustrated. "Give it time, though. There'll be an explanation. Maybe our intel was wrong. Possibly Raeder's cash is still in his hotel room. What matters is that Raeder's dead and his body will never be recovered—my four men will ensure that. The senator's just a bit jumpy, and it's in her interests to keep quiet about what we did. Today we just wiped out a piece of scum. The cash is irrelevant." Again, he tried Haden's cell. There was still no answer. He called the leader of the American team of assets at his disposal. "Everything under control?"

Jason Flail, a former Green Beret, replied, "Yeah. Body's in our truck. Target's car has been torched. We're moving now. No sight of the colonel. You told me he was to stay here until we'd sanitized the zone."

Kane ended the call. "Where the hell is Haden?"

Fox had a sinking feeling. "Are you thinking what I'm thinking?"

Kane rubbed his face. "Haden's stolen the cash and gone to ground."

"Yeah."

Kane shook his head in disbelief. "He planned this all along."

"Let's not jump to conclusions."

"No, let's jump to conclusions! We all agreed it was vital that Haden oversee the mission and remain in contact with us until the job was done. Now he's not answering his phone and Raeder's cash is gone."

Fox pondered Kane's observations. "Let me

know the moment Haden makes contact with you." He stood to leave but hesitated. "I'm worried about Sapper. Even if Haden has committed a crime, she'll keep quiet about what we did, providing everything is kept quiet about the hit on Raeder. But the moment there's a leak about the hit, she'll go public to save her neck."

After Fox was gone, Kane called Flail. "Are you confident the body can be disposed of?"

"Yes. My men and I will take it far from here."

Flail's men were also ex–Green Berets.

Kane nodded. "When you're back in the States, I want you to put a ring of steel around my team. You won't be able to track Cochrane. That doesn't matter. He doesn't know the full details of the mission and those involved. But I want you to put an intercept on Sapper's and Fox's cells, plus bug their homes. If you get a whiff that there are loose lips, let me know. You understand what I'm saying?"

The asset responded in the affirmative. "Is something wrong?"

"Maybe nothing. But Haden was supposed to stay with you and help remove the target. We have to assume something is wrong with Haden. And if that's the case, we can't have others breaking ranks and confessing to an illegal hit. You got that?"

"I got it."

Kane hung up. He considered what was happening. It didn't matter if Haden had stolen Raeder's cash, providing Haden went to ground and never reared his head again. That was the likely outcome, given he'd have no motive to return to the office or cause trouble. The problem was that Haden was as lethal as he was unpredictable.

ONE

Howard Kane made an urgent call to Senator Charlie Sapper. "Hold. I'm patching in Unwin Fox." When all three of them were on the line, Kane said, "I've just heard there's been a sighting of Mr. H. In the East Coast states!"

"Idiot. Why didn't he stay off the radar?" Fox was pacing in his office in Langley.

"Many possibilities." Kane felt agitated. "Maybe he's being careless. Maybe he's come back to see his wife. Or maybe . . ." He left the last sentence unfinished.

"What do we do?" asked Sapper.

"I don't know!" Kane composed himself. "The sighting is credible. Before taking over his job, I was duty bound to inform the military and the Feds that Mr. H was missing. Obviously they know nothing about Germany, but they've taken his disappearance seriously. The guy's a trained killer and carries category one secrets in his head. They don't want him on the loose. We do, but only if he doesn't come up for air and get captured. If that happens, certainly he'll use the Berlin mission to mitigate his crime of theft. Then we're screwed."

"You bastard, Kane!" Sapper was shouting. "It's one thing if the fallout had been only months after the hit. Three years makes it look like I'm a conspirator, trying to suppress the truth of a covert op. Mr. H, as you call him, can't stir things up this far down the line."

"I know, I know!" The last thing Kane needed was for the Berlin operatives to panic. "I have a plan. Let's meet at Charlie's house at nine P.M. I'll bring some of my men as protection. If I'm late, just wait there for me. I've got a lot of calls to make to the Feds and Homeland Security in the interim. But let's assume one thing: Mr. H is back and we are in severe danger."

Three years ago Haden was reassigned to the Pentagon from the army. Back then he was forty-one. He'd reached the rank of colonel at the remarkable age of thirty-six. Even more remarkable was that he'd done so in a career spent mostly in the special forces community. SF may have all the thrills and action, but it's a career killer for officers. They reach a stage where if they want to be promoted they have to leave SF and do their time in general service. That wasn't for Haden. He was a brilliant leader and soldier, and he'd probably be a brigadier or general by now had he not resolutely stuck to his Ranger and Delta Force units.

In order to progress his rapid ascendancy in the military, the Pentagon assignment was forced onto him by high command. He hated every minute of the job: wearing a suit, running a department, playing diplomatic politics—doing all of this when in truth he'd have rather been on a mountainside in Afghanistan calling in an airstrike or storming Taliban caves for up-close and personal head-to-head death.

Like many battle-hardened men, Haden was difficult to read. He did the job at hand, used brilliant tactics and unflinching bravery to destroy the enemy, yet nobody knew if he was a good man. He kept that hidden.

But there was no doubting his effectiveness. Or his ruthlessness.

This was what scared and confused most of the others in the Berlin operation. They didn't know if he was on their side. Now three of them knew. The truth was terrible.

The colonel was tall and slender, had buzz-cut silver hair, arms like entwined cables of high-tensile steel, a gait that moved slowly yet could cover forty miles in record time with sixty pounds on his back, and a hand that was as steady as ice as it pulled a trigger and sent a projectile to the exact spot it needed to go. He was a very intelligent and highly trained killing machine. And a powerful one at that. Haden said little and did a lot. But there was no hiding that look in his eyes. It was a thousand-yard stare. Always looking over the horizon. And the blue eyes were dead.

Only the assassin Will Cochrane wasn't scared of him. That's because Cochrane was infinitely worse. He was the one man Haden feared.

But even Cochrane didn't know where Haden was now.

The Berlin mission had happened like clockwork. Haden tails target; Cochrane shoots; proof of death confirmed; body extracted; job done.

Haden saw the shot. But he never came back to America after it happened. He vanished.

Three years later, it seemed that he'd returned to U.S. soil and was intent on killing all those involved in Germany.

When on active duty, the colonel had caught some of his Delta colleagues about to conduct a summary execution of five Taliban prisoners. They were on an Afghan escarpment, high wind and searing heat blasting the faces of the prisoners, all of them bound and on their knees. No doubt they deserved worse than death. They'd been caught raping, pillaging, and murdering a village. The whole village would be dead were it not for the bravery of the four-man Delta unit that was about to put bullets into the backs of their skulls. The colonel knew they'd get away with it. No one out here lived by rules. It was bandit country. The Wild West. A depraved and scorched stretch of hell where life had little meaning and death no consequence.

But the colonel was wise and had to show his men that barbarity meant nothing unless it had purpose. He told his men to stand down as he walked along the line of prisoners and gave his Delta operators a lecture on humanity. For once, he spoke at length.

"These men are scum. And we fight them because we are not scum. Don't get me wrong—I don't give a shit if they die. I don't care if these cunts get blown to pieces. But I do care about us. When we get back to Fort Bragg, we'll have a beer, get laid, watch a movie, vote on who we like and don't like in our shit-storm government, and breathe the free air. It's why we do this." He smiled as he spoke in fluent Pashto to the Afghan prisoners: "You guys seen *Sex and the City*? It's a bit too faggoty for my tastes. But I'll tell you what I like about it. It's about people working out their fate. Doing it themselves. No one telling them what they should think and feel. No frickin' imam giving them scriptures. It's why me and my men fight jerks like you. We make space for *Sex and the City*. We make people free."

The Taliban looked terrified as he unholstered his sidearm.

"My men want to kill you. Can't say I blame them. You punks are just like every other young man. You should be out every Friday night getting wasted, fighting, screwing, and ending up in a hospital until you get your testosterone out of your system and learn your lesson. Trouble is, you picked the wrong bar today."

He walked along the line, shooting four of the men in the head.

The fifth man was quaking and sobbing.

Haden looked at his Delta comrades. "This is the lesson. Toss me a tourniquet."

One of them did so.

Haden withdrew his military knife and sawed off the man's forearm. He applied the tourniquet. "Not sure if he'll live. Don't care." He cut loose his ropes and said to the screaming prisoner, "Get your ass out of here. And if you make it home tell your pals that there are devils in the mountains."

That was Haden.

His men never breathed a word about what they'd seen. They admired their commander way too much. And they saw a man capable of transcending evil and beating it at its own game.

They thought he might be a psychopath. But in war you work with the men who do what's necessary. Haden wanted to kill. It was fortuitous that he was killing the right guys.

It seemed that had changed.

Seven P.M., Charlie Sapper's house.

She was alone in the luxurious and tastefully decorated place on the outskirts of D.C., getting changed out of her suit, preparing for Kane and Fox to be there in two hours. A single woman, she loved the fact she had enough cash to own a property that was almost three times the size of the homes belonging to families who lived nearby. It was her finger to conformity. She had independence, a career that few could dream of, and an intellect that could outsmart most on Capitol Hill. To some extent, love was anathema to her at this stage, though she did wonder about having a man in her life at some point. Maybe when her career didn't matter. She was getting to the point where the aspirations of love versus job were at loggerheads. Having kids was no longer an option, but having a partner still was, providing she didn't wait too long. She was a looker and spent a lot of time fending off male advances.

Despite her wealth and faux internalizing that she was better off than the families around her, she knew she was missing out on family life. The nearest house to her was two hundred yards away. A family of four lived on that property that was half the size of hers. They had it better; she had it worse.

Now was not the time to dwell on such matters. Soon she'd see Kane and Fox. She hadn't had contact with either since the Berlin operation three years ago. There'd been no need. But it seemed Haden was back on U.S. terra firma. Kane hadn't fully articulated why that might be the case, but Sapper knew what the Pentagon staffer was thinking.

Haden was back to kill all those involved in the Berlin job.

Sapper wished she'd never gotten involved in the operation. She knew the mission was justified and that Raeder posed a major threat to Western security. If everything had gone according to plan and the assassination were leaked to U.S. officials, she, Fox, and Kane would have their knuckles rapped, but privately those in the corridors of power would hush up the mission and congratulate her on a job well done. It wouldn't be a career killer; if anything it would prove to others that she had the balls to do what it takes to remove scum off the earth. But things were different now. Almost certainly she'd been taken for a fool by Haden; Fox and Kane had also been duped. A Senate inquiry would determine they'd been wittingly complicit in an illegal murder and unwittingly complicit in a heist. They'd forgive her for the former; they'd damn her for the latter. Her career would be screwed.

For the last three years, she'd prayed that Haden was sipping cocktails and spending his loot on a tropical island somewhere, causing no one any problems. If that was the case, everyone was happy. The nightmare scenario was that Haden reemerged and caused trouble. And the worst place for that to happen was in the States. Here, he would be arrested and forced to explain his disappearance.

She checked the time. Fox and Kane were due here soon.

The doorbell rang.

Standing by the inside of the door, Sapper called out, "Who is it?"

Outside, a person held up a cell phone and pressed play on an audio recording. "It's Fox," said the recording.

Cursing, Sapper muttered, "You're early," as she unbolted the door and opened the entrance. "What the . . . ?!"

A man was standing before her with a silenced pistol.

Before Sapper could do anything about it, the man shot her in the chest, stood over her prone body, and shot her twice in the head.

The killer closed the door and left the premises.

Kane cursed as he wove his car between other vehicles as he exited the center of D.C. It was dark and raining, traffic was heavy, and he was certainly going to be late getting to Sapper's house. He called Jason Flail and explained his predicament. "I'll be with you soon."

Unwin Fox parked outside his home. Located in a quiet suburban part of Vienna, with a large yard in the rear, the house was way too big for a bachelor on a government salary. He'd inherited it from his deceased parents and had rattled around inside it for years, paying little heed to the repairs it needed or suggestions from casual female acquaintances that his books and academic papers would look better if not stacked haphazardly in most of the rooms. He bolted the front door behind him, one thing he had to thank his security-conscious father for: heavy-duty locks everywhere, iron bars on windows, every nook and cranny sealed up like Fort Knox. His face and open shirt soaked, he pulled the curtains closed, then peered out through the crack between fabric and one window. The street outside was empty, darkness pervading all but the surroundings of streetlights and the glow from other residences. A dog barked. That would be Jack, the mongrel belonging to the Terrences three doors down.

Jack often barked. Usually at strangers.

Fox weaved among piles of obscure volumes about geology and architecture, and went to his bedroom to change. Feeling refreshed and ready to make the drive to Sapper's home, Fox returned downstairs and decided he had time to make a coffee.

The front door handle turned, the door juddering as someone tried futilely to force it open. Fox froze. "Who is it?"

No one answered. But the door handle was still juddering.

He wondered if this was him.

Haden.

The locks would hold—he was in no doubt about that. And upstairs was just as secure. Short of Haden using breaching equipment, there was no way in.

The handle stopped turning. Fox stood in the center of his living room, rotating 360 degrees while listening for signs that the front or back doors were being forced. But all was quiet. Had Haden gone? Fox pulled aside curtains on a window facing the yard. That's when he saw him: one man, just standing and staring at his house. It was impossible to discern his facial features. But there was no doubt the man had a physique matching Haden's.

The man threw stones and didn't stop until every rear-facing window was smashed.

Fox paced back and forth, urgently trying to decide what to do. Was the man outside going to kill him? He couldn't risk getting the answer to that wrong. He called Sapper's cell. No answer. He called Kane.

The Pentagon official answered.

"There's a guy outside my house! Could be Haden!"

Kane was still stuck in traffic. "Shit!"

"He's smashing my windows. A random burglar doesn't do that."

Kane honked his horn in a futile attempt to get traffic moving. "Can he get in your house?"

"No. Bars on the windows. Specialist locks on the doors. So why's he smashing windows?"

A thought occurred to Kane. "Call the cops and the fire department now!"

"Fire department?"

"Now!" Kane hung up.

Fox dialed 911 and reported an intruder on his property. The operator told him to stay calm and that a squad car was on its way. Imploringly, Fox requested that more than one car be sent. He didn't elaborate that two cops in one car would be no match for the man outside.

Everything went quiet. The man in his yard had vanished. Maybe he'd seen Fox on the phone and realized that he'd called the police. But something didn't feel right.

All reason was gone as Fox sat at his computer desk and typed an e-mail to Will Cochrane.

My friend—

You saved my life in Syria and Moscow. You're the only person I can truly trust. But they say you died in the fall or drowned. If not, we need to meet tomorrow. What happened in Berlin was a lie, a sleight of hand by the colonel. Haden's back. I don't know why. But you can stop him. Meet me at four P.M. in D.C.'s Rock Creek Park. Find me.

The CIA officer added a landmark, pressed send, and glanced into the yard. The man was back there. He picked up an object. Fox couldn't discern in the darkness outside what it was. That changed when it was illuminated.

A firebomb.

It was hurled through a shattered window.

The bomb smashed against the floor, spewing blue-tinged flames across wood, furnishings, and the stacks of papers and books. It was too fierce and rapid to be ordinary gasoline. This was aviation fluid. More bombs were hurled through other windows.

Fox ran haphazardly. The heat was intense, the fire racing and devouring his parental home. Soon he'd be dead.

Sirens.

The front door his father had built out of a dying oak tree was blasted open by a shotgun. A cop ran in, ill equipped to deal with the inferno but unflinching in his duty to get Fox out of the blaze. He grabbed the CIA officer and ran him out of the house.

Another cop was outside, standing by his squad car and speaking on the radio.

Fox was coughing as he said, "One man! One man!"

Within ten minutes there were multiple sirens in the distance. Fire trucks, more cops, and an ambulance. They'd be too late. Fox's home was now completely alight. Everything was being rendered to ash.

The cop who'd rescued him and his partner made a sweep of the grounds. They returned and told him that the perpetrator was nowhere to be seen. They asked him if he had any suspicions as to who had done this.

Fox lied. "None whatsoever." Out of earshot of the cops, he called Kane and explained what had happened. "I'm aborting tonight's meeting—I have to be interviewed by the police. Be very careful at the senator's house. He's come after me. And that means he's after you and Sapper."

Kane stopped his car outside Charlie Sapper's house. There was an SUV also parked, belonging to one of Jason Flail's team.

The asset met him at the door. "She's dead. Shots to chest and head."

Kane rubbed his face. "No doubt you're wondering what's going on. It all has to do with my former boss—Colonel Haden."

"Okay."

"But I can't and won't tell you more."

The asset and Kane entered the house. Kane knelt down by Sapper's dead body and stroked the beautiful woman's bloody face. "She was on borrowed time."

"Your instructions to my boss?"

Kane replied, "Tell Flail that law enforcement

can't be brought in. This is a matter of national security. I want the body removed and the crime scene sanitized. Get your men to help."

"I'll call them now."

"No one else must know what happened here."

"How big a problem is Haden?"

"As big as it gets. My endgame is to make him dead. You're going to help."

The asset tried to ask more questions but Kane held up his hand.

"The less you know, the better. We're cleaning up a mess. This mess. Other messes. And I need you guys to do exactly what I say. My future instructions might sound confusing to you. And dangerous. But trust me, you don't want the information Fox and I have in our heads." He looked at Sapper. "She also had that information. Now she needs to disappear. Get it done."

TWO

It was past midnight as wind and rain pounded the exterior of the tiny bookstore in Chicago. The store was closed and its owner was sitting at his desk checking the week's receipts. The task wouldn't take long—his store specialized in rare works that he sourced from around the world. He had some loyal customers, but they were few. This week seven people had made purchases.

The only light in the room came from his green desk lamp, old-fashioned in design to match the ambience of the shop. Aside from some electronic devices on his desk and recessed lights that cast a discreet yellow glow when turned on, the place looked like it could have been a purveyor of fine works established and unchanged since the eighteenth century. He'd constructed it that way: dark maple bookshelves; many of the books leather bound, all of them hardcover; two armchairs for customers to sit in when perusing potential acquisitions; an urn for his more discerning patrons who valued his loose-leaf tea collection; and a cage for his two lovebirds.

He was an old-fashioned guy at heart.

And though he could have done with more cash coming in, he'd deliberately established a business and identity that drew little attention. He playacted a shy man, his trimmed beard intended to put up barriers between him and others, his shoulders artificially stooped during the day as if he were ashamed of his six-foot-four physique, his cropped blond-and-gray hair functional because he had no woman in his life to impress, and his unneeded glasses covering one green eye, one blue. He was always in a smart three-piece suit because the attire was good at hiding his athletic frame and scars. Customers thought he was Edward Pope, a gentleman scholar from the South. They'd probably estimate his age was late forties. They'd be wrong about that and most other things. He'd led a hard life and was forty-five.

His name wasn't Edward Pope.

It was Will Cochrane.

The assassin. The one Sapper and Kane were terrified of.

He wasn't from the Deep South. He was raised in Virginia and earned a double first-class degree at England's Cambridge University. And he'd been a bookseller for only under a year.

But he had to be Pope. In the eyes of the world, Will was a murderer. He'd killed people as a special forces French Foreign Legionnaire and assassinated targets in French intelligence black operations. He had been the West's prime joint operative with the CIA and Britain's MI6 for fourteen years, until he went crazy and killed a lot of cops and civilians in the States before throwing himself off the Brooklyn Bridge and dying.

His death was essential. He was America's Most Wanted. He wasn't what some thought of him—a psychopath. But he was a former special operative and killer. Had been all his adult life. It started when he was seventeen and walked in on four criminals suffocating his mother and about to kill his sister. His mother died; sister didn't, because he grabbed his mother's carving knife and ended the criminals' lives before fleeing to the Legion. He wished he didn't know how many people he'd killed since. It would be a lie. He knew every victim. Their souls lingered around him, taunting him, reminding him of who he was.

All 263 souls.

But the souls of the people they say he killed in the States didn't hassle him.

Because he didn't kill them. He never killed innocents, only those who needed to be killed.

But in the eyes of the law, that's not the case and that's why he had to fake his death and re-invent himself. A year ago, his situation was desperate, despite all of his training and covert operations experience in hostile countries. He'd received only one bit of help, but it was signifi-

cant. Russia's most formidable intelligence officer, code name Antaeus—now, thanks to Will, a
defector living in the States—had cleverly managed to get $300,000 into Will's pocket. Will
didn't know exactly why he'd done it. After all,
Will had accidentally killed his family with a car
bomb when in fact he'd intended only to kill the
spy. But he suspected he knew why the Russian
had become his benefactor: Antaeus wanted his
generosity to plunge the knife that was Will's
guilt deeper.

Regardless of Antaeus's motives, the cash helped
set up Will's new life.

Will's family and close acquaintances were all
dead. He'd be given the needle if cops found out
who he was. The West he'd served with unflinching duty had hung him out to dry. He thought
of himself as a scavenging dog, kicked out of its
owner's backyard and left to fend for itself. He
was resigned to that, every day expecting the
Feds to rush into his store and put a bullet in
his skull. That's what they'd do. No attempt to
arrest. No negotiations. Execution only. Will
wouldn't blame them. They knew he'd cause carnage if given the slightest of chances.

He finished his accounts, took a swig of Assam
tea, and frowned as he heard the female lovebird
make an unusual sound. Like her male compan-
ion, she resembled a small parrot, her plumage
green and yellow, face and beak red, large eyes
pure white with black pupils. He'd taken the birds
off the hands of an old lady who frequented his

store. Her son, a merchant marine officer, had brought them back from exotic climes, though she couldn't remember where because she was suffering from dementia. And she could no longer look after them, particularly now that the male had broken his wing. Will hated seeing animals in cages. But the female wouldn't leave the male's side. And for the time being, the male had to be kept in the cage until he was fully recuperated. Then Will would release them to a large aviary or the wild.

Their previous owner couldn't remember their names, so Will called the male Ebb and the female Flo. Flo was now agitated, hopping about as opposed to what she usually did, which was nestling her face against that of her lover. Will opened the cage, knowing Flo wouldn't go anywhere while Ebb was there. The former special operative bowed his head. Ebb was all wrong, flopping on the base of the cage, his good wing twitching, his broken one immobile. Will knew he was dying and there was nothing he could do about it. What goes through a bird's brain? He didn't know. And he didn't know whether lovebirds were in fact lifelong lovers or if that was a myth. But Will knew how he felt. He had to give Flo closure, let her be free, not allow her to think there was hope that Ebb would return to her. Gently he lifted Ebb. His body was warm but now limp. He carried him to the store's backyard. Flo followed him. Will had hoped she would.

Will looked at Flo, who was perched close

by on the branch of a tree. She was watching. It seemed she and Will didn't know what to do.

"I have to let you know this is the end," Will said to her. Actually, he was saying it to himself.

He snapped Ebb's neck and buried him.

Flo looked at him before flying into the darkness. As tears ran down his face, he wondered if she hated him. Or maybe she understood. Of course, he'd never know.

He returned to his desk and stared at the birdcage. After brushing soil off his fingers, he looked at his laptop and saw he had a new e-mail. Nobody sent him mail apart from spammers.

But this one was different. And shocking. It was from CIA officer Unwin Fox, the man who, alongside Will, had been one of those involved in the Berlin operation. Aside from Colonel Haden, Will didn't know who the other people on the small team were.

His heart was beating fast as he read the mail. Its tone was desperate. There was no way Fox could know that Will was alive. Something was terribly wrong. Fox wanted to meet. Tomorrow. In Washington, D.C.

In all probability it was a trap. Lure Will out, then bam! Swooped on by cops. But then again, Will knew what happened in Berlin. The law didn't. This would have been far too implausible a tactic to entrap him.

What to do?

He looked at the lovebirds' empty cage. The door was open.

He glanced at the entrance to his store.

What to fucking do?

He opened the drawer in his desk, pulled out his handgun, grabbed his bag containing all he needed if he ever had to run, and left.

He knew he'd never return.

THREE

Will Cochrane drove the car he'd stolen from an American assassin who'd tried to kill him a year ago. Its owner was now at the bottom of a lake in Virginia, decayed, his chest cavity sliced open and filled with rocks to weigh it down. Will had done that.

The vehicle contained Will's only bag of clothes and other items, plus all the remaining cash in his life.

Edward Pope no longer existed, though his fake ID might prove useful. His shop would be repossessed by the landlord and Chicago city council after a period of absence and closure, his precious books parceled up and sold or burned. Will was once again on the road, free from his cage, a man who would be gunned down by any-one and everyone if they knew who he was.

He parked outside D.C. and took the Metro

to Rock Creek Park, setting off on foot and constantly aware of the ordinary folk around him on the beautiful trails that navigated their way around hardwood trees, brooks, and the occasional rocky outcrops. Picnic areas were strewn with families enjoying a balmy late-autumn Saturday afternoon. There was laughter, kids running barefoot over grass, guys drinking beer while their wives laid out tablecloths on the ground and unpacked food, and a general ambience of joie de vivre. Families that had no care in the world. This was their weekend. Will walked among them.

Hidden under his belt and T-shirt were his handgun and spare magazines. His scant other belongings were not required. No one needed much cash and any spare clothes on such a day. He walked along a trail, a relaxed smile on his face, probably appearing to be a veteran who'd made peace with the horrors he'd seen. Families barely glanced at him and none of them was scared. He matched the bigger guys in the park and was too far away from other humans for them to notice his eyes. Up close, the eyes were the one thing he couldn't disguise.

He made it to one of the thirty picnic areas in the park and leaned against a tree, watching, knowing this might be the time the FBI's elite Hostage Rescue Team or SWAT swooped the area and dropped him to his knees. If that happened, he'd put many of them on their asses. But they'd be wearing Kevlar. Inevitably Will's face would smack the ground dead.

The picnic area was brimming with locals and tourists. A gunfight here would be disastrous, because the collateral would involve carnage. None of Will's bullets would strike a civilian, but he couldn't trust the police takedown squads. They'd be armed with Heckler & Koch submachine guns and would be so pumped up with adrenaline that their kill lust would consume their more measured drills. Will couldn't allow that to happen. He'd wallop the ones who looked most likely to make a mistake.

There was no sign of any of that happening. All that could be heard was laughter, men bantering, with the occasional bark of mothers scolding their kids. The air was rich with the scent of sausages, burgers, and steaks.

Will had walked through similar scenes so many times before all over the world. He'd never felt part of them. He had no one to love, no days off, no nothing. He was a fallen angel; a man dislocated from the world, sent here to save people who never rewarded his bravery with kindness; a person alone. He thought of Ebb, his broken wing emasculating his prowess and causing him to give up on life. Will understood that feeling. If something similar happened to him, he hoped a kind soul would snap his neck.

Long shadows struck him. Children raced close to him, cooked pork in their hands and mouths, giggling and gleeful. He was like that once, a freckled and blond five-year-old, his grin accompanied by a belly laugh and dimples that made adults stop and go, "Ah, shucks. He's such a cutey."

That year his smile vanished when his father, a CIA agent, was kidnapped and later slaughtered in Iran. Tears followed immediately, together with a burning sensation in his stomach that abated only when he fell asleep and dreamed of being a grown-up and hurting the bad men who'd sliced up his beloved father.

Back then it was a cathartic and juvenile fantasy designed by an immature brain to get him to sleep in the same way a child dreams of beating up the playground bully. But Will grew up. He butchered every man involved in the butchering of his father. And he didn't stop there.

He watched everyone in the picnic area closely, also scouring gaps in the distant trees and listening acutely. Elite police units move fast and silently when approaching a target. But up close they have to shout, because their primary purpose is to uphold the rule of law and arrest perpetrators, and they must call out warnings to nearby innocent civilians. Special forces guys like Will just kill and walk away, for the most part without anyone knowing apart from a distraught wife shrieking over the mashed and bloody face of her husband as he lies dead in his favorite armchair.

In the picnic area he was watching for undercover spotters; in the tree line, men in fire-resistant black or green coveralls running in the flat-footed way that minimized the sound of their footfalls and maintained their ability to fire accurately if needed.

No one came for him. Will moved on.

Unwin Fox had told him to head directly to the northern area of the picnic spot. Will didn't do that. Instead he went east, then north, and then south, so that he was looking at the same meeting point from the other direction. Would he shoot cops in the back? Of course. Any man or woman who's been in lethal situations will tell you the same—you kill or be killed. But this was different. Will didn't kill cops and knew their body armor would save them; no, he hoped it would give him enough time to vanish again. But cops were the least of his problems.

There was one thing for sure. He had to help Fox. The CIA officer was one of the few people Will trusted at the Agency. When Will was an operative for the CIA, Fox had stuck his neck out to support Will countless times. Because of that, Will had risked his neck several times to rescue Fox from dire situations in hostile countries.

He watched again before climbing a tree and squatting on a branch. Men rarely look up when going for a kill. They look straight ahead. He waited, patient, calculating hundreds of possibilities. If he got out of here, he'd sleep in his car somewhere rural, wet wipes his savior against BO, soap his remedy for dirty clothes. He didn't like that way of life. But he did what was needed.

A man walked along a trail, two hundred yards away. Will pulled out binos to observe him. The man was suited, his hair matted, his face downward. Another man was behind him—shorts and

T-shirt, baseball cap covering his upper face, a father no doubt—but quickly catching up, holding something that looked like a BBQ skewer, a grin on his face as he headed to a family.

Will immediately jumped down and ran to the first man he'd spotted.

Unwin Fox.

The CIA officer saw him running toward him on the trail and smiled. Cochrane was alive. Thank God.

Fox had always thought it was highly unlikely that Cochrane would have taken his own life. But facts were facts. There was no doubt Cochrane jumped off the Brooklyn Bridge. The event was captured on camera by the media. And that fall would have crushed most men. What had nagged Fox during the last year was that Cochrane would have made that jump for a reason—not suicide, but rather to fake his death. But, my goodness, Cochrane had taken an almighty risk.

The sight of him now warmed Fox's heart. Cochrane had fooled everyone and survived. And now he was racing toward the man he'd saved countless times. Cochrane scared most people. Not Fox. The CIA officer recalled when he'd crashed his car in pursuit of a double agent in Mozambique. Cochrane had been following. Battered and bloody, Fox had crawled out of the wreckage, gasping for life. Cochrane helped him get to his feet.

"Now is not the time for pain," Cochrane had

said as he withdrew his handgun. "This is a setup by the Russians. They're coming for you now. You're a dead man if you stay here. Get to the U.S. embassy. I'll hold them off."

As Fox ran through the alley, he looked back. There was a cacophony of gunfire. Cochrane was on one knee firing at encroaching hostiles. He didn't flinch as he held off the assault while Fox escaped.

As far as Fox was concerned, no man on the planet was more magnificent than Cochrane.

In the park, the man behind Fox drew nearer. He raised the metal stick in his hand.

Ten yards.

Five.

Then he was right behind Fox.

On the stick was a needle on its tip, a canister, and a trigger at the back.

Fox was oblivious to the man's presence.

The man jabbed the needle into Fox's calf and pulled the trigger.

Fox grabbed his calf. It was a tiny sting. A fly or wasp did this, he suspected. He carried on walking.

The man behind him grinned and walked away.

When Will got close to Fox, the CIA officer called out, "Back from the dead."

Will didn't smile and didn't stop running until he was very near to the Agency operative.

A few yards away from Will, Fox staggered and collapsed. Will grabbed him before he hit the ground. He held him close as he whispered, "What happened?"

Fox asked, "Just now?"

"What happened in Berlin?"

Fox's face was ashen coupled with red blotchy spots. "Berlin. It was a setup. Haden wanted you to kill Raeder so Haden could steal Raeder's cash." He was breathing fast and shallow. "What happened just now?"

Will spun around, watching everything. People were staring. Women had hands to their mouths. "You were poisoned."

Fox convulsed, his hands squeezing Will's oak-like arms. "Yes . . . yes. Shit! It was Haden."

Will scoured the area for the man with the BBQ tool. "He's gone! You'd have a puncture mark on your leg or back."

"I . . . I felt something. A sting. Didn't . . . didn't think anything of it." Fox vomited on the ground, his face now gray. Families nearby were exclaiming disgust about a drunk in their midst.

Will held his head. "Whatever's in you is too strong. I'm sorry, Fox. This is not looking good."

"Antidote . . . ?"

"Whoever did this knew that the very best D.C. hospitals wouldn't be able to reverse it." Will gently cupped Fox's head as the CIA officer started frothing at the mouth. At the same time, Will's eyes were frantically looking around. "Looks like you'll be dead in minutes, maybe less. I can't save you this time, my friend."

Fox spat blood over his chin, and his eyes almost rolled back completely. "Shit, shit!"

"I'll find Haden and make him pay."

"No! Too . . . too dangerous!"

Will lowered Fox's head to the ground. "We're both dead men. What's there to be scared of?" He smiled even though he felt tremendous sadness. "We've both been through so much. I'm going to help you one last time."

Fox grabbed Will's arm. "Besides you, Haden, and me, there were two others involved in Berlin. Get to them, and you'll get closer to Haden." He was wheezing. "They want him as much as . . . as much as I do."

Urgently, Will asked, "Names?"

Fox tried to speak but couldn't, more blood ejecting from his mouth and striking his chest, and then he was gasping for air, his whole body shaking. Will knew he was going to die in agony and could no longer speak or think. Alongside drowning, being poisoned is the worst way to die. Will had the choice of letting it happen until the end, or doing something to stop the terrible downward spiral.

"You want me to end this?"

Fox nodded frantically.

Will thought of Ebb and momentarily bowed his head. "I'm sorry."

He put his knee on Fox's throat and pressed down with all his might.

Fox's back arched.

Will laid the CIA operative's head fully on the trail. Fox was dead.

It was time to leave. But four big men were advancing on him. They were part of a nearby extended family, had shirts and shorts on, and had discarded their drinks. Behind them was a woman with her cell phone camera pointing at him.

The guys were telling him to stay on his knees until the cops arrived. The men were shouting and angry.

"What did you do to him?" one of them exclaimed.

Will stood up and said nothing as he looked at the encroaching group.

"Get on your knees or we'll make you do it!"

Will had to get the camera off the woman. If he didn't, the world would know he was alive. Then all hell would break loose.

"Don't come closer," Will said, standing stock-still.

The biggest of the men sneered. "You armed? Going to shoot us?"

"I'm not going to shoot you."

"Then you're screwed, buddy. Me and my pals are ex-marines. We know shit."

Will nodded. "Thank you for your service."

He rushed them. They were fast and organized. But the highly trained former special forces operatives were not comparable to Cochrane. The assassin jabbed a knee in the nearest man's ribs, tossed him aside like a rag doll as he took two steps forward and poleaxed the second man in the throat, slapped a palm into the face of the third man, crushing his nose, and punched the biggest with sufficient force to lift him off the ground and jam him back down with enough energy to dislocate his spine.

Blood was everywhere. Children were crying.

Will moved closer to the woman with the video camera that had recorded the explosive encounter. He stopped when she picked up her baby.

"Please don't, mister."

Will was still.

"Please don't!" she implored.

He looked at the baby. The men were on the ground behind him, writhing.

"My husband and brothers were just trying to do what was right. Please"—she rocked the baby—"I don't mean you any harm."

Will kept his eyes on the child. It would be easy to get the phone off the woman. Too easy. The child was looking at him, quizzical and afraid. It had cute dimples and freckles.

"I want your cell phone."

The woman was crying. "Please! It's got videos and pictures of my baby shortly after he was born. I haven't uploaded them yet. They're all I have."

Will glanced over his shoulder at the four men who'd come for him. They'd live.

He looked at the woman. "What will you do with the video of me?"

"I'll give it to the police." Her bottom lip was trembling.

"I thought you'd say that." He nodded at the baby. "The videos of him are more important."

He turned and ran.

FOUR

Will took the subway to traverse D.C. and get back to the place he'd parked his car, rapid thoughts cascading through his mind, his handgun ready to take down cops who might board the train and search for him. Every nerve ending in his body was alert to the possibility of threats, every neuron in his mind and torso communicating to each other that their carrier was now a coiled spring ready for combat. The nerves and neurons were well practiced in this maneuver. It was second nature.

Still, he couldn't have been tenser. There was no doubt that his real identity would soon become known. When that happened, he'd have to go to war.

He moved through the subway car, avoiding eye contact but seeing everything. People watched him, but he had an idea what they were thinking—big guy, ready smile, eyes glistening with intelligence, no hint of being a lonely monster.

The people around him were normal Americans—mothers, sons, commuters—solid people. These were the type of compatriots he'd protected all his life.

He passed the folk without them having the slightest inkling of what was happening.

Howard Kane watched his four men chop Charlie Sapper into manageable chunks and feed her body parts to boars. Jason Flail tossed Sapper's hand into the boar compound and watched the swine squeal with delight as they charged at the flesh. The Virginia farm was Flail's, bought with his savings and Green Beret pension. The three men helping him with his task had served with him in hellholes around the world. They weren't on the full-time payroll of Kane, but now and again they assisted him with stuff. They were his blunt instruments. And Kane had no problem with their methods.

"What about DNA?" Kane was wearing a crisp white shirt and slacks. "This won't get rid of DNA."

Flail, forty-six, was blond haired, six feet, and wearing a frogman's outfit. The three men with him, now standing close to the boar pen, were wearing the same. Flail smiled. "Depends if someone comes here to check. Why would they?"

"They might." The sight of Sapper being eaten didn't bother Kane in the slightest. Clearing all traces of the Berlin mess was what counted.

The former Green Beret shrugged. "You asked us to do this."

"As long as you know what you're doing."

Flail threw the last bit of Sapper into the pen. "The pigs eat. They shit what they don't need. We burn the shit. We burn the ground underneath the shit. We rotavate the soil underneath the burned crust. No DNA."

"But what about the boars? Won't Sapper's DNA be in them?"

Flail shrugged again. "Maybe. But pigs are on this earth to be slaughtered and eaten. I was due to kill them anyway. Plus, I'm a businessman. I've already negotiated sale of produce to fifty fast-food joints in Richmond, Columbus, Philadelphia, Cincinnati, and D.C. I get ten cents on every three-dollar burger they sell that contains my pork. Makes commercial sense. And it'll make me a lot of cash."

Kane laughed. "You're feeding Charlie Sapper to the East Coast?"

"You got a problem with that?"

"No."

Flail looked at the rolling hills and forest around him. "I don't need to know why Sapper was killed. In fact, I don't want to know. But I'm guessing it was vital her mouth was shut forever. Correct?"

"Yes." Kane swiveled to face the cool Virginia

wind. "I want Haden dead. Under no circumstances can he be captured alive. But this is a very complex task. Haden's got information that could bring down me and everyone who knows me." He looked at Flail. "That's why I've been asking you to do these tasks."

"To save your neck?"

"No. I don't care about that. My priority is national security. People like me come and go. National security doesn't. You got that?"

"Sure thing, boss."

Kane pulled Flail away from his men. Quietly he said, "There's more work to be done. Are you up for that?"

Flail nodded. "You're playing a mighty complex and odd game. But I'm willing to do my bit."

Kane returned his gaze to the hills in the distance. "Haden's out there. I have to be smarter than him. This is all about deflection. Don't let me down."

Will Cochrane stared at the assassin's car while recalling the first time his father had allowed him to sit on his lap in the driver's seat and grip the steering wheel. Will was barely five. His father gently depressed pedals and kept his hands hovering near the wheel just in case. They were on an open stretch of road. Back then Will was fearful of the law and rules.

"We shouldn't be doing this, Pa," he said.

"Yes, we should," his father had replied.

"Why?"

"Because there are no rules."

Will wished that memory could make him smile as he unlocked the car and drove fast.

He wondered what his father would think of him now. James Cochrane was such a steady hand, bright, descended from persecuted French Huguenots who fled France for America in the sixteenth century, his ancestors changing their name so it suggested they were Scottish. James was a wise and calm man. God knows why he joined the CIA. He should have been a professor.

But instead he wore a suit and sometimes held a gun.

Even at the age of five, Will knew it made his father sad to be that person.

Jason Flail was satisfied that Sapper was now fully eaten. "I've just heard that Fox is officially dead."

"I know. I have my sources in D.C. PD."

Flail smiled. "Maybe one day you'll tell me what's really happening."

Kane looked up at Flail. "It's all about the colonel."

"What's Haden done?"

"You don't need to know! But he's back and I don't fully know why. I suspect he wants all traces of Berlin neutered. Sapper's dead; Fox is dead; Cochrane's been dead for a year. All that's left is me. Thing is, unlike you, Haden's not selling consumed human flesh to burger flippers. He's far worse. Bear that in mind if you ever meet him."

What Kane didn't tell Flail was that there was

a reason events were unfolding three years after the Berlin hit. And it had to do with Otto Raeder.

Two weeks before the Berlin job, Haden drank whiskey, the aroma of oak cask alcohol hitting his nostrils and palate. Haden had three rules when drinking: one glass only, always when the body and mind were not fatigued, and never in the company of others. Whiskey, Haden reasoned, was a man's drink designed over centuries to allow their brains to settle without hearing the clatter of others, most of all women. A woman in the company of a man and Scotch was a deadly combination, because men get angry when it is their never-to-be-disturbed prayer time.

But only one glass. Haden was many things but was never a victim to other influences. Haden was always in control. Whiskey was a momentary pause for thought. And right now Haden's thoughts were alive.

Unwin Fox, Charlie Sapper, and Howard Kane had bought into the premise of the Berlin mission, but if anything went wrong the colonel could deal with them.

Though he'd never met him, Haden had heard that Cochrane was in a whole different league—too smart, too capable a covert operator.

Haden smiled. Cochrane's capabilities would ensure he'd get the job done.

FIVE

Special Agent Marsha Gage was the FBI's best man hunter.

To her husband and two kids, she was an adorable and stoic prime example of the very best a woman could be. To her colleagues, she was a dogmatic pain in the ass who never stopped.

The forty-one-year-old black-haired woman was sitting at her desk in her Bureau office, alone, late at night. Recently, she'd been tasked with only a handful of mundane jobs, the Bureau having decided that she was burned to a frazzle and needed some downtime. But Gage didn't do downtime. She ignored the dictate and focused her relentless energies on the one thing that had been plaguing her mind.

Will Cochrane.

Once, she'd pursued the operative from Norway to D.C., after he disobeyed orders in a CIA operation that required him to sacrifice an American agent. He'd refused to make that sacrifice. The CIA went after him. Or so it thought. More accurately, he went after the CIA and it ended badly for everyone involved except Cochrane. It culminated in him putting a gun to Gage's forehead. As petrified as she was at that moment, she had the deepest respect for the assassin. But she was a member of the law and didn't let respect get in the way of police work. Plus, later Cochrane proved to be a cop killer and a slaughterer of civilians. People believed he was dead. Gage wasn't so sure.

Above her desk was a large whiteboard with newspaper clippings, handwritten notes, photos, and arrows linking one image to another.

The board was her visual collation of all matters Cochrane. Her notes next to the images were erratic and constantly updated. There were many. Some of them were the following:

Murderer? Good man? Crazed? Child kidnapper? Did that happen? Why did he kill these cops? Why didn't he kill these American cops? Troubled youth. Compassionate. Hates dishing out death. The very best killer. Dead? Faked his death? Never does anything without a reason. Outsmarts everyone. Don't let him get up close to you again. Way too dangerous. Unpredictable. Worse than you think. No, he's not.

In the center of the board was her written question.

WHERE ARE YOU????

She looked at the board, her desk lamp the only source of light in the room. The information on the board had been collected and assembled over months. She hadn't been involved in the investigation a year ago to try to bring him to justice for the alleged murders and kidnapping. That investigation belonged to the NYPD. But from a distance she'd watched closely, always wondering why Cochrane fascinated her.

Bo Haupman, a bear of a man and her boss, came into the room holding two mugs of coffee.

"I'm going to get really damned pissed off with you," he said as he put the mugs on her table and sat on a chair next to her.

"I don't care." Gage was looking at the board.

"I'm your superior."

"No, you're not." Gage wiggled a finger in her searing-hot coffee.

Haupman smiled. "*My* superiors think otherwise. They think you need to be kept on a leash."

"But you don't and that's all that matters." Gage smiled because she didn't want to be too hard on Haupman. He was full of admiration for her and always went out of his way to protect her from others in the Bureau so she could do what she did best: brilliant law enforcement. He was a kind man who'd gratefully hung up his pistol a long time ago after decades of doing things he found distasteful. Her gaze on the whiteboard unbroken, her tone was more sympathetic as she said, "You still need to go up two shirt collar sizes. You look like you're being strangled."

"Mrs. Haupman—"

"Loves you for who you are."

Haupman nodded. "It's because of that I wish

I was the shape I was in on prom night. She deserves better."

"She deserves you." Gage's voice hardened. "You here to give me some chickenshit job?"

"No. There's been a killing in Rock Creek Park. Right now we don't have jurisdiction because it's a local law matter."

"So why bother me with it?"

"The victim's CIA. That means—"

"The Feds have to monitor the investigation. You're asking me to be a caretaker to an investigation Washington PD is perfectly capable of conducting." She pointed at the board. "You should be putting me on Will Cochrane."

Haupman sighed. "Marsha, please listen to the facts. Cochrane's dead, his body swept out to sea."

Gage swiveled in her chair. "Where's proof of death?"

Her boss was exasperated. "Come on, Marsha. He jumped off the Brooklyn Bridge a year ago. The Coast Guard confirmed there was a massive riptide that night. There's no way they could find the body. So I should be asking you, where's proof of life?"

Agent Gage tapped her desk, deep in thought. "For special operatives, the sea is the worst place to work. It's too unpredictable and unforgiving. Yet Cochrane survived that crazy twelve-month training program MI6 put him through, part of which was survival in the North Sea during winter. Later, they shot him out of submarine torpedo tubes so he could swim ashore in the Med and Siberian Sea to execute targets. There're so many other examples. A man like that knows the sea." She was earnest as she said to Haupman, "He's operated in every harsh climate known to man. He knows the elements. He knew exactly what he was doing when he threw himself off the bridge."

Part of Haupman agreed with Gage. But if he presented her assessment to Bureau directors, it would make her sound paranoid and disengaged with reality. Her seniority would suffer. Right now her career was deliberately on hiatus, but she was a rising star and tipped to one day be the first female head of the Bureau. Haupman never wanted to reach those dizzying heights. But he knew enough about Bureau politics at the top to realize that Gage could easily derail her ascendancy if she was too bullheaded. "Leave this alone. It's not good for you."

"It's not in me to leave things alone," she said quietly.

"I know." Haupman touched her hand. "That's why I'm here, to shield you from the shit. But one day I won't be here. Shark-infested waters at the top and all that. How will you manage without me when you haven't got a political bone in your body? And plus, maybe we should just let Cochrane rest."

The last comment got Gage riled. "Look at the board. They say he murdered his sister in the Waldorf Astoria hotel; assaulted two NYPD officers on an Amtrak train, easily unarming them and putting them on their asses without pulling a weapon; commandeered a civilian's vehicle at gunpoint and held the weapon to the driver's head as they fled; killed two uniforms at the house outside Roanoke, two detectives as well; murdered the homeowners—the great-uncle and -aunt of the ten-year-old twin boys Cochrane expected to adopt; kidnapped one of the boys, Tom Koenig, the son of Cochrane's former CIA colleague; gunned down in cold blood two Lynchburg cops who'd tried to arrest him; and then held an entire restaurant at gunpoint before tying them to each other and leading them to the bridge in front of hundreds of cops and the media. All of that one year ago and over just two weeks. Cochrane must be brought to justice. He can't rest."

Haupman looked at one of Gage's handwritten board notes.

I think he's innocent.

"Agent Gage, this is becoming an obsession."

"To get to the truth!" Gage withdrew her hand.

"You want to prove he didn't do those things?"

Gage shook her head. "I want to prove what happened, whether that means setting him free or putting a needle in him."

Haupman smiled. "Always the black-and-white objectivity?"

"It's what I do."

"And if he's alive and guilty?"

"I'll kill him."

SIX

Josef Kopański—Joe to his colleagues—was a silver-haired fifty-year-old with not an ounce of fat on his rangy frame. Hands as strong as clamps, the NYPD detective was renowned for his ability to put a bullet exactly where it needed to be put, with unflinching nerves and without the need for backup. Joe Cop Killer, his colleagues called him, though never to his face. The nickname derived from the moment he shot a sheriff in the head because the sheriff was holding a gun to his wife while intoxicated. A widower, Kopański had no woman in his life. He wasn't looking for one. Even if he were, it would have been difficult. Half of his face was good-looking, the other half deformed after a crack addict threw nitric acid at him. He didn't care. He'd gotten used to being a loner. Police work, he frequently incorrectly told himself, was all he needed. And alongside his detective partner, he broke more murder cases than anyone else in NYC.

He pulled out his gun in Queens and wondered if hatred was about to undo everything he'd worked for and pledged.

Kopański didn't give a rat's ass. This was more important. He grabbed his cell phone and called his partner.

The death factory in Queens was a sensory overload of noises, smells, and images. Cows were moaning, aware that something was badly wrong. Calves were being taken from their mothers. Mothers were also victim to the conveyor belt. One by one they were being electrocuted to knock them senseless yet still alive. Stupefied and prone, the bovines' arteries were sliced open, some of the cows unaware of what was happening to them, others vaguely conscious and screaming. Rivers of blood were directed to troughs by men in overalls and holding power hoses. The air was rich with the scent of musk, shit, and uncooked flesh and blood. Those beasts still alive used their hooves or heads to try to break free. They stood no chance of escape. Cows were brought here, processed, inspected for diseases that might contaminate humans, put in their cells, and sliced open. This was a Queens slaughterhouse.

The sight of such systematic killing didn't bother Joe Kopański because he'd already imagined this was how it was done. The detective had seen too much suffering in his career and personal life to be shocked by yet more pain and death. Plus, he had something else to worry about. He had a gun in his hand and was searching for a piece of scum.

The Polish American moved through the large room, workers looking at him, the cacophony of death all around the detective. But he did not slow his pace.

Finding the rapist was all that mattered.

"Where is he?!" he shouted as some of the spray of water mingled with blood hit his face and shirt.

The workers didn't respond. They had no idea what was happening.

He ran to the end of the factory, conveyor belts above him rotating massive carcasses on hooks, blood dripping from partially severed heads. That's when he saw him: the butcher, slicing his blade through a suspended cow's throat, his white apron splattered crimson.

The man looked at him and instantly knew the detective was here for him. Kopański gave no warning as he fired his gun. The bullet would have hit the butcher in the forehead. But the butcher swung the carcass between them, the detective's bullet striking the dead cow's heart. The butcher ran. Kopański pursued.

They raced out the rear entrance of the factory and into the darkness, Kopański catching only white flashes of the butcher.

Kopański's limbs ached as he chased the younger man. He didn't worry. He knew he had something the butcher didn't have: no fear of death.

They ran through side alleys, streets; past hookers, lovers, drunk kids chowing down on falafels, and crazies strung out on whatever it was that got them through the night. The butcher leaped over barriers in alleys and kept running. Kopański shot him in the leg.

The cop saw the butcher limp into a doorway, his hand shaking as he inserted a key and unlocked a door. The butcher entered his apartment block. Kopański followed.

Blood droplets were all over the stairwell as Kopański ascended to the top floor. The trail led him to the home he had been watching for weeks. The butcher's home. It took minimal effort to enter. The detective found the rapist in the corner of his bedroom, clutching his leg, whimpering.

Kopański took off his jacket and rolled up the sleeves of his bloody white shirt.

The butcher grinned between gritted teeth. "The pictures."

"Maybe." Kopański knew his career was about to die. He hadn't built enough evidence against the butcher. But it didn't matter. The women on the wall were good women.

They deserved peace.

The butcher pushed his hand against his leg, his face desperately trying not to display the agony he was undergoing. "You can't prove anything!"

Kopański walked to the wall displaying the photos. He placed a finger on one of them. "You raped my daughter."

The butcher could not move but abject fear was writ across his face. "I . . . I had no idea, I . . ."

Kopański strode up to him, lifted him with one hand by the throat, and tossed him across the room like a useless rag doll. The butcher bounced off the opposite wall, displacing most of the photos, and hit the floor screaming.

"You did it on prom night. You and my Susan. Same class. Same dance. Ten years ago. That's when it started. And it didn't stop. One woman a year ever since. But now you're speeding up."

The butcher spat blood. "Get me a lawyer!"

"There's no need for that." Kopański raised his gun. "See, a man like you deals with flesh all the time. You're numb to it. You don't think of it as living. All that matters is what it can give you in return. You don't need a lawyer."

The butcher spat. "So what are you then? Judge and jury?"

"Right now I'm a father who found his daughter screaming in a ditch. It's a shame for you that happened."

He blew the butcher's brains out.

Thyme Painter was Joe Kopański's NYPD detective partner. The former Black Hawk helicopter major hobbled as she arrived at Hunts Point. Her prosthetic limb had been expertly fitted after she'd deliberately flown into the path of a SAM missile in Afghanistan to save another helicopter that was carrying SEAL Team Six. But sometimes the limb felt like it was gnawing at her stump. The svelte, black-haired, single woman often joked it kept her weight down and stopped her from having to worry about sex and men. In reality, the limb had become an intrinsic part of her, as much as Kopański's mottled face helped define his mind.

Painter's parents were investment bankers; she was a Harvard and West Point grad, top of her class at both institutions, with postgraduate options on Capitol Hill. But like Kopański she always wanted to do things different. She'd been on the force for fifteen years and could have been fast-tracked to deputy commissioner had she not been a rebel who favored pure police work rather than careerism.

It was nearly two A.M. as Painter arrived at Hunts Point. The vast building was abuzz with workers sorting produce in the 328-warehouse complex, which was divided into fruit and vegetables, meat, and fish. It was the Fulton Fish Market segment that Painter headed to, though she didn't enter. Instead, she waited outside the massive warehouses, watching people in hard hats driving forklifts and huge trucks, entering barricades to unload fish caught near Long Island.

She was hunting the female criminal who'd lured victims to the butcher—victims including Kopański's daughter. The enabler would be driving one of the trucks. She always arrived in the early hours. Painter was here for her.

A fine rain drizzled vertically, highlighted by the beams of work vehicles, the droplets soaking Painter's hair as she stood adjacent to her vehicle, her hand on her holster.

Kopański had done his bit. Now it was time for her to do her share of the work. Even if it meant she'd get kicked out of the NYPD. Six months ago, Kopański had told her not to get involved. She knew he secretly loved her, not that he'd ever revealed that emotion. But because of that knowledge, she was here to avenge the trauma he'd had for so long. It was the least she could do.

Tonight they were taking out the trash.

A truck stopped by the security booth. Painter couldn't see the driver or the plates because of the headlights. But no doubt it was one of the vehicles heading to the market, capable of carrying thirteen tons of red snapper, bream, cod, and other species. Its engine roared as it was allowed to proceed. Painter waited.

The truck pulled up outside the warehouse where Painter was positioned. Its driver didn't notice Painter. It was too dark and bustling with night shift workers who were desperate to get everything set up for the morning's trade with wholesalers. The night shift was a race—get produce ready, find out what each vendor was prepared to sell for, adjust prices accordingly so other vendors weren't undercut, and make sure everything was pristine and fresh. Once, the market was America's biggest. Gang wars among vendors and the aspirations of realtors drove the market to the Bronx. The place was still worked by tough men and women who'd seen thieves and competitors shot in the head. They were used to violence.

A woman got out of the truck. She was wearing jeans and a windbreaker, her blond hair tied in a ponytail. Under other circumstances Painter would have envied her good looks and attractive frame. But under these circumstances she just felt revulsion.

The detective walked up to her. "Margie Bane?"

Margie looked quizzical. "Yes."

"Are you carrying a piece?"

"Of course not."

"Yes, you are." Painter used her gloved hand to pull out a Smith & Wesson sidearm she'd seized off a perp a year ago. "This is your gun."

"What the hell?! It's not my gun!"

Painter's expression was cold. "The butcher raped. But he was only able to do that because you enabled his actions. You brought him the women. Got drunk with them in bars. Befriended them. Asked them back to your place so you could party. Enabled. And that's when you got off watching the butcher raping the people you brought him. You're a damn bitch."

Margie looked venomous. "Are you a cop?"

"Yes. But tonight I'm off duty." For the benefit of any potential witnesses, Painter shouted, "Gun! Gun! Put it down!" She shot Margie in the head, hunched over her, placed the spare pistol in her hand, and radioed the NYPD.

SEVEN

Washington, D.C., cops took Unwin Fox's body to the morgue and submitted it to analysis. The room was brightly illuminated by ceiling spotlights and had huge drawers for cadavers. Four people were in the room: two doctors, a D.C. detective, and Marsha Gage. On the slab in the center of the room was Fox's naked body. On other slabs next to him were bodies of criminals and prostitutes, all of them sliced open to reveal their lungs, the folded-back flaps of flesh making them look like grotesque angels.

The air was rich with the scent of formaldehyde and decay. One of the spotlights flickered and buzzed like a fly that was hoping to nest maggots in the most rotten elements of the dead.

It was three A.M. The doctors and D.C. cop were tired but focused. Gage, however, was irritated to be here. This wasn't her case. It belonged to D.C. and she was present only to ensure Fox hadn't been killed to jeopardize national interest. She'd never met Fox and she'd avoided spooks. The CIA, she'd long ago concluded, was an institution filled with overqualified underachievers.

Only one spy she'd confronted was very different and filled her with dread. But Cochrane was dead. Allegedly.

The senior doctor spoke calmly and with command. "Severe bruising to the neck. A witness caught the attack on camera. The assailant was male and placed his knee on the victim's throat."

Gage asked, "Did it cause death?"

"Yes." The senior doctor glanced at the cops. "Death by asphyxiation. Odd way for a man to be killed in a park."

Gage asked, "An altercation that got out of hand?"

The D.C. detective answered, "Could be. Very hard to tell from the witness's cell phone camera. It looks like the assailant and victim spoke briefly first, but despite our efforts, we can't pick up audio."

"Where's the video now?"

"We're processing it. Trying to identify the perp."

The senior doctor continued. "This is nagging me."

The D.C. detective asked, "Why?"

"Because I've done this for thirty years. Strangling is always rare. It's an unpremeditated crime of impetuosity."

Gage interjected. "You're sure the contusions are the cause of death?"

The senior doctor nodded. "Yes. The larynx is crushed."

Gage was now alert and focused. Like the doctor, something was nagging her about the death. "How long for the blood test results?"

"We're running them now but it'll take a few hours."

"Your laboratory needs to move quicker." Gage moved closer to the body. "What if the killing wasn't the only crime?"

The senior doctor didn't follow. "We know what killed Fox."

"Do we?" Gage stared at the body. "You're working on the assumption that the killer was out of control. But what if the killer had a very rational mind and was covering something else up. Or . . ." Gage's mind was racing. "Or his act was mercy."

"Mercy?"

"A mercy killing."

The doctor glanced at his medical colleague. "The victim had a fatal physiological condition?"

The junior doctor shook his head. "Strangling someone to save him from a worse fate means the condition would have to be sudden, rather than progressive. Otherwise the killer would have found a more humane way to kill."

The doctors spoke fast:

"Heart attack?"

"More preferable to strangulation, plus people can recover from heart attacks. There's no mercy in killing someone with a weak heart."

"Stage four cancer?"

"If someone cared about a terminally ill cancer patient, he'd have made better plans to end his misery."

The junior doctor shrugged. "So let's wait for the bloods, but here and now this looks like a fight. Two guys who lost their temper. Something like that."

Gage wouldn't let it drop. "What if he was poisoned? The strangulation was to kill a worse killing."

Both doctors shook their heads. The senior doctor said, "Death by poison, no matter which poison, shows up quickly. Skin discoloration. Change of color to the tongue. Contortions. Variations in pupil dilation. Other obvious symptoms."

Gage agreed but had experience the doctors didn't, including knowing the more insidious ways states sponsored death. "Does he have any lacerations?"

"He's got a cut on his calf. Tiny puncture mark. Probably an insect did it. But we're not taking it for granted. The tests will give us clarity."

Gage had already thought about something that had happened in London in 2006.

The killing of former Russian spy Alexander Litvinenko.

She asked, "Have you got a Geiger counter?"

The senior doctor said, "Are you crazy?!"

"You don't have one?"

"Of course we do!"

Gage pointed at the corpse. "I reckon you might want to run a test."

The junior doctor returned two minutes later and ran the counter over the corpse. "Holy shit!"

His superior snatched the Geiger from him and read the display. "Everyone get out of the room right now!"

Thunder boomed as Will Cochrane headed to west D.C. through a ragged forest on a deserted road, his windshield wipers on full, a flask of black coffee nestled beside him. His thoughts were racing.

Haden poisoned Unwin Fox—but why?

He should have just stayed low and enjoyed his stolen cash.

There must have been a trigger, something that happened very recently, to bring Haden out of hiding.

What was the trigger?

For now, Will concluded it didn't matter.

A lightning bolt struck a tree and sent it crashing across the road. Will carried on, swerving past it, his thoughts too preoccupied to worry about the sometimes angry confluence between the heavens and earth.

Haden. All roads led to Haden.

A man who was a superstar in the military; he would have been the next chairman of the Joint Chiefs of Staff if he hadn't let his machismo get in the way of leadership. Nevertheless, an undeniably brilliant yet incredibly ruthless commander.

Haden was the problem. Will was going to sort that out.

The scientific department of the FBI had taken over jurisdiction of the morgue containing Unwin Fox because D.C. cops didn't have the expertise to deal with the situation. The Feds were dressed in white NBC suits as they descended the stairs to the morgue. Fox was still in the center of the room, surrounded by other dead who'd been torn apart by the doctors.

Once in the room, the Fed scientists moved slowly while Gage and the senior doctor who'd conducted the autopsy watched through a one-way mirror, having been tested for radiation and cleared.

"What's happening?" asked Gage.

The doctor pressed a finger against the glass. "This is the first time for me. The guys in there know what they're doing."

"Which is what?"

"They're pursuing your very clever lead." Though he'd never conducted an autopsy on a person with polonium poisoning, the D.C. doctor had some knowledge of the effects. "If you hold a piece of polonium in your hand, it's obviously radioactive. But it won't hurt you in the short term. However, if it's converted into a soluble compound it can have catastrophic effects."

"What compound?"

"Salt. The big problem with radioactive salts is that they dissolve in liquids."

"Water?"

"Also blood." The doctor was glad to be behind the glass. "When I was a professor in med school I used to put a Geiger counter near Brazil nuts in lessons to show students how radioactive they are. Nut trees in Brazil absorb via their roots the natural volcanic radiation in the water."

"Your point?"

"My point is that radiation is all around us, but we can live with it. But what happened to Fox was on a whole other scale. I can't give you a time frame, but I can give you an end result. Polonium mutates cells extremely rapidly. It's worse than cancer. You die in agony." He was somber as he added, "Your colleagues are testing to see whether the tiny lesion on the back of Fox's calf was the point where polonium was injected. If so, goodness knows how it was done."

Gage knew. "It would have been done with a special contraption. A rod, no longer than an umbrella, probably disguised to look like an everyday item that would have blended into activities in the park. The tip would have been spring-loaded. The murderer places the tip against Fox's calf and pulls a trigger at the other end of the rod. The tip is so fine and strong it would have punctured Fox's pants and would have only felt like a tiny pinprick. Probably, he thought nothing of it and carried on walking. Problem was, he now had a huge dose of polonium inside him."

The doctor nodded. "Like darting an animal. How did you know to call for a Geiger reading?"

"I didn't *know* anything. It just occurred to me." Gage's mind was racing. "Whoever killed

Fox had no reason to do so if he was the one who darted Fox. This *was* a mercy killing. But for that to happen, it means the man who crushed Fox's throat knew exactly what had happened. We're dealing with someone very different. Skilled. Unusually so." She knew the killer was a highly trained professional. More than that, someone who knew the dark arts of assassination. "I need to see the video of the assailant."

Will arrived at the burned-out shell of Fox's house in Vienna. He hadn't anticipated the CIA officer's home would have been destroyed, instead believing it might have been burgled and torn apart by men looking for something. Fox was carrying a secret that made men kill him. Fox would have known that possibility. He'd have stored his secret somewhere in case his mouth was permanently shut. His house was the obvious location.

But now it was a blackened shell, the smell of cinder and smoke still evident despite the rain and a wind that was swirling aimlessly at three A.M.

Will parked three hundred yards away.

Close enough to reach if he needed to bolt.

Far enough away to allow him to approach the building without others noticing.

On the other side of the street, he watched everything around him. He knew what he had to do.

He walked into the ruins, ducking under police tape, his sidearm tucked into his waistband.

Smoke was still coming off the shell, walls and roof nearly gone, clumps of siding, brick, and wood dropping to the floor because they no longer had anything to adhere to. Everything was burned to a crisp, the remnants of furniture reduced to ugly molten vestiges of what they once were. Rain drizzled through the open roof. The whole place would have to be pulled down to make space for a new home.

He moved through the ruins, his brain processing everything and imagining Fox living here. The key question was where Fox would have stored the evidence that something was wrong with Berlin.

The cellar door was nearly off its hinges, a crumbling black shadow of its former solidity. It resembled a shield that had failed to protect its master in battle, broken and impotent.

Will descended to the basement, a flashlight in his hand, and saw a wooden chest in the center of the bare room. The chest was ravaged by fire. Will ripped off the lid. Inside was nothing but ashes. He gathered some of the ashes in his hands and rubbed them between his fingers. Burned paper or cardboard, he decided.

"What the hell are you doing in here?"

Will turned to face the man who'd asked the question. The man was standing next to three others. All were wearing suits. Will's eyes took in everything he could see. "I'm a friend of the man who lived here. Who are you?"

The men pulled out their guns and pointed them at Will.

Will let them.

"We're cops and you're trespassing in a crime scene."

Will stared at them, saying nothing.

"This is a D.C. crime scene!"

Will nodded. "Yes, it is. So why are you here?"

"What?"

"Why are you here?"

"We're detectives!"

"No, you're not."

The men glanced at one another. Their leader said, "We're here on official duty."

"Of that, I'm certain." Will kept his eyes on the guns as he scooped a handful of ash out of the chest. "It's just ash. Nothing more. There's no reason to pull triggers for ash, is there?"

He held their gaze as he walked past the men and exited the house.

Marsha Gage entered the D.C. detective's office. "My people have ascertained that without question Fox has been assassinated. But someone close to him put him out of his misery. Something is going on here that's way beyond a murder."

"A cover-up?"

"Could be." Gage could tell there was a degree of territorial hostility in the D.C. detective's tone. The murder was being transferred to the Feds. He didn't like that one bit. Gage didn't care.

"Perhaps Fox was injected and then strangled to make sure of death."

Agent Gage shook her head. "Why not just strangle him in the first place?"

"He was injected to weaken him first? That way the killer could move in and finish him off."

Gage didn't buy that. "You saw the crush to

Fox's larynx. It's massive. Whoever ended his life could have done so on a healthy three-hundred-pound WWE wrestler."

"I agree. In my entire career, I've never seen such damage." The detective inhaled slowly. "The cell phone's on its way here. I've watched the video. The guy who ended Fox's life looked like he was killing a child. But what he didn't look like is someone who'd stop."

"He's killed before?"

"Without doubt."

"Your assessment?"

The D.C. detective pondered Gage's question. He said, "I'm used to dealing with perps who use guns or brawl or just go crazy. This is something else." To Gage's surprise the detective walked up to her and shook her hand. "This needs to be your case. I'm out of my league. When the cell phone arrives, take a look at his eyes."

"His eyes?"

"Yeah. I can't figure them out."

Will reached his car and looked back at Fox's decimated home. He pulled out his handgun and kept it low, scouring his surroundings. The four men who'd confronted him in the house exited. At this distance it was impossible for most men to fire a handgun and kill. Will could. He'd done similar in Bogotá, Hong Kong, and Mexico City. Dropped people like flies.

The men sauntered to their vehicles. They were officials, of that Will was in no doubt. But they weren't bad guys, Will imagined. They were on the payroll of someone good. Even though they weren't cops.

He replaced his gun and got in his car.

Marsha Gage watched the cell phone video and then paced back and forth in the D.C. detective's room.

"See what I mean?" said the detective next to her.

"Shut up!" Gage didn't care what anyone in D.C. PD thought right now. "Nine to get an outside line, yes?"

The detective looked quizzical. "Yes, but . . ."

"I don't care." She rang Bo Haupman from the detective's landline. "I need everyone, and I mean *everyone*, who's seen this video to be told by you to keep their mouths shut." Her heart was beating fast. "I want them gagged. Nothing, repeat nothing, to the press or official. The last time we made that mistake we lost. He won."

Haupman sighed on his end of the phone. "Is this what I'm thinking?"

Gage replied, "You better give me the goddamn resources I need. And I need my shooter." She felt breathless. "This is the worst-case scenario. A CIA guy was killed in a D.C. park by a guy who we thought was dead."

She glanced at the detective; his face was pale.

EIGHT

Howard Kane answered his cell phone at 3:24 A.M. while in bed. "This had better be good!"

Jason Flail responded, "Me and my guys found a snooper at Fox's place. Don't know who he is. We pretended to be detectives. He saw through us."

"What did you do?"

"We let him go." The former special forces operative hesitated. "Actually, it was more complicated than that."

Kane was fully awake now.

"What do you want us to do about it, sir?"

"Just keep an eye out for him. We don't like snoopers, do we?"

"No, we don't, Mr. Kane."

Kane sat upright in bed. "The snooper's description?"

"It was dark in the basement where we confronted him, so difficult to be precise. But he was a big guy. And . . ."

"And?"

Flail took two seconds to answer. "Mr. Kane, I've worked with a lot of tough guys. They still get scared when the shit hits the fan. We all do."

"Get on with it!"

Flail said, "There were four of us. We had guns out. We knew what we were doing. We had the snooper cornered in a basement. No way could he get past us. But here's the thing."

"The thing?"

"The thing, Mr. Kane." Flail sounded uncharacteristically uneasy. "The snooper wasn't scared. Not at all. He just walked past us and left."

Will Cochrane drove through the night amid a torrential downpour, his sidearm rubbing skin off his hip as he wrangled his vehicle to keep traction on the Virginia road that was surrounded by forests.

The constant specks of rain played havoc with his eyes, making visibility tenuous and plagued by a lack of discernible landmarks. He was like a skier who no longer knows if he's moving due to the plainness of his white surroundings.

But he kept driving, no chance of stopping to relieve the tension on his eyes, his desire to get to Colonel Haden overwhelming.

Will had executed the Berlin job. And now

he knew he'd killed a major terrorist so Colonel Haden could profit from the action.

Marsha Gage was back in her FBI office in D.C.'s J. Edgar Hoover Building. She hadn't slept all night, fatigue writ across her face, sun rising and reminding her that she needed to call her husband and tell him that today was soccer day and both their kids needed to pack their uniforms before school.

She stared at the whiteboard above her desk, her head giddy from tiredness and excessive mental stimulation.

Everything on the board was about Will Cochrane.

And all the data on the board seemed cluttered and confusing.

Gage knew he was a killer whose body count was off the scale. And his intellect frightened her. But he wasn't a psychopath and didn't have any other mental disorders she was aware of. It seemed to her that it was inconceivable he'd gone on a rampage a year ago in the States and killed innocent civilians. And yet the evidence to the contrary was palpable.

And now it turned out he was alive.

She tried to understand how that made her feel.

Even if innocent of the alleged crimes, Cochrane was a massive conundrum for society. He protected people and served the West with distinction, and yet he was too highly trained and capable.

But she'd once looked into his eyes and saw a good man, while he charmed her by speaking fluent Latin. Why did he have that capability?

Agent Gage rubbed her face and decided she needed to reapply makeup and clean her Glock sidearm.

She wanted to look the part when she confronted Cochrane again and make a decision as to whether to pull the trigger.

It was seven A.M.

Thyme Painter and Joe Kopański were sitting outside of an internal affairs office in one of Manhattan's precincts. They were wearing the same clothes they'd worn the night before: Kopański in his white shirt mottled with bloodstains; Painter in her black trouser suit that smelled of cordite.

Inside the office was an IA officer who was unshaven though dressed in a suit. He'd been woken an hour earlier and told to get to the precinct ASAP.

He put his head around the door and addressed NYPD's finest detectives. "Get in here now."

Kopański and Painter said nothing as they entered.

"Sit."

They did so opposite the IA man, a desk in between them.

The IA officer briefly riffled through the reports that Painter and Kopański had written. He addressed Kopański first. "You killed the man who raped your daughter."

Kopański didn't respond.

The IA officer looked at Painter. "And you shot the woman who got the butcher his female victims."

Painter was still, her eyes shining and defiant.

"You took the law into your own hands," the IA officer concluded. "I'm suspending you both because I think you executed the butcher and his partner."

NINE

Four hours later, Marsha Gage was in Quantico. In the control center with her were three men: Bo Haupman, Jack O'Connor, and Pete Duggan.

Duggan was a team leader on the FBI's Hostage Rescue Team. A former SEAL Team Six operative, he was without doubt one of the best combatants in the United States. He was the shooter Gage had wanted on her team. Duggan and Gage had worked together before, when both had confronted Cochrane and lost.

O'Connor was as senior in the Bureau as Haupman. He was head of the Critical Incident Response Group and was Duggan's boss. HRT was CIRG's last resort if things went south in a serious situation. When that happened, Duggan was always O'Connor's first choice as the man who brought criminal matters to an end.

Gage was in control.

She pointed at Duggan. "Under the direction of the head of the Bureau, I'm requisitioning Duggan to be part of my task force."

O'Connor didn't like that one bit. "He's one of *my* men!"

Gage's expression remained neutral. "Sign this." She slid across a sheet of paper. "It's telling you to keep your mouth shut about what you're going to hear."

O'Connor read the formal document. He shrugged and put his signature at the bottom. "Guess I don't have an option."

Duggan said, "You need me to sign one as well?"

Gage shook her head. "You're going to be a major part of the plan. Signing stuff won't help." She clasped her hands together. Her fingers were ringless, despite her being married for fourteen years. She hated that. But her job required her to have minimal personal accoutrements in case she was caught by perps and tortured. "Will Cochrane is alive."

Duggan frowned. "He killed himself a year ago."

"He faked killing himself." Gage stared at the table. "And now he's been captured on camera killing a man who'd been injected with polonium."

O'Connor asked, "He injected the victim?"

"I don't think so. He placed a knee on the victim's throat and squeezed the life out of him. If—"

"—he was the poisoner, why bother doing

that?" O'Connor had to tread carefully with Gage. Though she was junior to him in the Bureau, she was way too successful in her job to be browbeaten by her seniors. Plus, he deeply respected her intelligence and lack of ambition. If, as predicted, she made it to the top of the Bureau, she'd be the first director who got there without a damn care that she was running the show. Power was not her thing. Getting the job done was. "We can't have Cochrane loose on U.S. soil. I thought that had been tied up."

"Apparently not." Gage said to Haupman, "Bo, fill in some of the gaps for the benefit of Mr. O'Connor."

Haupman felt uncomfortable being put on the spot. "You know about the killings Cochrane is alleged to have done near Roanoke and in Lynchburg. And you know some of his background— English/American; French Special Forces; Cambridge University; intellect through the roof; lead operator in MI6 then joint with CIA; left service two years ago. Came up against"—he glanced at Duggan—"Pete three years ago."

"Not exactly." Duggan was still. "I never met him face-to-face. All I saw was the wreckage he caused. The only Fed who confronted him was Agent Gage."

Haupman nodded. "I stand corrected." He undid the top button of his shirt, his flabby throat feeling constricted. "This is what you don't know." He eyed O'Connor and Duggan to make sure he had their full attention. "Among many other things, when he was an operative Cochrane saved the lives of Western and Middle Eastern premiers' wives, plus three thousand child musicians, who were subject to an attempted bomb attack in New York; he prevented an unwanted war between America and Russia and a massive chemical attack against China that would have resulted in millions of dead civilians; caught traitors; stopped the Middle East from imploding; and"—he paused—"left all that behind him to do the honorable thing and adopt the twin boys of a fallen U.S. SEAL comrade."

Everyone in the room was silent.

Haupman continued. "But Cochrane is a problem for us for three reasons. The first is he can outthink us all. The second is he has shown that he always does the right thing. Or so we thought. The final reason is he's most likely the world's deadliest killer."

O'Connor smirked. "Don't be melodramatic."

Haupman was sweating because of the heat in the room and his overweight physique. "In many ways, I wish I was being melodramatic." He looked at Gage. "Tell them what you told me. Your analogy."

Gage hesitated. "It sounds silly to repeat it in this room."

"It's not silly. It's the most accurate way I could think of Cochrane."

Gage leaned forward. "We start with wolves. Their bite strength is ten times that of a dog. And there's dispute as to whether dogs derive from wolves. Doesn't matter. This is *my* analogy so I can tell it how I see it. So we domesticate

wolves and turn them into dogs. But some of us
want them to be wolves again. Idiots breed that
back into them. So imagine the worst dog. What
is it?"

Duggan answered, "A pit bull. They never let
go when they bite. They're designed to attack
bears."

"No." Gage was worried about the impact
of what she was about to say. The analogy now
seemed absurd, yet so real. "Any dog is like a female lover. It's loyal to the death providing you
care for it. But if you turn your back on it, hundreds of years of breeding it to be domesticated
don't mean a thing. It reverts to a wolf in a nanosecond. Cochrane was a loyal dog. *Any* dog. But
we turned our back on him. Now he's a wolf."

Duggan retorted, "But wolves are pack animals."

"Not when they've been kicked out of the
pack. MI6 and the CIA did that. And when
that happens the wolf becomes infinitely more
terrible. Its back is in a corner. It forages. Kills
things it wouldn't ordinarily kill. Its intelligence
increases exponentially because it can no longer
rely on others. It becomes a survivor and absolute killer."

Duggan unfolded his arms. "And you want me
to go after him?"

Gage hesitated. "When I've tracked Cochrane
to a place where he can be cornered, I need a
hunter by my side who can go in to finish it."

Duggan glanced at O'Connor. O'Connor said
nothing, his head bowed.

Gage added, "But I can't lie about the risks. I'm not setting up a big task force. This has to be under the radar. Pete, you and I both know that the more visible this manhunt becomes to Cochrane, the worse it gets for us."

"You want me to go after Cochrane? With no backup?"

Gage considered the question. "There will be four of us hunting him. No more, no less."

Duggan imagined coming toe-to-toe with Cochrane. "Agent Gage, I—"

"Are you accepting the assignment or not?!"

Duggan never swerved from his duty. "Of course, ma'am. But who are the two other members of the team?"

Gage prodded the nondisclosure document O'Connor had signed. She said to the head of the CIRG, "Not one word to anyone, you hear?" She addressed Duggan. "To get to Cochrane we have to understand his motives in Roanoke and Lynchburg. You're the heavy hitter. When it comes to a head, you go in and put him on his ass. And you have my authority and the authority of the attorney general to shoot first and ask questions later. But to get you there, I need detectives. There are only two in the States who are capable of helping me. Don't underestimate them. They pull triggers too. And their minds are as sharp as scalpels."

TEN

Agent Gage knocked on the door of the house in New Jersey.

Joe Kopański opened the door. "Miss Gage."

"Mrs."

"I don't give a shit whether you're hooked up or not, or a dyke, or some dumb feminist who doesn't want to be labeled. Come in."

Gage entered the house. It was clear it was once a family home—pictures of Joe and his daughter and deceased wife everywhere, the place immaculate, floral scents in the air, an overall ambience that a wife and daughter would be returning soon. Four cats were in the living room, emaciated and with patchy fur.

Kopański gestured at them. "Hope you don't mind these guys and girls. I'm rehabilitating them. Found them on the streets. Trying to give them some life back. I tell myself that I'll release them when they're fit. But I know I'll keep them."

Gage sat on the sofa, the cats on either side of her. "When's she arriving?"

"When she damn well likes." He pointed at the cats. "Like them, she doesn't take orders. You want coffee?"

Gage nodded. "I'll have it with milk and—"

"I make it black. Take it or leave it."

Kopański disappeared into the kitchen and returned a few minutes later with a mug that he placed next to Gage.

He sat opposite. "So let's get this out of the way. I shot a woman's husband. She was strung out and pissed off when I tried to arrest her. She threw nitric acid over my face."

Gage hadn't wondered about Kopański's face, but she played ball. "Where did she get the acid from?"

"Hardware store, I guess." Kopański placed his tremendously strong hands on his immaculately pressed trousers. "But you didn't care to worry about my face."

"No, sir. I didn't."

"It doesn't frighten you?"

"I've seen far worse."

Kopański believed that. "Why did you join the FBI instead of proper law enforcement?"

Gage was motionless. "When I was a girl I read a book about the Pinkertons. That's all."

"Then you should have joined the Secret Service. Protection and anticounterfeiting are all they do. Much like the Pinkertons. You made the wrong choice in career."

Gage smiled. "Detective Kopański, are you deliberately trying to antagonize me?"

"No. Today's the anniversary of my wife's death. It means I've got other things on my mind."

Gage hadn't anticipated that. "I'm sorry."

"You have nothing to be sorry about. You didn't invent cancer." Kopański sighed. "I'm not busting your balls."

The doorbell rang. Twenty seconds later, Thyme Painter was sitting in the room. "I've heard of you, Gage. On the fast track apparently. Are you trying to be a man? Beat them at their own game?"

"No, Detective Painter."

"Then what are you doing?"

"I'm trying to raise two kids."

"Then get a job in your local twenty-four/seven." Painter looked at Kopański. "You okay, Joe?"

The huge detective wasn't going to get emotional. "I'll go to bed tonight. Tomorrow, everything will be different."

"It will." Painter stared at Gage. "You picked a bad day."

Gage was struck by the bond between the two detectives. "You both executed two perps. You're suspended. I thought that was as bad as it got."

"Then you know shit." Kopański stood.

Painter pulled him back down. "We're under investigation by internal affairs. We're on half pay while that investigation is ongoing. Joe's daughter was violated by a butcher. She's never recovered and won't speak to Joe, for the simple reason she's confused and can't stand the sight of men. She blames Joe for letting her go to the prom ten years ago. I've been trying to talk her around and I'm making progress. But meanwhile, Joe has been living in purgatory. He wants his daughter back. He's the greatest father and man on this planet." She took no heed that her words might be embarrassing Kopański. "I confronted the butcher's accomplice. What do the Feds want with us?"

Gage was unperturbed. "The evidence against you looks bad. The butcher was immobile when Joe met him. And he had bruising on his back and neck that suggested he'd been severely beaten." She looked at Kopański. "Or thrown against a wall." She returned her attention to Painter. "The woman was unlikely to pull a piece at the Fulton Fish Market. Statistically, female shooters are so rare that the probability of your account is crap."

"I'm a female shooter. So are you."

Gage took a sip of her coffee. "I'm not investigating either of you."

Painter and Kopański exchanged glances.

Gage continued: "You cannot practice law enforcement in the NYPD while under investigation. Correct?"

"Fucking correct." Kopański looked at his partner. "My daughter gets raped. I meet the guy who did it. I'm suspended."

te1
9

Gage turned her attention on Painter. "You were special forces."

"I was a helicopter pilot."

"But a Night Stalker. That's almost impossible to become. A major. Lost your leg in combat."

Painter didn't respond to that. Instead she stood and hobbled across the room. Picking up a picture, she said, "To my knowledge, this is the only picture in the house of Joe without his wife and daughter. The guy on the left you know— former commissioner of the NYPD. The guy on the right looks like shit." She winked at Joe. "He was in uniform because he was receiving the Medal of Valor. Now he's at home looking after stray cats. Times change."

Gage agreed. "Are you both happy to be sitting on your asses?"

Kopański snapped, "What do you think?"

"I think you'd prefer to be working." Gage studied the two detectives. "The issue I have is whether you're able to work on a team."

Painter asked, "A team of what?"

Gage replied, "Me, an HRT specialist called Pete Duggan, you, and Kopański."

"We're suspended!"

"Not anymore." Gage pulled out two leather wallets. "I've ensured that the deaths of the butcher and his enabler can't be pinned on you. I've told the chief of the NYPD that you've resigned and can never be tried in court. And now I'm employing you." She tossed the wallets to the cops.

They flipped them open. They were FBI shields.

Gage smiled. "You're now officially FBI agents."

Painter frowned. "You must have some major-league clout to pull this off. But for what reason?"

Gage walked to the door and turned. "Duggan and I once met a man who scared the daylights out of us. A year ago, you and Kopański met the same guy. The four of us are uniquely placed to track him."

Kopański couldn't believe what he was hearing. "Cochrane's alive?"

Gage nodded. "Report to my office in the morning. We capture Cochrane if he's innocent. We kill him if he's not."

ELEVEN

Kay Ash took an elevator to the fifth floor of the CIA headquarters, walked down a corridor, and entered a room without knocking.

Most rooms in the CIA HQ were functional, with very few personal effects on display because officers couldn't be bothered at the end of each day to clear their desks and store items in secure cabinets. It was one extra chore they didn't need, and to have left a room unattended with even just a framed photo of loved ones would have constituted a security breach.

But the room she was now in was different. It was big—way too big for one man and yet that's all it housed. It had paintings, bonsai plants, a shoe rack containing expensive loafers bought on Fifth Avenue, a humidifier that changed color every five seconds and puffed out the scent of lime, books adorning shelves (all the volumes eclectic and in foreign languages), a chalkboard containing handwritten algorithms, and a framed photo of a man receiving the CIA's highest award from the president of America—the über-rare Intelligence Cross.

But what was most striking about the room was the number of wall-mounted TV monitors. There were thirty of them, all active.

Hessian Bell had his back to Ash, standing with his arms folded, in suit pants but barefoot, watching one of the monitors. "Miss Ash. You didn't knock before entering." His Bostonian accent was clipped and precise.

The deep-cover CIA officer responded, "No, sir. I didn't."

Bell still had his back to her. "Because to have done so would have made you feel deferential. And you don't do that, do you?"

"That's not strictly true." She moved to his side and studied the monitor. "What's happening?"

Bell pointed at the monitor. "I've got a gang down there. Boys aged ten to thirteen. They live on the streets and survive however they can. They're my eyes and ears."

"Syria?"

Bell nodded. "Aleppo. They're tailing a bomb maker."

"Why don't you neutralize the target?"

"A dead terrorist's of no use to me. Plus my boys think the target has developed a conscience. I'd like to talk to a man like that. Walk with me."

He guided her to a leather armchair and sat in

the lotus position opposite her on what looked like a shrink's couch. "Now I can examine you."

This was the first time Ash and Bell had met. He was to be her new controller, her previous one having retired.

He stared at her. "I've only glanced at your file."

"Why not read it properly?"

"Because it will be filled with anodyne lies." He smiled. "What do you make of me?"

Ash thought fast. "You're single. No, your wife died. You"—she looked at the monitors—"you use your mind to grab the world."

Bell's eyes twinkled. "More please."

Ash frowned. "There's something in here. An aura." She couldn't put her finger on the ambience.

"You'll work it out. I don't ever leave this room when working."

"You have others do the running while you're thinking?"

Bell gestured to the photo of him and the president. "I once did the running. Big time. But you know, there are barbarians out there. When they capture someone, they feast on him."

Ash frowned.

"I was shot four times. Every shot was from a military-grade assault rifle. The bullets entered and exited without disturbing vital organs. It was deliberate and precise. The idea was agony, not death." Bell smiled as he put his fingertips together, his gaze penetrating. "Kay Ash. Kay Ash. What to make of you."

Ash sat still in front of the diminutive fifty-eight-year-old whose body was as subtle as his mind.

Bell's head, covered with cropped black-and-silver hair, was motionless. "You too are single. Highly educated. Dysfunctional family I'd hazard to guess. You've killed people. You don't know how that makes you feel. You were engaged once. He . . . no, you broke it off. You were once a smoker but no more. And you have no idea why you ended up in the Agency."

All of this was true, but Ash wasn't going to give Bell the satisfaction of knowing he was right. "What about you, sir? Where do you fit in here?"

"I don't fit in. And that is precisely the point."

"You must have a boss."

"If I do and you find out, please let me know."

Ash was puzzled. "You have no chain of command?"

Bell laughed. "Below me, yes. Above me?" He left the question unanswered. "Management has deliberately forgotten about me. Perhaps they find it uncomfortable that—"

"You're the only living Agency officer who has the Star."

"Maybe. Are you in awe of that?"

"No."

"Nor am I." Bell chuckled. "It's just a piece of metal. I suspect you've done braver things than me."

"I doubt that, sir."

"Kay Ash, if we are to get along, you will stop calling me 'sir.'"

"What do I call you?"

"Hessian's not a bad start." Bell uncrossed his legs. "Everything is different for you now. I'm your controller. That means I'm going to give you access to my mind."

Ash's IQ was measured at a whopping 180 during her last assessment. But she was struggling with Bell. "What's your job . . . Hessian?"

Bell grinned. "I collect waifs and strays." His smile vanished. "Why did you request that I become your new controller?"

Ash pondered her next words. "I asked for you because you're the smartest man in the Agency. And you don't give a shit about that."

"So you seek a rebel?"

"I . . . seek someone who thinks like me."

"A contrarian soul?"

"A person who doesn't conform." Ash wondered how Bell worked here undisturbed. "What do you have over them?"

Bell examined his fingernails. "In grade, I'm equivalent to the director of the CIA. Yet I have never sat in on a board meeting. Never want to. Instead, I sit here. I have nine hundred and sixty-three assets who work for me. They're spread across the globe. I'm their father. We get along just fine without interference."

"Your private army."

Bell waved a hand dismissively. "I serve the American people. There's nothing *private* about that. But I concede I have a different modus operandi from most." He smiled. "What do I have over senior management? Knowledge. I know them inside out. Everything. Their professional lives. Their private lives. They know I know. And they dare not touch me as a result."

"So you're a blackmailer as well?"

Bell's hand was still as he held it outstretched toward Ash. "Jettison all of the labels you've hurled at me. I'm someone who worries about his street urchins in Aleppo."

"I'm sorry, sir, I—"

"You can't be sorry for something you can't compute. I don't blackmail. To do so would be crass. But I do retain information in case of need. The people at the top need checks and balances. They must be held to account."

Ash looked around. "Your output is exponentially outstripping all other departments in the Agency. The president takes a personal interest in everything that comes out of this room. Without leaving this space, you spy better than anyone."

"And you want to be part of that road show?"

Ash considered the question. "No. You and I don't like glory. We want privacy."

"Yes." Bell's expression softened. "Privacy is the nub of it all. Without it, we achieve nothing. *You* don't want adoration."

"I don't."

"That's a good thing. You'd be out the door if you did."

"Sir . . . Hessian—what do you want me to do? I have no cases at present."

Bell placed the tips of his fingers back together. "Unwin Fox. Do you remember him?"

"Vaguely. About three years ago I handed him intel about a terrorist financier in Germany. That's the only contact I've had with Fox."

"You were deep cover in Berlin at the time."

"I couldn't break cover. So I handed what I knew up the Agency food chain."

"And then you were pulled out and placed on another assignment in Moscow."

"I thought you hadn't read my file."

"Only the bullet points about your work. Nothing about you as a person. It's for me to decide who you really are." Bell gestured to the door. "There are many people in this building who think I'm a renegade. You must decide if you're comfortable with that before you agree to work for me."

Ash shrugged. "I've never had a problem with breaking rules."

"Good." Bell nodded in understanding. "Unwin Fox was recently murdered. We don't know how or why. The FBI has jurisdiction and is being very tight-lipped about events. Of course, I've made inquiries, but even within the Bureau very little is known. I suspect they've set up a tiny task force and are restricting all information about the killing to that force."

"Who's in charge of the investigation?"

"Agent Marsha Gage."

"Haven't heard of her."

"You're not a cop—no reason you would have. But if you worked in law enforcement anywhere in the States, her name would mean a great deal to you."

"She's good at her job?"

"Impeccable."

"How old is she?"

Bell grinned. "You want to get the measure of her, woman to woman?"

"Partly, yes. But I also want a mental image of her."

"Forty-one. Married, two kids. Slim, brunette. Yale educated. Four-point-oh GPA in law. Top of her class. In fact, top grades in the university for decades. She's a star. But she has no political aspirations. She just wants to solve crimes. She's like you."

"I'm not domesticated."

"Despite having a family, neither is she. Don't underestimate her."

"Then what should I do to her?"

Bell picked up a pen and scrawled something on the white cuff of his shirt. "I want to know why Unwin Fox was murdered."

Anger welled in Ash. "I can't put the squeeze on Gage. That would be fundamentally illegal, dammit. Nor can I work the margins to get data. The Bureau's in lockdown. And even within the Bureau most people know nothing about Fox. I'm good at my job but this is a fool's errand!"

Bell stood and stared at his monitors. "I don't want you to spy on the Bureau. Sometimes all we can do is watch and wait."

"I don't understand."

Bell spun around. "Consider this. Three years ago you gave Fox intelligence about a financier in Germany who was planning to courier his money to Munich. Since then, Fox has done nothing. Nothing! Or so we think. Let's use our imagination. What if Fox spent the last three years being busy? It all has to do with Germany. What if there are skeletons in the closet? What if Fox was murdered because of them?"

"What if Fox was killed by a mugger?"

"And the Bureau is involved in that because . . . ?"

Ash said nothing.

"No. Agent Gage is involved because this is a hot potato. The Feds wouldn't waste such valuable talent otherwise." Bell sounded like he was addressing a class of new CIA recruits. "But there is a problem. What is it?"

Ash thought fast. "Unwin Fox was a senior CIA officer. If it was a state-sponsored murder, details of the investigation would have to be shared with the Agency. But they're not being shared."

"Ergo?"

"Ergo it's a criminal matter, not a spy matter."

"Of course. In their eyes at least. But do we trust the Bureau to make that judgment?"

"Yes. The Bureau is world-class when it comes to solving issues. If it thinks this is a criminal matter, it is. Plus, they've put their best bloodhound on the case."

"I concur." Bell wondered if Ash was thinking what he was thinking. "There are, however, blurred lines. What are the odds of a senior Agency official being murdered for petty crime reasons?"

"Slim to dim."

"*Slim to dim.*" Bell liked that phrase. "I think there is more afoot here than meets the eye."

"But I can't go deep cover into the Bureau. That's an impossible task."

"I'm not asking you to go deep cover. If I'm correct and this has to do with Germany, all I need you to do is stay still."

"Still?"

Bell didn't elaborate. "Just keep me informed if anything Fox-related rears its head. Aside from that, I have no tasks for you. Protocol dictates a minimum of three weeks' decompression after deep cover. I'm adhering to that. I want you to rest and lead your daily normal existence. When I have something substantial for you to work on, I'll give you a call. Meanwhile, you can come and go in this building as you choose." Bell walked right up to her. "You've just completed a rather dangerous assignment in Seoul. You need to rest. Three weeks. Theater, cinema, bars, men, gym—whatever floats your boat. Decompress. You'll know when you need to find me."

"Know?"

"Know." Bell's demeanor changed to one of absolute calm. "Something or nothing always happens. If I'm right and it's something, run here as fast as you can."

TWELVE

Kay Ash entered the digital key code to access the communal hallway of the apartment block she lived in within Bethesda. The residential district was popular among CIA officers due to its proximity to Langley. As a result, the Agency ensured that the buildings housing its best officers had top-notch security. It had to be that way. Operatives like Ash were away for long periods of time. When they came home they needed a secure refuge where the troubles of the outside world didn't intrude on their rare downtime.

Ash walked up four flights of stairs and unlocked three state-of-the-art dead bolts in her apartment front door. It was seven P.M. and she could hear her neighbors' voices and the *chink* of dinner plates. Outside was pitch-dark. Inside, there was the dim glow of the hallway lamps and the occasional flashing of a red light in a smoke detector. Ash was the only Agency officer living in the twelve-apartment building. Single CIA officers were never housed together in case of acts of crime, fire, or terror attacks.

Ash was glad of that. The last thing she needed was to come home and encounter other Agency officers who'd pry about where she'd been and why. Her solitude was sacrosanct, particularly after deployment in hellholes around the world or with people who'd slit her throat given half a chance.

She was typically away for months and in one case two years. Her apartment, she'd long ago decided, was her safe place. When she'd had guns pointed at her, men gripping her throat, U.S. drones dropping precision missiles near her, and a shovel in her hand while she dug a shallow grave, she told herself that her apartment was her safe place.

Ma and Pa hadn't given her hope. Physical and mental abuse was rife in her family, and she bore a lot of the brunt of hostilities. Ma was a fiend when intoxicated with gin. Pa had been sober since he was twenty-four years old, but he lashed out when stressed. They were dysfunctional. They should never have gotten married and had kids. But she couldn't forgive them for that. When you're twelve and you haven't been fed dinner by your ma and your father comes home and whips your ma because she's drunk and irresponsible, love goes out the window.

She was sure that was why she felt no fear.

When all constructive love is stripped away, there is resigned calm. Nothing was worse than or even comparable to her childhood.

She entered her apartment and locked the bolts behind her. Breathing deeply and with relief, she wondered about ordering pizza. First, she needed a shower. She moved through the tiny one-bedroom apartment and stripped off her clothes. It was her ritual: cleansing herself of her job.

She placed her gun in the living room and stood under steaming water in her bathroom's shower. Soaps, shampoo, and conditioner applied and rinsed, she wrapped herself in a white towel and reentered the living room.

That's when she sensed his presence.

She flicked on the overhead light but it didn't work.

She dashed to a lamp and turned it on. The light worked and shone across the room, showing a shadow in the corner where a man was seated in her armchair. His upper body was in darkness.

She picked up her gun and pointed it at the shadow. "Whoever you are, you picked the wrong house!"

The shadow said nothing.

"I'm an agent of the United States government. That means I can shoot you with zero worries about a trial."

Her voice was the only sound.

"If you're here to rob me, rape me, or kill me, know this: I'll put a bullet in your head without hesitation."

"Try." The man's voice was calm, yet commanding.

Ash hadn't expected that response. She pointed her gun one foot away from the shadow and pulled the trigger. *Click.* A misfire. She tried again. Same thing happened.

"Weapons are of no use with me." The man's voice was deep, yet beguiling. "They're crass tools. I make it a habit to ensure they mean me no harm."

Urgently, Ash stripped the weapon. The firing pin was missing. "I didn't aim at your head. Think about that."

"I already have."

"I don't know who you are or why you're here!" Ash tossed her useless gun to one side. "If I scream, the door will be kicked in within seconds."

"Because you think you have people nearby? Laughter and the sounds of dining can easily be placed on a recorder. Your neighbors are sleeping. They'll wake in a few hours, alive but bruised."

"I don't believe you." Ash glanced at her phone.

"The cable's cut. Even if it wasn't, it would take the cops at least three minutes to get here. And when they enter the door, it would be over for them."

Ash wondered about running to her kitchen and grabbing a knife. "You don't scare me! You picked the wrong woman!"

"I picked the right woman." The shadow asked, "Why aren't you scared?"

Ash tightened the knot in her bath towel. "Because I deal with punks all the time. And I've survived all of their crap."

"Turn on the overhead light."

"I did. It doesn't work. You've removed the bulb or tripped the switch."

"Try again."

Ash hesitated, then flicked the switch. The room was bathed in light.

There were no longer any shadows.

Ash stood stock-still. "You!"

"You know me?"

"Yes. Your face. I know you."

"My name?"

Ash held her ground, wishing she had a backup weapon. "It's a dead name."

He stood. "And you fear the dead?"

"No." Ash braced herself in case he attacked her. "We thought you were dead. We hoped you were dead. You should be dead."

He strode up to her and placed her gun's firing pin in her hand. "You don't need to fear me."

"I don't fear you. But it stands to reason that I don't want you, of all people, in my apartment."

He caressed her face. "I'm not here to hurt you."

"You kill people." Her voice was cold. "You always kill."

"Not today." The man towered over her. "Instead, I'm here to work with you. Say my name!"

Ash spat, "You could just walk away from here. I don't need to tell anyone about you."

"That comment undermines your intelligence.

No way would you keep our little encounter to yourself. Who am I?!"

"Go to hell."

"I've been there. And now I'm back in the land of the living."

She looked at his blue and green eyes and for a moment wondered what it must be like to look out of them and see the things he'd seen. "You don't wish me harm?"

He shook his head. "I'd have killed you in the shower if I'd wanted to."

For some reason, the thought of him observing her naked perturbed her more than death.

He sensed that. "Don't worry. Your dignity is intact. I'm a gentleman. I averted my gaze."

"You're anything but a *gentleman*! But . . ." Was she seriously considering thanking him for not gawking at her naked body? "How did you get in here?"

"I've infiltrated prisons, military bases, embassies, and other high-security facilities. This was child's play. Get dressed." He backed away and retook his seat. "I'll wait."

"My bedroom's out of your view. I could run."

"Yes, you could. And I wouldn't pursue."

Her towel started to loosen. She grabbed the knot and held the garment firm.

"For the sake of avoiding both of us blushing, I suggest you get into something more substantial." The man was so still it was unsettling, his eyes fixed on hers. "Will you return to your living room? Or will you run?"

Ash felt like she was entranced. "One is a dumb option. The other is astute."

"There is a third way. You're a spy. Intrigue interests you."

"Yes, it does." She recalled what Hessian Bell had said to her and now understood what he meant. He'd told her to do nothing because she didn't need to do anything. He'd made her a tethered goat, knowing Fox's murderer would come after her. *Clever bastard*, she thought. But should she trust the man in the room? Or turn and bolt? Or risk her life and stay to find out what was going on? She made a decision. "I'll get dressed and return."

"That's the right choice."

She hesitated, the hand holding the upper hem of her towel dropping to her side. "Your name . . ."

"Yes?"

"Your name is Will Cochrane."

THIRTEEN

Eight miles south of D.C., the smells of dying rosemary and basil and the sight of bare flames from torches on Howard Kane's rooftop apartment in Alexandria barely registered in his mind.

For years, Kane had cultivated the rooftop to comprise troughs of manure-infused soil containing tomatoes, corn, beans, flowers, and chilies. But a frost was upon Alexandria and he had neither the inclination nor the expertise to extend the growing season. He always harvested, then let the plants die in the first cold snap. Then he lit the flames atop the roof as if they were a symbolic farewell to life that had existed for only two seasons. And in spring he'd replant new shoots.

Dark now, Kane watched nightlife twenty-one stories below him. Car horns honked as vehicles traveled slowly, headlights on full, a fine icy drizzle doing nothing to dampen the torches.

The son of a highly skilled welder who married a breast surgeon, Kane was brother to two men and one woman: a merchant navy captain, a priest, and a doctor. The four children were naturally gifted, exceeding their parents' intellects in leaps and bounds, though they lacked the physicality of their father and the precision of their mother. Kane was the brightest of them all, despite a cleft palate when he was young that his mother cut out, and being wrongly diagnosed as autistic by shrinks and a foot shorter than his father and brothers. He was loved by his parents and siblings because he could perform magic tricks and cook Lebanese meze.

He recalled three years ago being in Haden's Pentagon office. Fox and Sapper were with him.

Haden had said, "I've called this meeting in strictest confidence. Nothing we speak about must leave this room. If anyone objects to that, exit now."

The room was silent.

Haden proceeded. "Fox, tell them what you told me."

The CIA officer said, "One of my deep-cover officers has located the financier. He's in Berlin and plans to travel to Munich with five million dollars. There, he'll hand the cash over to a terror cell."

"What are you going to do?" asked Sapper.

Fox looked at Kane. "Are you sure you're cleared for this discussion?"

Haden interjected. "He's my deputy. We don't hide secrets from each other. Plus, I need his brain."

Fox had looked uncertain as he continued. "Officially, there is only one thing we can do. We notify the Germans and let them deal with the matter. But . . ."

"But?" asked Kane.

"But that means we lose control. The Germans will seek to enforce due process of law. There's nothing illegal about couriering cash. They'd have to prove his purpose."

"We know his purpose!" snapped Sapper. "We've been trying to get this guy for years!"

"*We* being America. Germany is a different jurisdiction. And it has a more liberal judiciary. Our suspicions and evidence will not carry much weight in their courts. There's every possibility the financier will get off."

"That can't happen!" Haden paced back and forth. "Otto Raeder is an anarchist for hire. He funds whichever terrorist group takes his fancy at any one time." He pointed at Fox. "I remember the Agency's assessment of his motivation—he's a mischief maker, is what you said. He wants to see the world burn."

Fox nodded. "Tracking him has been the problem. This is the best lead we've had and our best opportunity to stop him once and for all. The intel says Raeder can't make the cash-run for a few days, because the terror cell's not yet assembled in Munich. Regardless, we have to move fast and make a decision now."

Haden stopped pacing and asked Sapper, "The likelihood of Capitol Hill authorizing a covert U.S. assault on Raeder on German soil?"

"Zero." The senator adjusted her chiffon scarf. "And if I take this to the Hill, this will be blown wide open. We'll lose control and have to trust the Germans to get it right."

"And Germany will not hit first and ask questions later." Fox was deep in thought. "Raeder is a German national. Most of the evidence we have on him has not been shared with the Germans. They'll take this as a cold case. Bureaucracy will kick in. Raeder will at best be arrested or at worst vanish."

"Shit!" Haden started pacing again. He addressed Fox. "Why did you bring this to us? By all accounts, my spec op units can't be involved."

The CIA officer replied, "Because we think the same."

Sapper laughed, making no effort to hide her sarcasm.

Fox was unperturbed. "I didn't say we *liked* each other. But if I wanted to have a conversation about Raeder without Congress, the White House, the Pentagon, and the CIA knowing, then this is the room I want to be in."

Haden frowned. "You haven't told the CIA what you know?"

Fox shook his head. "I brought this to you first. The Agency deep-cover officer—her name's Kay; I'm not giving you her surname—has relocated to another assignment. That's how it works. Her intel landed on my desk in CT."

Counterterrorism.

"I sat on the data for a day. Now I'm here."

Haden glanced at Kane. "Thoughts?"

Howard Kane looked around the room. Beautiful yet vicious Charlie Sapper. Untrustworthy Unwin Fox. Insane Colonel Haden. That's how he thought of them right now. But that didn't influence his thinking. Instead, he was focused on getting a solution to the problem of Otto Raeder. "You will not be the only person in CIA HQ who knows about the Raeder intel," he said to Fox.

"No. There are a handful of people who will have been privy to the information. But it's off their desks. And now they've got a thousand other terrorists to worry about. Raeder's my problem. They've forgotten about him and moved on."

"And your deep-cover officer, Kay?" Though only a few years younger than Fox, Kane wondered how the senior CIA officer felt being asked questions by a Pentagon staffer who was two grades beneath him. "You're sure she's out of the picture?"

"She has to be. New identity. New mission. She gets intel, passes it on, goes dark again, moves to other assignments."

Kane was pulling the strands together. "So this room is where information is kept and decisions are made . . . or not."

Sapper, Fox, and Haden were silent as they watched him.

"And we have three stark choices: inform the Germans about Raeder; do nothing; or do something."

Sapper raised an eyebrow. "Do *something*?"

Kane didn't know how far he should push this. Haden was staring at him like a creature that would strike him if he did the wrong thing. "The problem is Raeder. We don't benefit from him, do we?"

Fox laughed. "No, we don't."

"His money kills lots of people, yes?"

The CIA officer agreed. "A shit ton."

"He has financial resources that we can't quantify, but let's assume it's many millions."

Fox said, "Hundreds. Maybe much more."

"So he's virtually unstoppable."

"*Virtually?*" Haden was deliberately being antagonistic to his protégé because Sapper and Fox were in the room, but he was intrigued to hear what Kane meant. "Are you saying what I think you're saying?"

Kane smiled. "The solution is obvious. We kill Raeder. And no one outside of this room need ever know."

"And how do we do that?" asked Sapper.

Kane looked at Fox. "There's one man who could do it. We both know who he is. My question to you is can he be activated?"

Fox was silent for thirty seconds. "Yes. But only I can activate him. I act as cutout. He's a friend of mine. I don't want to give him any details other than those essential to the mission."

Kane agreed. "The less he knows the better. The four of us take what we know to our graves." He looked at Haden. "Sir, I have a team of four ex–Green Berets at my disposal. They're efficient and don't ask questions. They can dispose of Raeder's body. But I'm not a military man. Can you tell us how we kill Raeder?"

The ex–Delta Force colonel replied, "Raeder needs to be put under surveillance for a few days. We watch for patterns of behavior. At some point he'll do something out of the ordinary. That'll be when he does his money run. We bring in Fox's shooter. Your Green Berets can tail Raeder and provide the shooter with proof of ID. The shot needs to be outside Berlin, somewhere remote. Your team then grabs Raeder's body and burns his car."

"That sounds watertight." Fox looked at Sapper. "What do you think?"

The senator shrugged. "How it's done is not my area of expertise. What happens if things go wrong is. Just make sure he's dead and there are no traces that lead to us."

"Then it's agreed." Haden was commanding as he said, "Mr. Kane, I'm relying on you to spot any flaws in my plan."

Kane was deep in thought. "Central to this job is minimizing information to any others involved. My assets are good. They will need to know that Raeder is the target, but at this stage I don't want them to know this isn't state sanctioned. I want them to mop up the mess, but I'd prefer they didn't call the shot. That would make them complicit in murder. I trust them, but it's always a numbers game. There are four of them. There's always the danger one of them will talk. I can't look you in the eye and say hand on heart that I can guarantee absolute secrecy. Therefore, I'd rather they didn't call the shot."

Haden agreed. "I'll do it. Beats hanging around here in a suit."

Kane was delighted with the colonel's conclusion. "Plus you have the training to follow someone without him knowing you're on his tail. It's settled. Colonel Haden follows Raeder until the financier makes his cash-run. He tells the shooter to make the kill when there's guaranteed proof of ID. My team grabs Raeder. The colonel makes sure my team covers up all traces of the kill. The shooter exits Germany. And no one but us on either side of the Pond will ever know what happened."

Under the command of General Stanley McChrystal during his tenure as head of the ultrasecret activities of Joint Special Operations Command in Iraq, Haden had been in charge of one of the task forces responsible for door-kicking missions. Based on CIA and JSOC intelligence, night after night he and his Delta, SEAL, and British SAS and SBS colleagues went out into urban and rural locales and hunted down insurgents. And though a senior officer, Haden made a point of always being on at least one of the daily missions. It gained him enormous respect from his men, though some of them wondered if it was bloodlust. Officers were on the ground to strategize and command from JSOC bases, not smash through entrances and shoot occupants.

Frequently, he flagrantly disobeyed orders and rules of engagement, though his successes were so significant that nobody questioned his methods. Except on one occasion.

He and a four-man JSOC team had entered a dwelling in Baghdad to capture or kill an Iraqi who'd blown up three marine vehicles. But the terrorist wasn't in the building. Instead his wife and two children were there eating supper. The colonel hadn't hesitated. He went up to the mother and smashed the butt of his rifle into her face, rendering her unconscious. Then he turned on the young adolescent kids. They were crying and in shock. Haden was screaming at them, trying to ascertain the whereabouts of their father. They were shaking their heads, blurting out in Arabic that they didn't know. Haden pulled out a length of rope and made it into a hangman's knot. After stringing it to the ceiling, he forced one of the boys to stand on a chair with the noose around his throat.

To the other boy, Haden said in Arabic, "You choose. You tell me where your father is, or I kick the chair and let your brother dangle."

Haden's men had tried to interject, but Haden ignored them.

"Tell me where the asshole is or your brother dies!"

This carried on for ten minutes, both brothers petrified and having no knowledge of where their father was. Exasperated, Haden kicked the chair. The boy's legs flailed frantically in the air while the other boy screamed. But two of the JSOC men rushed to the rope and cut him down while the other two trained their guns on Haden.

"Not on our watch, sir," said a seasoned SEAL Team Six operative.

"And I'll shoot you, pal, if you lay another hand on them," added a veteran SAS soldier.

The hanged boy had bruising around his throat but would live. It would all have been different for him within seconds had the two U.S. operatives not cut him free.

Haden was furious and pulled out his side-arm, pointing it at each of his men respectively. "You think I give a shit about your consciences?! I could have you court-martialed!"

One of the men replied, "We're witnesses. We could have you court-martialed."

Haden went up to the man and shoved the muzzle of his pistol against his head. "I answer to the president and God. And I'm on friendly speaking terms with both. You want to try your luck in a military court?"

The man said nothing.

"Give it a try! Let's see who comes out on top!"

The incident was never mentioned by the four men, though they stayed on for two more years in JSOC for one reason only: to keep an eye on Haden.

Years on, Haden was no longer their problem. But he was a massive problem for Kane and Cochrane.

FOURTEEN

Ash wondered what the hell she was doing as she finished getting dressed and reentered her living room.

Will was still in her armchair, no visible weapon, his eyes following her as she took a seat opposite him.

She asked, "What do you want?"

"I want you to break rules."

"You've misjudged me."

"Have I?" Will leaned forward. "Deep-cover officers serve no one. They survive by their wits. And when it all goes tits up, they get scant support from their employer. You don't have loyalty to the Agency. You're simply on its payroll."

"*Tits up?* Seems you've dropped your American predisposition."

"English was always my first language." Will smiled. "You once served undercover in London, spying on our economic strategies with the European Union. You know our terminology."

"How did you know I served there?"

Will waved his hand. "Irrelevant. What's pertinent is the here and now."

"Which is what?"

Will gestured to the walls. "Framed quality posters of Rembrandt, Renoir, Caravaggio, and Degas." He swept his hand. "Sculptures from Tibet, Peru, and Java. A mounted Arabic dirk. A library of jazz vinyl and Iranian poetry. That's a lot of effort for a woman who's rarely here. You see and embrace the world but you don't like the prism that gives you that knowledge. Yet you collect beauty when you can. You're an adventurer, not a spy."

This was true. But Ash said, "You know nothing about me!"

Will shook his head. "Is that true?"

Ash kept her mouth shut.

He looked like he was mentally undressing her. "Three years ago you were deep cover in Berlin. You secured evidence about Otto Raeder. You passed that evidence to Unwin Fox. As a result, I was brought in. My mission was clear: exterminate the financier. The morality pertaining to that mission was unquestionable. Raeder was couriering five million dollars to jihadists in Munich. They were going to use that money to set Europe ablaze. I got in the way."

Ash frowned. "I didn't know what happened after I handed my intel over. It wasn't my job to know."

"But now you know."

"And I don't see a problem with what you did."

"Nor do I, on paper. But here's the issue: the mission wasn't officially sanctioned. Fox took your intel to a guy in the Pentagon called Colonel Haden. Have you heard of him?"

"Of course. The Delta Force commander. A big name. A bit crazy, I heard. But supremely effective."

"A bit crazy?" Will smiled. "That's an understatement. More important, why would Fox go to him rather than his superiors in the Agency?"

Ash thought fast. "This is fishy."

"Yes, it is."

"And you didn't know at the time?"

Will was forthright. "No. Like you, I was brought in to do a job and then vanish. But *think*. Why did it happen this way?"

"You sound like my boss!"

"Who is . . . ?"

"Hessian Bell."

"Ah, Mr. Bell. I pulled bullets out of him once. He started breathing again. Send him my regards. He'll remember me." Will turned serious. "Bell is a very decent man. Treat him right. He's smart, and his heart is exactly where it should be."

"As smart as you?"

"You be the judge of that."

"And your heart?"

"It's where it's always been." Will thought Ash was a beautiful woman, but she clearly put up defenses—probably the reason she was alone.

"The question still is: Why did Berlin happen this way?"

"Sanctions from Capitol Hill to do a hit on German soil were impossible. The mission would have to be handed over to the Germans. Somebody in the States decided to keep this off the books."

Ash asked, "Haden?"

"I believe it was my friend Unwin Fox's idea. But I also believe he lost control of that idea when he brought Haden and others into his confidence."

Ash frowned. "Where is Haden?"

"He vanished on the day I killed Raeder."

"In Berlin?"

"Yes. He was tailing the target in his car. His job was to call my shot."

"How far was he behind Raeder?"

Cochrane answered, "Haden was in front. Distance varied, but never farther than a few hundred yards."

"Close enough to get to Raeder's dead body and take his cash before the cleanup team moved in to dispose of the body."

"Clever, Miss Ash."

"And that was the last we heard of Haden. I can see where your thinking is going. But there's no proof of any of this."

Will stood. "Unwin Fox is dead."

"How?!"

Will sighed. "He was dying and in agony. There was no way back for him. He asked me to put him out of his misery." He stared at the wall as he whispered, "He was my friend."

Blood drained from Ash's face. "So, you're still the same man you always were."

Will's voice steeled as he returned his gaze to Ash. "He was poisoned, but not by me. But he managed to tell me that what happened in Berlin was a lie and Haden was behind it all. Alongside Fox and Haden, there were two others involved in the Berlin operation. In order to get to Haden, I need their names. They may know where Haden is."

"If I do that I might be committing treason."

"But you might not be." Will pointed at her. "None of what happened in Berlin was your fault. But like it or not, you set the ball rolling."

"I have no reason to work for you!"

"You do if in any way you want to understand the events that happened after you handed your Raeder intel to Fox." A thought occurred to him. "Tell Hessian Bell about this meeting and our conversation. He might put the cops on me, but I'm willing to take that risk. See what he says before making a decision." Will picked up his coat and walked to the door. "I've left my cell phone number on your bedside table. I'd like you to call me when you find anything out. First, I need you to establish the address of Haden's wife."

The comment surprised Ash. "And if I agree to this, what are you going to do?"

Will didn't say that he was certain his captured image in the D.C. park had been escalated up the law enforcement food chain to the Feds; that zero press releases and media coverage meant he was being hunted off the radar; that he suspected he knew whom he was being hunted by and that the female FBI agent had not a hope in hell of tracking him unless he gave her a trail. Nor did he say that the trail had to help him clear his name while also confuse the Feds. Instead, he said, "I suspect misdirection is at play. But I can play that game as well."

Ash stared at the handsome man and saw something she hadn't seen before: sorrow. "I don't think you killed the people they say you did in Virginia."

Will smiled, though his expression was resigned. "Does it matter whether I killed anyone there? I've killed so many others. Bad guys and girls for sure. But maybe if I let them live they would have changed."

"Or maybe not."

Will looked at Ash's art. "You have a nice apartment. But it doesn't feel like your home."

Ash stood. "You wish me no harm?"

"Why would I?"

"Because you kill. We made you into this."

"Killing is not my favorite job." Will's eyes seemed distant. "They could never get to all of me."

"*They?*"

"My masters. And now I have no masters." He took a step forward again.

Ash recoiled.

But this time Will didn't step back. "I didn't kill the people they say I did in Virginia. Others, yes, but they were the kidnappers of a ten-year-old boy. I slaughtered eight men and women who did that. Does that worry you?"

"Yes."

"Then you're not me." Will stood right in front of her. "It's my burden."

"We all carry burdens."

Will wondered if he could trust Ash with what he was about to say. "When I was in British intelligence, I was put in a top-secret training and selection course. It was twelve months long. Only one person at a time was allowed in the MI6 Spartan Program. They all died on it or were invalided out. Somehow, I got through."

Ash was stationary in front of the big man. "It broke your mind but not your body."

Will answered, "No. It's more complicated than that. They tried to snap everything in me and carve me into what they wanted. But I clung on. If a person loses all vestiges of himself, he becomes inhuman."

"Robotic?"

"A slave." Will touched her hand. "I answer to no man or woman. Will you help me?"

"I *may* try to help you. But what are you going to do?"

Will pulled out his handgun and tapped it against Ash. "I'm going after Haden. And then I will get the truth."

Marsha Gage, Thyme Painter, Joe Kopański, and Pete Duggan assembled in a house on Gloucester Drive in Lynchburg, Virginia.

The place was a detached residential building, four bedrooms, and in an area of the city that was suburban and quiet, though there were other residences spread along the street. It looked like a normal home belonging to a family who parked their two black SUVs in the driveway and kept to themselves.

Inside was tastefully decorated yet functional, and way too immaculate for a family who used the place on a day-to-day basis. It was a Bureau safe house, maintained by a housekeeper on the Feds' books who'd vacated the building to make space for the tiny team hunting Will Cochrane.

"Why do we have to be here?" growled Kopański as he watched Duggan stripping and cleaning a submachine gun.

Gage replied, "To minimize leakage. We don't want tongues wagging in the Hoover Building. This is a safe house for a reason." She withdrew her sidearm and handed it to Duggan.

Kopański walked up to Duggan and looked at the array of weapons next to him on the sideboard. "What are you doing, son?"

The weapons were four apiece: Springfield Custom Professional 1911-A1 .45ACP pistols, MP5/10 submachine guns, and Remington 870 twelve-gauge shotguns. Alongside them was a single Remington 700 sniper rifle, covert communications equipment, hundreds of laundered hundred-dollar bills, zoom lens cameras, police radio intercepts, body armor, flash-bang grenades, photos of Cochrane, and a letter from the

attorney general—countersigned by the director
of the FBI and the president—saying that Gage
had full authority to do whatever the hell she
liked to bring Cochrane to justice.

Duggan picked up the sniper rifle. "This is
mine. The rest are upgrades for the team. I need
your and Painter's sidearms. In return, you get
the ACPs. They're elephant killers."

Kopański pulled out his Webley .455. "I once
used this to knock a three-hundred-pound man
off his feet. His mashed skull disintegrated on a
sidewalk in Charlestown. If you don't mind, *boy*,
I'll keep it."

Duggan held out his hand. "Can I look?"

Kopański hesitated, then handed his beloved
weapon to the former SEAL Team Six operative.

Duggan weighed the heavy pistol in his hand.
"It's a superb hostile-stopper. But my God, it re-
quires strength to fire. You sure about this?"

Kopański nodded. "It's killed things."

Duggan checked the workings. "You keep it
excellently prepped."

"I'm older than you, Duggan. Men my age get
achy after a while. Keeping a gun clean and well
oiled is all we have."

Duggan saw no evidence of weakness in Kopański. On the contrary, the tall man looked like he
could snap the HRT leader's neck if his mood
took him that way. "Where did you get this? It's
British World War II issue."

Kopański was granite still. "You know your
weaponry."

"You haven't answered my question. And I thought your weapons were requisitioned by the NYPD, pending investigation."

Painter walked up to the sideboard. "Joe always has contingency plans." She placed her backup weapon on the table. "Me too. I'll take your ACP. Leave Joe to shoot his own gun. It never fails him."

Duggan smiled. "Agent Painter, I just need to know we're properly equipped."

Painter took the ACP and spare magazines. "We know. It's just . . . Joe and I have worked so long together without backup. This is new to us."

Duggan returned his attention to Kopański. "Where did you get the Webley?"

It was Painter who answered. "Joe's father was Polish and worked for the British Special Operations Executive. He was parachuted into France and the Netherlands in the early forties and rallied resistance. He blew up German trains and bases, and hunted down Nazis." She touched Joe's gun. "This never left his side. You have your elephant killers. Joe has his Nazi killer."

Duggan nodded slowly. "The Webley has a hell of a recoil. I've only fired it on one occasion on a range. Couldn't hit the damn target at first. But when I did it made one god-awful mess of the target." He handed the weapon back to Joe. "It's a six-shooter revolver, but you'll only need one bullet. Even a leg shot will kill an enemy. The Webley is yours. It will do the job. Just don't miss."

"He never does," said Painter.

Gage had been watching the exchange, silent. Now was time to exert her authority. She summoned them over. "On two occasions we tried to flush Cochrane out with massive media exposure. Both times we failed because he outplayed us. So this time it's just the four of us doing the hunting. How do we capture him?"

Duggan replied, "He was last spotted in D.C. so this is the reason for the safe house in Virginia. We're nearby. You think he might still be local."

Kopański added, "But he might be a thousand miles from here. This could be a wild goose chase."

Painter touched Kopański's hand. "Two things keep Cochrane rooted here. The first is his alleged crimes. The second is Unwin Fox. Cochrane's not a psychopath. He wants answers. And he won't stray until he gets them."

"Answers to what?" asked Duggan.

"Answers to why he had to put Fox out of his misery." Painter addressed Kopański. "Josef, what makes Cochrane tick?"

The Polish American glanced at Gage by his side, then looked back at Painter. "Some people burn from the inside. Good and bad people. It defines them one way or the other. I think Cochrane's a good man, but I won't gamble my new badge on that. Cochrane is an angel."

Painter frowned. "Meaning what?"

"He's fallen to earth, but he's not one of us. He's here to make sense of it all. Shepherd us; protect us; punish us." Kopański pulled out his Webley and spun the chamber. "The Brits have a problem. Out of a population of sixty million, or whatever it is, they choose just seven hundred who are the top of the tree. They turn them into MI6 operatives—angels. But those seven hundred don't really like each other because angels aren't designed to rub shoulders. They tolerate each other. They're not pack animals. They're loners. And they look at the rest of us like we're victims or trash. They save or kill. That's Cochrane."

Gage shook her head. "I've looked Cochrane in the eye. He doesn't view anyone as trash."

Kopański disagreed. "He kills trash."

"Yet it saddens him."

"Because he wishes there was no trash."

"Yes." Gage checked her ACP. "Tonight we're going to kick a door down. Pete will be taking point. Make no mistake—this is going to be very tricky."

It was nine P.M. and dark as Kay Ash entered the CIA HQ in Langley. Wearing the same jeans and sweater she'd changed into when confronting Will, she walked through the largely deserted building and entered Hessian Bell's office.

The CIA controller was in a black tuxedo suit and bow tie. "This had better be good" was all he said when he saw her.

Ash hesitated. "I'm sorry I disturbed your evening."

Bell didn't like that comment. "I was on a first date. Middle-aged woman. Same interests as me. We met on a dating site and she told me she liked

La Traviata. So I thought I'd take her to the Kennedy Center tonight for the opera. We were at intermission when I got your call. I had to leave her there. Guess I'll never see her again." Bell looked wistful. "It was my first date since Maureen died."

Under other circumstances and with other men, Ash would have been tempted to apologize. But Bell wouldn't have taken kindly to that. "If you give me her number, I'll call her and explain. It might sound better coming from a woman."

Bell eyed her. "I might hold you to that. Right—get on with it."

"You set me up."

Bell was silent.

"Something or nothing always happens, you said. And you thought that in the case of Unwin Fox's murder it would be something. You positioned me as bait."

"And clearly *something* has happened. This evening."

Ash folded her arms. "Perhaps it happened quicker than you anticipated."

Bell leaned against his desk. "I don't have enough facts to make time-sensitive predictions. I made a guess that Fox's death had to do with the German intel you supplied. Was I correct?"

"Yes."

"And you know this because someone involved in the operation approached you this evening."

Ash nodded.

"Then we have a tangled knot to untie. Give me details."

Ash took a seat on an antique chaise longue. "How much do you know about what happened after I supplied the intel about Otto Raeder?"

"Nothing."

"Are you sure?"

Bell stood. "Yes, I'm damn sure!"

Ash could see that he was telling the truth. "Then we have a big problem."

Bell waited expectantly.

"The man who murdered Unwin Fox visited me this evening. He told me to speak to you."

Bell frowned.

"He said that in doing so he fully realized you might turn him in to the police. But he also said he once dug bullets out of you. I presume he saved your life."

Bell rubbed his face. "A tall man? Half-English? Half-American? Built like a prizefighter? But extremely smart?"

"Yes."

Bell sounded distant as he said, "It was in Hong Kong. Kowloon, to be precise. Eight years ago. I was deep cover, trying to get alongside Asia's biggest arms dealer. My cover was blown by an asset who was working both sides. The dealer's men punished me and dumped my body in the estuary. It was too complicated for local CIA assets to get to me. So Cochrane stepped in and did the job alone. He pulled me out of the estuary and performed emergency medical care. And he shot a few people to get to me." Bell pointed at the framed photo of him receiving the Intelligence Star from the U.S. president. "I'm not the

only living spy to have the Star. For his actions
that night, Cochrane was awarded the Star."

"But he's a Brit and back then wasn't joint with
the Agency. He was purely MI6."

"It didn't matter." Bell picked up the photo off
a shelf. "Given what I've just told you, Cochrane
would have deserved our highest award. But here's
the thing: after he got me to the embassy, he
turned around and went back to the arms dealer's
men. I don't know how many men he killed, but
it was a lot. He should have gotten a second Star
for that." Bell placed the photo back down. "Cochrane is alive. He killed Unwin Fox. He visited
you tonight." The controller stared at Ash.

"Correct."

"Motive for killing Fox?"

"He said it was a mercy killing, that Fox had
been poisoned by someone else."

"How is Cochrane alive?"

"He faked his death."

"Accurate." Bell started pacing. "He was involved in the German operation. I suggest he
was brought in to kill Otto Raeder."

"And yet no one in the Agency knows what
happened."

Bell stopped moving. "What did Cochrane
say to you?"

Ash felt like she was in the presence of an unstoppable intellectual force. "He said that my intel was taken by Unwin Fox to Colonel Haden in
the Pentagon."

Bell's expression was neutral. "Cochrane won-
ders why that breach of protocol occurred. He

also suspects one or two others were privy to your intel. He wants their names."

"He also wants me to give him the address of Mrs. Haden."

"Give it to him."

"What?!"

"Give it to him." Bell sat again on his desk. "Cochrane used you to get to me, and I'm using you to get back to him. Don't get prissy about that fact. You know, I know, and Cochrane knows what we're doing. In fact, Cochrane has orchestrated this. I told you there are two CIAs: the one outside my door and the one inside this room. Tell no one about what's happened. Trust no one apart from me and Cochrane."

"Trust Cochrane?!"

"Yes. He needs our help. You're my insider. This is what you do best. You got that?"

Ash pondered this assessment. Being deep cover was her lifeblood. She smiled. "Damn right."

"Good." Bell glanced at his watch and sighed. "You may have to call my date. She's a lovely person." His expression steeled. "Find out everything you can about what happened after you handed your intel over to Unwin Fox. Give that data to me and Cochrane. From here on in, carry a sidearm at all times."

FIFTEEN

It was close to two A.M. when Gage, Painter, Kopański, and Duggan pulled up in their SUV on a residential street in Queens, New York City. The sound of traffic was in the distance, but the road they were on was quiet and deserted. Streetlamps were on, so too some house lights, though the majority of the street was bathed in darkness. Gage told Duggan to stop the vehicle and extinguish the headlights.

She peered over her shoulder at Kopański and Painter. "Now that we're here, I can tell you why. But first I have to make a call." She hit a number on her cell. "This is Agent Gage. Cut surveillance with immediate effect and get out of the zone. We're taking over." She ended the call and addressed the former NYPD detectives. "In the house behind the sixth streetlamp away from us is an extremely dangerous man. We've been watching him for a year. So far he's done nothing wrong. Probably that means he knows he's being watched. Why he's here interests us. And we have a theory why he's here."

Painter asked, "You think he's relevant to getting to Cochrane?"

"He's as relevant as can be." Gage pulled out her ACP handgun and addressed Duggan. "Don't take any chances."

Duggan nodded. "Yes, ma'am."

"Don't call me ma'am." Gage returned her attention to Kopański and Painter. "He's on his own, though he's got a dog called Mr. Peres. The dog's no threat. He's a mongrel and as docile as they come. Plus he has arthritis in his back legs. His owner is thirty-five but looks ten years younger. He's six foot and has long blond hair. He's built like a sprinter—not obviously muscular but certainly as athletic as they come." She looked at Painter. "You and I would probably not be able to take our eyes off him if we saw him walking into a bar. Don't let that get in the way of things. He's killed as many people as Cochrane."

Painter asked, "Who is he?"

"He's a former Israeli Mossad assassin. We think he's here to find out what really happened to Cochrane. He and Cochrane worked together, though at first they tried to kill each other. The fact he's in the States led us to believe that he suspected Cochrane wasn't dead. I've had him under Bureau surveillance ever since. But he's extremely canny. My agents have got nothing on him. Every morning and evening he walks his dog in a nearby park. In between, the man disappears. We try to find him but our best experts can't get close." She said to Kopański, "I need you to back Pete up at every step of the way. This isn't an NYC perp we're confronting. We're dealing with an incredibly dangerous and highly trained killer."

Michael Stein emptied the remains of his beef casserole into a bowl, stirred handmade roughage into the broth, and placed a second bowl of fresh water next to the meal. Both were on the floor of his tiny studio apartment.

"There we go, Mr. Peres," he said to his aging dog. "Dinnertime. It's a bit of a treat tonight. Real meat. Not the normal crap."

The mongrel limped to the kitchen and started devouring the food, while Stein stroked his neck.

"We'll be back on the kibbutz soon. We just have to get you through quarantine first." He thought about his passport. "Me too for that matter. The Americans don't like me. We might have to take a different route out." He crouched down and gave his dog a hug, knowing that there was no way the dog would make the return journey to Dalia, the kibbutz in Israel where Stein worked in a soap factory, having eschewed his life as a Sayeret Matkal special forces operative and Mossad Kidon assassin. "It's okay, boy. We'll get through this together. I won't leave your side. Ever."

Mr. Peres wolfed down his meal, his arthritic back legs shaking as he did so.

Stein had owned the dog since he rescued him as a stray on the streets of Tel Aviv. Back then Peres was one year old. Now he was thirteen, his once golden fleece now white and gray. Probably he was a Labrador cross, though it was difficult to tell. But he was medium-size and had the appetite of a champion.

"I'm going to have to take you out for a pee after you've finished eating. Cold, dark, and wet out there. Not good for your legs, I know. But rules are rules and your bladder isn't what it used to be."

The meal complete, Stein attached a lead to Peres and carried him down four flights of stairs. Outside, he gently lowered him onto the sidewalk and walked him to the park.

"This time of year it's warmer in Israel. Better for your legs. Do you remember, Mr. Peres? I'm sorry I had to bring you here. I had to find the truth about something. And I just couldn't leave you on your own."

They walked for twenty minutes in the park, until Peres started whining.

"Time for home is it?" Stein about-faced and walked his dog toward his apartment.

But before he exited the park, three men approached him out of the darkness. All were in hoodies and winter coats; two of the men black, one white.

The tallest of them, a black guy, said, "Cash. Give it to us or we'll snap your dog's legs."

The men pulled out knives.

Stein was motionless.

"Cash," the lead mugger repeated.

"I have no cash on me."

The men laughed.

Stein told Peres to sit and said to the men, "I'm walking my dog in a park. What would require me to consider carrying sufficient funds to placate a robber? Do you think I'm that dumb?"

The white mugger strode up to him and put a knife against Stein's throat. "Don't mess with us!"

Stein remained still. "I'm walking my dog" was all he said.

The man moved to the dog and put his knife against Mr. Peres's back right leg. "You want me to saw this off?"

"No."

"Then give us what you have."

"Okay. So long as you back away from my dog."

The mugger looked at his leader, who nodded. "All right. But make this fast." He walked back to Stein. "All you need to do is reach into your pocket and give us what you have."

Stein put a hand into his jeans, withdrew a clenched fist, and opened it in front of the man's face while saying, "Poof. Magic. Nothing in the hand."

"You goddamn—"

Stein grabbed the man's head with two hands and tossed him to one side, causing the man's skull to smack on the concrete path and render him unconscious. Stein advanced on the other two. "You chose the wrong man tonight. You threatened my dog."

Both men lunged at him with their knives.

Stein slammed his palm into the nose of the first, splintering cartilage. A nanosecond later he swept his leg and upended the second, before stamping repeatedly on his face. Both men were writhing on the ground in agony from the blisteringly quick assault.

Stein calmly picked up Mr. Peres's lead and led him back to the apartment. "Not our normal routine," he said as he towel-dried Peres from the rain. "What did you see out there?"

The dog was shivering as Stein got him dry.

"Shall I tell you?"

Peres nuzzled his nose against his beloved master.

Stein walked to the only window in the living room. "I'll tell you what I saw out there. Absolutely nothing. And that's a problem."

Gage said to Duggan, "For the benefit of Agents Painter and Kopański, run through the drill."

Duggan swiveled around. "It's a fast snatch. The target's name is Michael Stein. We grab him and question him. Here." He tossed Kopański a pair of plastic cuffs.

Painter asked, "Will he be armed?"

"We have no evidence one way or the other."

"Unarmed combat capabilities?"

"The best."

Painter addressed Gage. "You may have noticed that due to my leg I don't do anything *fast* these days."

Gage was indifferent. "We'll get the guys to do the heroics. You and I will use our brains when we've got Stein somewhere private." She checked her ACP handgun. "Time to get this done."

Mr. Peres was curled up in his bed, snoring and with his front paws twitching fast as if he was dreaming about chasing a rabbit. Stein smiled at the thought of his dog running free in a field, younger, with the energy that he probably never had due to malnourishment as a puppy. He brewed a pot of coffee and looked at the window. The curtains were closed. He dared not open them even an inch. Thermal imagery would catch him if he just got close to the pane.

"The Feds have gone," he whispered to his sleeping dog. "Either they're bored of me, or something's about to go down." He picked up his tiny hemp satchel containing his passport, wallet, and other essential items, slung it over his shoulder, and said in a loud voice, "I sweep this room for bugs daily. But I know you guys have long-range audio equipment these days. I stand no chance against that. So if you're listening and about to do something idiotic, know that I'm unarmed."

He picked up two small metal objects and attached them to the door with twine. There was nothing more that could be done. He placed plugs into his ears and Ray-Ban sunglasses over his eyes, sat next to Peres on the floor, and waited.

Duggan and Kopański moved quickly down the street, avoiding lamps and other sources of light, their handguns secreted under their jackets.

Many of the residential dwellings around them were dark, their residents long asleep. But there was nothing to disturb the two men as they raced to the front door of the apartment building.

Duggan pulled out a key, but said nothing.

Kopański knew the Feds had somehow gotten a copy to the communal entrance.

Duggan nodded at his colleague and opened the lock. He held four fingers up.

Four flights of stairs.

The men ascended.

Stein stroked his dog. "Catch that rabbit, my friend. Maybe we could have it for supper." He stared at the door. "Ninety-nine times out of a hundred, nothing happens. But now and again it all goes wrong. I always hate the quiet. It means something's not right."

He watched the metal objects on the entrance.

Duggan and Kopański reached the fourth floor. Duggan pointed at a door, his expression totally focused. "No key," he whispered. "You choose who does this."

Kopański didn't hesitate. He strode up to the door, gun in hand, and kicked the door open and immediately swung left so that Duggan could enter and he could follow.

One second later the stun grenades Stein had attached to the door went off, causing brief deafening noise and light. Duggan and Kopański reeled as if they were blind drunk as Stein picked up Peres and sprinted past them, leaping down the stairs and out into the darkness of the street below.

It took the Feds ten seconds to recover from the devastating onslaught on their senses.

Kopański yelled, "The dog's not here. It's fled or Stein's taken it with him."

Duggan screamed, "Move!"

They leaped down the stairs, Duggan on his cell to Gage. "He just sucker punched us! We think he may have his dog with him. No idea on direction."

Gage told Painter to unholster her weapon and stand in the center of the street before Gage sprinted to the other end, her ACP in hand. "We can't see him!"

Duggan and Kopański exited the apartment block.

"Where the hell is he?" muttered Duggan. "The street's covered. He's got nowhere to go."

Kopański looked up and down the street. Gage was motionless at one end, facing the men, her pistol held in two hands. Painter mirrored her at the other end. He spun 360 degrees. "The alley. That's where he's gone."

The men ran into the alley adjacent to the block. At the end was a seven-foot wall. They scrambled over it, landing in trash bins on the other side before continuing their pursuit.

In his fierce Israeli special forces training with Sayeret Matkal, a unit comparable to Britain's SAS and America's Delta Force and SEAL Team Six, Stein was the top of his class. He excelled at fitness, even though there were more muscular men in his batch. But carrying a load in front of your chest is hell. No man can go fast over long distances in that condition. But he wasn't going to let go of Mr. Peres. He breathed fast as he carried his dog while running as quickly as his legs and lungs would allow.

He could hear the rapid footsteps of the Feds behind him. They'd established he'd used the alley to evade capture. Now they were pursuing him down an adjacent street. He doubted they'd shoot him in the back. But he knew there was no chance of escape.

He slowed down and lowered Mr. Peres to the ground. "End of the line for us, Mr. Peres."

He faced Kopański and Duggan as they rushed to him, their guns at eye level.

Stein smiled while sucking in air. "Sorry about the flash-bangs."

Duggan yelled, "On your knees!"

The Feds were directly in front of him.

Stein complied and put his hands behind his head. "Mr. Peres is frightened by men with guns. Please don't scare him."

"That's the least of our concerns right now!"

"It should be. But he's old and dying. You're just doing your job. Neither of you look like unsympathetic bullies. Look after my dog."

Kopański cuffed Stein while Duggan kept his gun trained on Stein's head. "The dog will be fine. It's you who should be worried," Kopański said.

Stein looked at Kopański with an expression that suggested he was anything but worried. "Do what you have to. But I'll burn New York to the ground if you mistreat Mr. Peres."

Gage jogged back to the SUV as she saw her men escort Stein to the vehicle, Duggan walking Peres on his lead, Kopański gripping the straps of Stein's cuffs and holding the Israeli's arms high behind his back.

"No names!" barked Gage at her colleagues as Stein was put in the back of the SUV. She addressed both men. "You two in the back." She darted a look at Painter. "Time for the ladies to get to work."

Gage and Painter swiveled to face Stein. Along with a burlap shirt, blue jeans, and boots, his gorgeous looks were accentuated by his flowing blond hair. Mr. Peres was by his side.

Gage was completely composed as she said, "Mr. Stein, you are an assassin."

Stein smiled.

"You know the Federal Bureau of Investigation has been watching you for some time."

"A year to be precise." Stein's smile broadened. "I see them every day. But not tonight. Not until you turned up."

"Why do you think we turned up?"

"Because you want information about a man."

"Correct."

Painter asked, "Would it be foolish of us to assume you will give us that information?"

Stein turned his attention on the former detective. "Two big men are pointing their guns at me. It's a bit rude, don't you think?"

"So you won't talk while guns are pointing at you?"

"It's not the guns that bother me; it's the disposition it puts my mind into."

"It makes you angry?"

"It makes me fear for your friends' lives."

Gage and Painter exchanged glances.

Gage addressed her male colleagues. "Lower your guns. But if he does anything stupid, kill him." She said to Stein, "You are not under arrest, nor will we torture you."

"Tut, tut. Never reveal your weaknesses."

"But we will rendition you to Syria, where local authorities there will question you under more extreme methods because of at least ten assassinations you've committed in the country."

Stein shrugged. "Mr. Peres and I are a dying breed. How we go out is in the lap of the gods." His expression steeled. "*You* are playing God. But that doesn't scare me."

Gage retorted, "I want you to take a deep breath and think about your situation."

"I've done that already, *Agent Gage*."

Gage frowned. "Who is that?"

"She is you." Stein looked at the others in the vehicle. "I confess I don't know who your backup is." He returned his attention to Gage. "But I made it my business to know who you are."

"Which is what?"

"The person who broke the Frisco killings, the Baltimore massacre; dismantled the Russian spy ring in New York; and has a husband who works in an accounting firm at 2430 M Street

Northwest, D.C." Stein's grin returned. "I could go on. You've done so much. But your crowning achievement was bringing Will Cochrane to jail three years ago."

Gage had no idea how he knew this information, half of which was classified.

"And after all, Agent Gage, we're here to talk about Will Cochrane. Aren't we?"

"If I am who you say I am and have a husband in 2430, you'd better not touch him!"

"I won't. He seems like a nice man. He takes your two kids to school when you work nights. Your children seem so happy."

Gage snapped at Kopański and Duggan, "Raise your guns!" She lowered her voice. "You've been living in the States because you want to know what happened to Cochrane. You worked with Cochrane two years ago. I know this because I was given access to CIA files. You tried to kill him, then allied with him against a bigger threat. You saved his life, he saved yours. You feel a debt of obligation to him. You are trying to ascertain whether he really died a year ago."

"Bravo, Mrs. Gage. But in doing so I'm breaking no U.S. laws that I'm aware of."

"We don't take kindly to Kidon assassins being on our soil."

"I'm no longer Kidon. I work shifts in a kibbutz soap factory that exports to the entire Middle East. We transcend cultural divides more than diplomacy or politics. It's about societal necessity. It's a happy place to be."

"And yet you've been here for a year."

"I took a sabbatical."

"Once a killer, always a killer."

Stein looked at his dog. "We slow down."

"You're too young for that."

Stein laughed. "I've seen twenty-year-old men slow down because they have a knife to their balls and can't do anything about it." His face turned serious as he looked around the vehicle. "I see killers in here who know exactly what I'm talking about. Don't be hypocrites."

Painter leaned forward. "We're not. We just want to know what you suspect. We know something that you might not know. But we want your perspective. If Cochrane is alive, is he a threat?"

Stein pulled his arms from behind his back. They were uncuffed, causing Duggan and Kopański to immediately lunge forward. Stein held his grin as he stared at the men. "Don't be scared, gentlemen. It could have happened to you one minute ago. I decided not to." He stared at Painter. "I think you are a war veteran. Not infantry or navy. Aviation, I would hazard a guess." Attention on Gage. "You are the Bureau's best bloodhound. There's no guessing there. I did my research. Plus, I can see your intellect in your eyes. You're a problem." This to Duggan. "Ex–special forces, without a doubt. Now Hostage Rescue Team or SWAT. No, HRT. You've come up against Cochrane, haven't you? And you lost. So did Agent Gage." Finally he looked at Kopański. "You I can't fathom. Sorrow is in your face. So is death. It means we are kindred souls."

Kopański barked, "Shut your mouth!"

"As you wish." Stein stroked his dog. "I believe Cochrane is alive. I've not met him since his alleged death, nor have any evidence to support my assumption he's alive. But I know that he would not have killed himself. You know that too. You have proof he's alive, otherwise why snatch me?" He waved his hands. "I could have easily killed everyone in this vehicle and walked out with Mr. Peres. I chose not to. Know this"—Stein leaned forward, causing the men to place their fingers on their triggers—"I wanted to find him and see that he was okay. But I also knew I would stand no chance against him if he decided my approach compromised him."

Gage said, "He may have faked his death, but why is he alive again?"

Stein laughed. "I'm free to leave if I tell you the answer?"

Gage's heart was pounding. "Yes. You and your dog."

Stein looked at Mr. Peres. "He has cancer. The vet says he has days at best to live. When you kill people, you cherish life more than anyone. I cherish life."

"That's a noble sentiment, Stein, but it's not answering my question."

Michael Stein ran his fingers through the dog's fur and said, "Come on, pal. Time to go." He looked at everyone in the SUV. "Will Cochrane is not your enemy. But I know he's come back to life for a reason. It will have to do with something from his past. You will all die if you piss him off. Don't do that. *Please* don't do that."

He faced Duggan and Kopański. "I very much doubt you'd want to go up against me without a cancerous and lame dog slowing me down. But nothing slows Cochrane down. Think doubly hard if you're considering going up against him."

He exited the vehicle, carefully lifting Mr. Peres with him. Before slamming the rear door shut, he said to all, "I suspect what you did this evening was illegal. That matters not a bit to me. I'm very used to *illegal*. I will forget this ever happened." His expression turned cold. "If you put your Bureau surveillance team back on me, it will continue to be a waste of your time. It's in all of your interests to leave me alone. If Cochrane is alive and on the hunt, he'll scorch everything in his way. And I'll help him."

SIXTEEN

Will lowered his binoculars and watched Stein carry his dog back to his apartment. Will pressed numbers on his cell. "Miss Ash, you know who this is. I want you to tell me what you have."

Kay Ash sounded irritated. "It's only been a few hours!"

"You'll have met with Hessian Bell. What did he say?"

She was silent for a moment. "He said to trust you."

"I thought that's what he'd say." Will walked away from Stein's street. "There is a four-person FBI team hunting me. You know who they are?"

"Agent Marsha Gage is team leader. Don't underestimate her."

"I know she's team leader. And the others?"

"Bell and I don't know."

"I do."

"How?"

"Agent Gage and I go way back. She still looks as young as she always did. Alongside her are two NYPD detectives, Joe Kopański and Thyme Painter. They tried to apprehend me a year ago. Both are extremely accomplished. The fourth is an HRT shooter called Pete Duggan. He's ex-SF and won't stop until I or someone else puts a bullet in his brain. Gage has selected him for the team because he's one of the best killers America has to offer." He turned off the street. "Gage is doing this off the radar."

"You've been watching them?"

"Yes."

"Where?"

"Somewhere. With the help of your pals in the NSA you could triangulate this call to get my location, send a team in to get me. You won't see them again if you do."

"I'm not going to do that."

"Good." Will was walking fast. "Do you have Mrs. Haden's address?"

"Yes." She gave him the details. "But I don't have anything else yet."

"Do you know what's happening?"

"No."

"I do. It's imperative you get me the other names involved in the Berlin job."

"Why is this so important?"

Will stopped. "Think of this as a chessboard with three combatants. First, we have you, me, and Bell on our team. There are two others you don't yet know about who may be on our side. Second, there is Gage and her crew. Third, there is the major problem: Haden. But there are others in the mix. Thus, the issue is you and I don't know who all the chess pieces are. I'm trying to correct that. Tell Hessian Bell that an acquaintance of mine is almost certainly going to talk to Mr. A. Mr. A is a foreign national residing on U.S. soil. Say nothing more than that. And don't do anything stupid to corrupt that encounter. It's to our advantage."

Ash's mind was racing. "But what if there's a fourth side?"

"There is a fourth side. It's a corruption of what went down in Berlin. Keep your eye on the ball."

He hung up and got into his car.

Within the confines of his tiny apartment, Stein looked at his dog. "We've got to make another journey, Mr. Peres. Not too far this time. But it will involve a rented car and a road trip. I'll put water and treats in the back for you. Are you cool with that?"

Mr. Peres limped over to his master and licked him.

Stein stroked his dog while looking out the window at the night and artificial lights. "I'll drive carefully to try to avoid pain on your legs when I go over bumps. Sometimes the best of us start caving in because of our bodies. Don't fear that. Gage is right—I'm a long way off that. What she doesn't understand is that I've been witness to the end of life so many times. All of it by my hand. And I'm at my prime."

He picked up his satchel.

"This will be the last we see of this shitty place. Old man, you've been my savior. But now I need to get to work. It will be a hunt. Most certainly your swan song. Are you with me?"

Ash pulled up outside Hessian Bell's mansion in the outskirts of D.C. The place was palatial and accessed by a gravel drive. Exterior lights were dimmed, casting a golden glow over the building, which had been deliberately covered with vines and had been built in 1822 by a gangster who had garroted two men and dumped their bodies in baths of lime before getting the electric chair. Bell had bought the vast home for his now-deceased wife fifteen years ago after winning a long-shot bet on which bull would throw its rider in a rodeo. The billionaire who lost to him tried to extricate himself from the bet. Bell had pretended to acquiesce before showing the billionaire a picture of him and his mistress in flagrante delicto. Money was then wired to Bell's account.

It was now 3:30 A.M.

Ash rang the doorbell, wondering if Bell was still awake. She suspected that if he was not, he'd be opening the door soon. Bell never did deep slumber, she deduced. He was always ready for the unexpected.

The door opened. Bell was there in pajamas

and a robe that resembled a Victorian gentle-man's crimson smoking gown. "Twice in one night, Miss Ash. I'm beginning to regret taking you on." He gestured for her to enter.

Ash followed him into his living room, pass-ing ornate sculptures and framed oil paintings in the long corridor.

The living room fireplace had dying embers. Bell tossed kindling and logs on top and ges-tured to one of the five sofas for her to sit. The vast room was an eclectic mishmash of style and quirkiness: original drawings from Turner, photos of Scott's expedition to the South Pole, a cabinet containing first editions of Mark Twain's and Ernest Hemingway's books, a map that was framed in gold and had once been a top-secret chart of the Normandy landing zones in World War II, candles, indoor Japanese bonsai trees, French Renaissance furniture, oil lamps spread sporadically around the room, and, above the mantelpiece, a jar of Ottoman tobacco and bullet holes in the wall that spelled "CIA." A revolver was next to the tobacco.

What was missing in the room was a woman's touch.

Bell sat on a sofa opposite Ash and sensed her observation. "When Maureen died, I kept some things, got rid of others. I loved her too much to be reminded of her every day. Others would have done different. But I'm not others. Cochrane has been in touch with you again."

It wasn't a question.

Ash nodded and told him about the call.

Bell bowed his head, deep in thought. "Do you think Cochrane was watching Gage?"

"No."

"Excellent." Bell was pleased she had worked this out. "Extrapolate."

Ash stared at her controller, trying to scrutinize him. "He was watching someone else, and that someone is going to contact the aforementioned Mr. A. Who's Mr. A?"

Bell slowly lifted his head. "He is a version of me, but with a different first language."

"A spymaster?"

Bell smiled, though he looked wary. "Once he was. Now he's retired and living in Virginia. Cochrane made that happen. He brought him in from the cold. It was a brilliant tactic."

"Does Mr. A scare you?"

Bell considered the question. "No. I could crush him. He could crush me. I believe we are equals. What scares me is that we are both too competitive with our minds. One could always burn the other out if there is a confrontation."

"Then don't confront him."

"Maybe." Bell leaned forward, his hands clasped. "Do you have any suspicions as to who's going to see him?"

"No."

"Cochrane knows exactly who it is."

"He told me not to disrupt the meeting."

"Then we don't."

"Sir, I—"

"We don't!" Bell stood and walked to his fireplace. "Mr. A is a Russian, code name Antaeus. He was the most powerful intelligence officer in Moscow. Ruthless, ingenious, but with a heart. Cochrane mistakenly slaughtered his wife and daughter. Cochrane was racked with guilt. But then Cochrane discovered that Antaeus had an American child he didn't know about from a fling before he got married. Cochrane used the child to lure Antaeus to America three years ago."

"Callous."

"Clever." Bell picked up his revolver. "And kind. You see, Cochrane recognized himself in Antaeus. I feel the same about myself. We're kindred spirits, albeit truly isolated from humanity. Antaeus is a defector. He's given more secrets to the States than any other Russian in the last sixty years. And he's done so for the most laudable reason. What is it that spies yearn for the most?"

"Love."

"Correct. Love. We get it in spades from the assets we send to their deaths. Therein is the problem."

"It's like marrying your beloved childhood sweetheart and one day pushing her off a cliff."

Bell nodded. "Antaeus was the spider in the center of the web. He is not a man of action—he's a thinker." Bell prodded his gun against the bullet holes and placed it back down. "Cochrane was given very specific instructions to kill him. He was in MI6 at the time and his plan was ingenious. He tracked Antaeus and established he always drove to and from work alone. Antaeus never permitted his wife and daughter to travel

with him. So Cochrane had the green light.
He planted a bomb in his car. But that evening,
Antaeus's wife and daughter were shopping in
Moscow. His daughter sprained her ankle. As
Antaeus was driving home he got a call from
his wife. He could hear his daughter crying in
the background. The wife was imploring, saying they couldn't catch the train home. Antaeus
broke protocol and picked them up. One of his
assets got tipped off about the bomb and called
Antaeus seconds before the bomb was due to
detonate. Antaeus stopped to get his wife and
child out of the rear of the vehicle. But he was
too late. The car exploded. Antaeus was knocked
across the street. Still, he tried to rescue his family. Sadly, they were in tiny pieces."

"He got burned?"

Bell nodded. "It was impossible to do anything for his family, but Antaeus tried. It was the
most tremendous act of courage. But now he has
a droopy eye, a face that is mashed by unsuccess-
ful plastic surgery, a body lacerated by burn and
shrapnel scars, and he has to walk with a cane as
tall as his head."

"Where was Cochrane?"

"The other side of the city. He didn't know
what had happened until much later. Had he been
there, he'd have done everything to help Antaeus."

"Antaeus's age?"

Bell smiled. "Same as me. Fifty-eight."

"Your bodies are different but your minds are
the same. You both sit in the center of your webs."

Bell shook his head. "This is the remarkable thing. Cochrane used incredible subterfuge to get Antaeus to defect to America. But, and there is a *but,* Antaeus responded because of his thirteen-year-old American daughter, Crystal. He decided not to sit in the center of the web any longer. He cares for his daughter in Virginia and writes groundbreaking archaeological papers for Harvard and Stanford."

Ash walked to him. "You're still a spider."

Bell was silent.

Ash wished she could penetrate Bell's thoughts. "Antaeus is also still a spider. Whoever's going to see him knows that."

Bell noted the glint in her eyes. "Of course. So who's going to see him?"

"I told you, I don't know."

"You may not know the person's identity, but think it through. What is the *type* of person?"

Ash's mind raced. "Antaeus is disabled, he—"

"He walks twenty miles a day. He's anything but disabled."

Ash was unperturbed. "Nevertheless, he has limitations. He needs a doer."

Bell smiled.

"Someone much younger and agile."

"Go on."

Ash tried to picture the person. "A man. Not American. Not Western, in all probability. Someone with a track record respected by Antaeus. Someone who has a connection to Cochrane. A man who Cochrane would listen to." She looked at the bullet holes on the wall. "Why did you do that?"

Bell held her gaze. "When my wife died, I received no help from the Agency. I'm not a big drinker, but after her wake I came home and consumed two bottles of merlot. I took out my gun and wrote on the wall what I despised. Since then the anger's gone and I've adopted different strategies. I run my own show."

"The man seeking Antaeus is a spy."

Bell brushed his fingers against a bullet hole. "*Was* a spy and *was* an assassin. That's my bet. Put Antaeus and that man together and we have formidable opponents."

Ash frowned. "Then we have a problem. Because Cochrane said they might be on our side."

SEVENTEEN

One of Jason Flail's men watched the house through thermal binoculars. Secreted in a hedge in darkness, he was convinced no one could see him. It was six A.M. The birds and crickets that usually added ambience to the Virginia countryside were mute. A fine rain drizzled over his green Nomex coveralls, strapped over which were, among other things, a Glock handgun, webbing containing rations, and plastic bags with his feces, water, spare ammunition, and audio equipment.

He'd been here for twelve hours and was pissed off. Howard Kane had told him and the other ex-SF men to watch the house for two days. Each of the four-man unit had taken it in turn to do the task, and none of them knew why he was doing it or what was so special about the house. But Kane had given them a very specific instruction:

photograph anyone coming or going from the property.

In one hour the sun would be rising. An hour after that, another of Flail's men would take over duties.

He positioned his long-range camera at the house and continued watching the abode through the camera's lens.

Wolf Trap.

An area in northeast Virginia that had approximately sixteen thousand inhabitants. Among the houses there was one on the outskirts that belonged to Colonel Haden.

Will Cochrane parked his car nearby and went to the place on foot, seemingly oblivious to his surroundings, though that was a lie. Wearing the only suit now in his possession and an overcoat, he took in everything.

He rang the doorbell of the huge white wooden house that was far removed from others in Wolf Trap and waited. Around him, leaves from trees drifted slowly to the ground, and a fine rain sprinkled over an immaculate meadow that encased the property and ran for as far as the eye could see. Occasionally a car would pass on the adjacent road leading to suburbia, spraying water as tires moved through puddles, headlights on because of the dim light. The scent was rich with pine, the noise of vehicles accompanied by a woodpecker that was drilling holes in a nearby oak tree. Everything else was peaceful and quiet.

A woman answered the door.

Will asked, "Mrs. Elizabeth Haden?"

The woman was tall, svelte, maybe late forties, and had a platinum bob encapsulating a classically elegant face that did not detract from the sparkling allure of her eyes. In flared heavy cotton black slacks, classy shoes, and a crisp white shirt that would have been fashionable in the thirties and maybe was fashionable again among wealthy ladies, she looked every part the civilized yet cheeky party hostess who could charm her guests.

She looked him up and down. "When I saw you, I pressed a panic alarm in my house. It has a ten-minute delay and only I can turn it off. But I won't do so if you're here for anything other than good reasons. I'm Mrs. Haden. Who are you?"

Her voice was refined and from the South.

Will smiled. "My name is Edward Pope. I've worked with your husband. Is he here? May I speak with him?"

Will expected her to frown.

She didn't. Just held his gaze, exuding self-confidence. "Are you government? If so, which department do you work for?"

"Like your husband, we get moved around a lot. And that's why I'm here. I haven't seen him for three years. I wanted to tell him something private, if that's okay with you?"

"Something private?"

"Something private."

They both stared at each other.

"You expect me to let in a complete stranger?"

"Not if your husband's away. I can come back at a more convenient time."

A trace of a smile appeared on Mrs. Haden's face as she kept her eyes on Will's. There was something about her that intrigued him. She was too in control.

In the background, a maid and a handyman passed through the corridor to attend to their morning duties. Will saw them without moving his eyes.

"No need for panic alarms," Mrs. Haden said. "I'm guessing you now know I've got people here. But my husband isn't one of them."

"That's a shame, because it's been a long drive."

"Then where's your car?"

Will gestured. "Up the road. I needed to stretch my legs and get a bit of fresh air."

Mrs. Haden's expression didn't betray a thing. "All right. Come in."

He followed her into the house.

"You want tea or coffee?"

"That's kind, but no thank you."

"Your Virginia accent is good. Where did you learn it?"

Will smiled. "One time I lived near here. My father was from these parts."

"But you're no longer rooted here." She spun around. "Part of you is English."

"Part of me isn't. English mother. American father."

"And you think being part American gives you the right to ask about my husband?"

"No. We were former colleagues. I'm here because he's been missing for a long time."

"Yes." Mrs. Haden walked into the kitchen. "Colonel Haden is missing. And you want to know why."

Will watched her pour homemade lemonade into a glass. "I want to know what you know."

"You're not a government employee anymore. I can tell."

"How?"

"Your voice is too soft-spoken. You're alone. You're not throwing your weight around." She frowned as she took a sip of the drink. "But your hands are covered in scars. You're a brutal man."

"Not to you."

"Mister, men say that to gals all the time."

"I'm different."

She placed her drink on the work surface. "You a reporter?"

Will dropped his Virginia accent. "You wouldn't have let me in if I was."

"You speak nice in your own accent. It's musical."

"I like playing the lute. Its strings inform my vocal cords."

She grinned. "You play an audience."

"I lull them to sleep."

Mrs. Haden glanced again at Will's hands. "I can see that." Her expression turned. "Just before you kill them." Mrs. Haden cocked her head. "Do you know much about bees?"

Will playacted dumb.

"Let me show you. They love the sunrise." Mrs. Haden escorted Will into the vast back-yard.

Yew trees were there, also lavender bushes, birdhouses, and oaks dripping rainwater as if they were sweating. Now, it wasn't raining. The sun was doing its thing.

She pointed at a beehive. It was small, a waist-high wooden rectangle positioned on top of uncut lavish green grass covered with dew and traces of frost. "The queen bee waits in the middle."

"Her minions servicing her." Will crouched in front of the container. "Why do you keep them?"

"To recollect." Mrs. Haden put a hand on the hive. "They won't hurt me. They're docile this time of year, plus all they care about is waiting for spring to pollinate lavender and avoiding wasps." She pointed at a nearby tree. "I had to destroy a wasp nest two months ago. They're predators. Bees give back to society."

Will stood. "The point of all this is the queen bee."

"Yes."

"She is incredible, so long as she has the love of others around her."

Mrs. Haden laughed. "She's a woman. What do you expect?"

"The unexpected." Will lifted a docile worker bee onto his finger. "He is lost without his woman." He gently laid the bee back onto the surface and watched it fly into the hive. "Colonel Haden is lost without you."

For the first time, Mrs. Haden looked shaken. "You know nothing!"

"You showed a stranger your hive. It is a mechanistic exemplar of productivity. No humans are harmed. To the contrary, they coexist. But what happens if the queen bee is left exposed? The wasps get her." Will swiveled to face Mrs. Haden. "That's how you've felt for three years."

Mrs. Haden strode right up to him. "What's your name and who are you?"

"I told you. Edward Pope. Once I had dealings with the Pentagon. That's when I encountered your husband."

"*Encountered?* That's a word open to interpretation."

Will could almost feel her intelligence. "I never met him in person. We spoke on the phone."

"But you once worked for the government?"

"Yes." Will chose his words carefully. "Your husband and I collaborated on a project. The project was successful. Then he disappeared. Do you know where he is?"

Elizabeth Haden started walking back to the house. "No, I don't."

Inside the house, Will asked, "Have you seen him at all during the last three years?"

Haden drained the remains of her lemonade. "Do you know why I'm talking to you without the slightest evidence of your credentials?"

"The thought occurred to me."

She slammed the glass down. "It's because my husband couldn't keep his dick in his pants! To my knowledge, he screwed three Pentagon women. The only reason I found out about the cheating bastard was because one of the women turned up here and told me she was pregnant with my husband's child."

Will knew she wasn't lying. But something was nagging him. "Is he with one of the women now?"

Haden shrugged. "One of them, maybe. Or with another slut. Who cares?" She placed a finger on Will's jaw. "If you do track him down, you have my permission to punch him off his feet."

Will moved away from her and glanced around. "Do you have employment?"

"I look after my bees and this huge place. That's employment enough."

"I'm sure it is. Colonel Haden's salary couldn't have afforded a place this size and so distinguished."

"I . . . The money came from me. Inheritance. My parents were in the oil business."

"Ah, that makes sense." Will grabbed his coat. "You've been extremely gracious to talk with me. I must lay my cards on the table. If I track your husband down, I may do worse than punch him off his feet."

Elizabeth Haden smiled but said nothing.

"Three years ago, your husband brought me in to do a job in Berlin. He did so via a CIA officer called Unwin Fox. I watched Fox die days ago. Just before, he told me that he was killed because of your husband. What would you do if you were in my position?"

Haden looked hesitant. "I'd want to speak to my husband."

"Precisely. But what else?"

For the first time, Haden looked confused. "I've never heard of Unwin Fox. My husband never spoke about his work."

Will gestured to the meadow outside the kitchen. "There were worker bees involved in the mission I was brought in to execute. Probably not many. Nothing on the scale of your hive. The problem I have is I don't know some of them."

"The workers are protecting their king bee."

"There is no such thing as a king bee."

"Then have you considered the possibility of dissension in the ranks?"

"I have. Plus I've considered one other possibility."

Haden paled. "Get out of my house!"

Will nodded. "Good day to you, Mrs. Haden."

Outside, he glanced around urgently. Across the road, there was an escarpment covered in bushy foliage. Two hundred yards away from the main house was a garage the size of a cottage.

He walked casually in that direction.

Flail's colleague watched Cochrane through the lens of his camera, taking photos. Cochrane approached the garage and used a jimmy to force its lock. He looked oblivious to his surveillance, jamming open the garage door and entering. He disappeared from view.

Inside, Will saw three cars, all of them covered by dust sheets. He took off one sheet. Underneath was a Ferrari worth at least $400,000. Under the next was an Aston Martin in mint condition. The last was a Bentley. None of them looked like they'd been driven for some time, and in any case Mrs. Haden had a functional SUV parked outside the front of her house. These cars were boys' toys. Either the colonel had bought them using his wife's money, or there was another explanation.

He left the garage, walked behind it, and vanished.

Flail's special operative called Howard Kane. "I've just spotted the same snooper we met at Fox's house. I've got photos. Want me to do anything?"

Kane asked, "Why do you think he's there?"

"You're the one who should know the answer to that. You're making us watch her place. And I don't even know who *she* is!"

Kane was silent for a moment before replying, "She's Colonel Haden's wife. There's every possibility Haden will make contact with her."

The asset said, "Okay. I'm due to be relieved by my boss shortly. I'll upload and send you the shots from my camera now."

"Good. I want to have a look at this snooper."

An hour after the operative sent the pictures to Kane, the operative started packing up his things in anticipation of being relieved of his duties. He knew the snooper had long gone and there was little chance of catching anything new on camera. Plus, Kane was paying him only $500 per day for this short assignment. It was a lot of money on Civvy Street, but little when you were freezing your balls off in hedgerows for half a day.

But Kane had now explained his interest in Elizabeth Haden. The ex–Green Beret wondered if she was aiding her husband. The operative liked that notion. He'd always wanted to outcompete a former Delta Force commander. And he dearly hoped he'd be the one on observation duty when the colonel returned to his wife.

He picked up his phone to call Jason Flail.

But Cochrane punched him in the back of the head first. He pulled him up by the collar of his over suit. "Who do you work for?"

The operative swung a leg in an attempt to put Cochrane on his ass, but Cochrane jumped and the leg didn't engage.

Cochrane maintained his grip. "I knew you were watching me. It's my business to know. Who sent you?"

The operative punched at Cochrane with immense force but Cochrane dodged the blow, grabbed the fist, and flipped the man onto his front while maintaining a grip on his arm. With his mouth by the prone operative's ear, he whispered, "Who do you work for?"

His mouth buried in soil and grass, the operative spluttered, "You'd better let me go. I'm a cop."

"You and your colleagues tried that line when we met at Unwin Fox's house. It didn't work then. It isn't working now." Will wrenched the man's arm into a more painful lock.

"Fuck you!"

Will placed his foot on the back of the man's head. "You choose. I suffocate you with my foot, or I snap your neck."

"Okay, okay. There's no big secret. This is not about you, whoever *you* are. But I'm not doing this under duress."

Will wasn't going to trust the man, though he could see he was a tough operator who wouldn't crack in this style. He took the man's handgun, yanked him upright, and released him, before taking three paces back and pointing the handgun at the operative's head. "Talk!"

"There'll be no need for that." The new man's voice came from behind Will.

Will was certain it was one of the other men he'd met at Fox's destroyed house, obviously here to take over surveillance duties and armed with a gun pointing right at him.

Will didn't flinch. In a loud voice he said, "No one wins here. I'm a private investigator, licensed to carry and use firearms."

"Bullshit!"

"And you're allegedly cops, though we might have to agree to disagree on that assertion." Will's gun arm was motionless, his finger on the trigger, pointing at the sweating operative's head in front of him. "Why are you watching Elizabeth Haden's home?"

It was Jason Flail behind him. "None of your damned business."

"You work for the government?"

Flail placed the muzzle of his handgun against the back of Will's head. "You're not in a position to ask questions."

"I'm in a position where if you shoot me, my finger will pull the trigger. At best I'll hit your colleague in the chest or belly. At worst I'll put a bullet in his head before I drop. It's a bad situation for us all either way."

Flail circled around Will, maintaining his aim on Cochrane's head. Face-to-face with Will, he said, "What's your name?"

Will didn't blink. "On the ground next to your colleague's ankles is a long-range camera. Linked to the camera is a cable and cell phone. Your colleague has taken photos of me and uploaded them to someone. That someone will tell you my name."

"Private investigator?"

"Yes. That is exactly what I am."

"And your business here?"

"Mundane. Mrs. Haden wants to know if her husband's having an affair. She's my client. She wondered if the woman was someone in the CIA. She knew Unwin Fox and thought he might know something. That's why I was at Fox's house. I have no idea why it was a burned mess. Clearly, we're working very different cases."

Flail glanced at his colleague. Both men were uncertain. Flail lowered his gun. "Let's part company without drama."

Will edged away from Flail, keeping his gun pointed at Flail's colleague. "No drama."

Flail's cell phone rang.

It was Howard Kane. "The man in the photos is Will Cochrane! He's alive! Kill him on sight!"

Flail raised his gun.

But Will pointed his gun at Flail's head, backed away, and disappeared.

In his office, Kane paced back and forward, staring at the image of Cochrane on his phone. How had this come to pass? Cochrane was supposed to be dead. And he was the last man on earth whom Kane wanted to come back to life.

In Africa, wild dogs are an endangered species. No one really knows why. Specialist bush vets in South and Central Africa try to save them. They keep them in reserves. The problem is the wild dogs don't recognize humans. People are simply not in their food chain. They can't be domesticated. You can walk right past them and they won't give a damn.

That's Cochrane.

With one exception: he's evolved to put humans in the food chain.

And he killed the terror financier Otto Raeder in Berlin without blinking. Raeder was like a species that was simply in his way. That's why Cochrane was chosen for the job. He doesn't know what humans are, but he's willing to exterminate them with brutal efficiency.

The fact that Cochrane was alive again changed things dramatically. Kane had a plan to finish what Unwin Fox had started. But Cochrane could blunder into a situation he didn't comprehend and destroy everything.

Now, Haden had to be held up as the corrupt coward. Due process of law or a bullet in the head would ensure that.

Kane stood still and breathed deeply to calm himself.

He called Jason Flail. "We're now in a very dark place. Bigger things are in motion. Cochrane is a traitor and murderer. If you see him again, kill him without asking my permission."

"Are you going to report his sighting to the police?"

Kane considered this. "No. If I did that, Haden would go to ground for good. We have to let him come to us. But don't let Cochrane get in the way."

EIGHTEEN

The eleven-year-old twins Billy and Tom Koenig and their sole guardian, their aunt, Faye Glass, were in witness protection in Virginia, guarded by two detectives.

The Koenigs were the sons of Roger Koenig, a former CIA Special Operations Group paramilitary officer and SEAL Team Six operative who was a colleague of Will Cochrane's and was the closest thing Will had to a brother. Together, they'd conducted numerous overseas missions, each rescuing the other in trouble spots around the world. It ended when Roger was killed in Beirut. Will tracked down his murderer and shot him.

Justice wasn't to be had. A year later Will was framed for numerous murders in the States and the abduction of Tom Koenig. This was why he was still on the run.

Faye and the twins were in protection to avoid another abduction attempt by Cochrane. The two detectives guarding them were expert shots and excelled at close-quarter combat as well as thinking. They were renowned for their ability to not only put up defenses, but also gauge the mind-set of their charges. Often in witness protection, the hardest job was anticipating the idiocies of those in harm's way.

Tonight was like every other night during the last twelve months. Faye had cooked dinner, had put the boys to bed, and was in the kitchen washing dishes. She was a slightly portly forty-year-old who wore clothes that were frequently stitched and unstitched to accommodate weight loss and gain, and had the most beautiful jet-black hair that often was coiled atop her head as if it were a serpent. Faye prepared a pot of coffee and some cookies for the cops.

"I would like you to leave soon. Forever," she said to the detectives.

One of them answered, "Ma'am, we can only do that once we're satisfied you're safe. And that can only happen once our superiors believe there's no risk that Cochrane's alive."

"It's been a year!"

"I know, ma'am." The detective touched her hand. "We've been in this together throughout."

"Yes, yes, yes!" Faye started getting tearful. "We're all in prison because of a dead man!"

"*Possibly* dead."

Faye wiped tears off her cheeks. "He's dead. We all know that." She grabbed a cookie and munched on it. "I should have put more butter in the mix." Her eyes welled up again as she looked at the cops. "Murderer? Kidnapper? Does your department have any idea who Will Cochrane really is? He is not the man they think he is. But the only reason me and the boys have lived under these conditions for twelve months is because we know one thing—too many people want Cochrane dead; he attracts trouble."

The nearest detective smiled sympathetically. "Personally, I believe this has all been a waste of your time and our time. I'm pretty certain you'll be able to take the boys back to your home in Roanoke soon."

"What makes you so certain?"

"Virginia PD cutbacks. My bosses are having to prioritize expenditure. They'll review this case and conclude that me and my partner should be working other cases. Are you happy about that?"

Faye nodded. "Will Cochrane wanted nothing more than to be a father to the twins. I think someone set him up for the murders of my aunt and uncle and the police officers. But I also think he couldn't bear the idea that his reputation had been so catastrophically tarnished. What drove him throughout his career was to do the right thing. But people only remember the last thing about someone. In Will's case, it was murder of innocents." She took another cookie. "He killed himself. That's the end of the matter. Yes, I'd be happy if we could go home."

The detectives glanced at each other. "The house is all locked up. No one can get in or out.

My colleague will help you do the school run to-morrow."

The detectives withdrew.

Faye walked to the kitchen window and stared at nothing. Outside was only a small plot of land, but it was impossible to see given it was night and there were no exterior lights. Strange, she thought, that she was now fantasizing about see-ing Will Cochrane come up to the other side of the window and place his hand on the bul-letproof glass. He'd smile at her, she imagined. And she'd smile back because he'd be here to show that he hadn't forgotten the twins and was checking to see they were safe and well. All she'd have to do was nod at him. Then he'd vanish. But that would be enough. He'd be telling her that he was their guardian from afar.

She bowed her head and felt tears welling up again. How could this have been done to Will, such a good person, a man who was about to start a new life as a father and teacher at the twins' school? The police had forced her and the boys into witness protection until they had proof that Will was dead. But even if he was alive, Will never posed a threat to her, Billy, and Tom. On the contrary, he was the best thing they could have.

Now their world had been turned upside down. All Billy and Tom had wanted was for Will to adopt them. All Faye had wanted was to relinquish care of the boys to Will's charge and visit them every week. All Will had wanted was to do a very honorable thing and sacrifice his career for the sake of the youngsters and their fallen father's memory.

Her tears weren't helping. They were dwelling on a fantasy that would never happen.

Cochrane was dead.

Tomorrow she'd be escorted to the twins' school, and after that she'd go to the university where she lectured on mathematics and quantum physics. She came from an academic family, her uncle and aunt both having been university professors. Will was alleged to have killed them both. He didn't and wouldn't have.

She wiped away her tears and sighed. She had to be strong for the boys. Trouble was, two years ago her sister, Roger Koenig's wife, was brutally murdered in her house. Shortly thereafter, Roger was killed in Lebanon. It left the twins bereft of immediate family. And it left Faye suffering from PTSD because of her loss. But despite the gargantuan effort required, Faye's aging uncle and aunt—Robert and Celia—had rallied to provide a home for the twins, while Faye was too enveloped with grief to help. Eventually she overcame the grief and stepped up to the plate to care for the boys after her uncle and aunt were murdered.

But look where it left her now.

In witness protection.

Alone.

On a university lecturer's salary that barely paid off her overdraft on payday.

Her childhood sweetheart, a beautiful man called Brian, was allowed to visit her only on Wednesdays, because of Virginia PD rules that anyone over the age of forty would be blocked from her until questioned. Brian had been cleared by the police. But he was the only one, aside from her work colleagues.

She was constantly under police surveillance.

She was impoverished and in prison.

More important, the twins were too.

It would be wonderful if the detectives guarding her were right, that she could return home to Roanoke. Every day in the last year she'd imagined reentering her home and raising the boys. Brian, she knew, would want to be by her side. He was such a good man; not as clever as her but my goodness he had skills she didn't have, such as knowing how to repair a house and selecting produce from their local supermarket that could feed a family on forty dollars a week.

Brian had proposed to Faye last Wednesday and she'd gleefully accepted.

Trouble was, he was unemployed, having been fired from the construction firm he worked for. He was a fighter and a skilled artisan. He'd get work soon. But that didn't help Faye's bank account troubles right now.

It wasn't Brian's fault, her fault, or Cochrane's fault. It was the fault of life itself.

She forced herself to think of other matters: stripping the twins' beds tomorrow after work, washing clothes, what to have for dinner, whether the nice detectives guarding her had an opinion on what movie they'd like to watch tomorrow evening.

This was her life.

Today was Monday.

Two more days until she was allowed to see Brian.

But even then, what would they do? Between them they barely had enough money to buy a burger, let alone a fancy lunch.

She turned and walked back to the kitchen block and her plate of cookies.

She frowned.

On the plate was a beautiful red rose and an envelope that had the word "Faye" written on it.

It wasn't there a moment ago.

She wondered if it was from one of the detectives. Heaven forbid one of them had taken a shine to her. She was loyal to Brian, though she understood that close confinement over twelve months could produce confusing emotions. No, she'd detected no such boyish advances from the detectives. They'd always been thoroughly professional and had spoken with affection about their wives and children. Should she call the detectives in to look at the envelope? Maybe inside was something nasty.

She was confused but made a decision.

She ripped open the envelope.

Inside was fifty thousand dollars and a note.

Dear Faye,

I'm so sorry I couldn't reach out to you before. Things have changed. I've been spotted. But during the last year I have been checking up on you to make sure you're all fine. The two detectives protecting you seem like good

*men. That's been reassuring to me. The money
enclosed is all I can afford at present. I will
endeavor to earn more cash so I can send you
further funds in the future. Please tell Billy
and Tom I love them. It's up to you whether
you tell the detectives about this note. But
please don't tell them about the cash. They'll
confiscate it as evidence. I have to stay low
at present, as I have a very complicated task
ahead of me. But maybe when it's complete
I can come visit. I'd risk imprisonment as
a result, but twelve months away from the
boys has been too long. I'd happily have life
imprisonment for one minute with the twins.
Look after yourself. Brian is the perfect man
for you. He'll make you smile. The flower came
from your yard. You cut it. That's the line you
take with the detectives.*

*The cell phone number on the back of this
note is new. It's your access to me. Memorize
the number. Never store it in your phone.
Burn the note after reading.*

Always remember I'm watching over you.

WC x

Faye clutched a chair as she felt giddy and
feared she would collapse. She held the note to
her chest, breathing fast, mouthing but not articulating, "Thank God! Thank God!" She read
the note again, her eyes wide with disbelief. But
she knew this wasn't a trick. Cochrane had de-

liberately made no attempt to hide his distinctive handwriting. This was him. Putting his neck on the line once again. Telling her that the family he could never have was more important to him than his safety.

How he knew the location of the safe house was beyond her comprehension. How he knew about Brian was also a puzzle. Then again, Cochrane had peculiar skills and seemed to know a lot of things. She was glad. And what mattered was he was alive.

She looked at the corridor leading to the spare bedrooms containing the detectives. The TVs they were watching were audible. And when they retired to their rooms after dinner, they had a rule that they would give her privacy unless there was a problem.

Quickly, she hid the money in her handbag, grabbed a box of matches, and burned the note over the sink. She placed the rose in a wineglass and wept.

Will watched Faye from the yard. Next to him was the rosebush. The flower he'd cut from the bush was his way of saying she was a great woman and was loved by all. His lip trembled as he saw Faye in tears. He wished he could go to her and give her a hug. So many times in the last year he'd watched her and the twins from a distance, making sure they were okay. Tonight was the closest he'd gotten. But he'd arrived too late to see the boys. That broke his heart.

He meant what he'd said in the note. When this was over, he'd come see them, even if it meant he was killed as a result.

The senior White House adviser to the president had whimsically given himself the code name Deep Throat. But he wasn't a benign informant, driven by a conscience to blow the whistle on unsavory activity on Capitol Hill. On the contrary, he was a bastard who needed power around him. The right kind of power. He'd never be president; long ago he'd realized that. There were too many skeletons in his closet, too much bad media claiming he was a fascist who wanted to influence the president toward isolationism by shutting down borders and freedom of speech. So he'd come up with a plan: get someone into power who was like him, a power-hungry politician who'd tread over everyone to get to the top.

Deep Throat picked up his phone in his office in the White House's East Wing. "This matter better be solved soon," he said.

"There's a complication. He's alive."

"He?"

"I'm not going to say his name on the phone."

Deep Throat thought a second. "Does his name begin with *W*?"

"Yes."

"How do you know he's alive?"

"I just know. Don't ask me how."

"We had this covered. W will mess this up," Deep Throat responded.

"He won't mess it up. He's the only person who could untangle it."

"Same thing." Deep Throat looked around to ensure he wasn't being overheard. "You have procedures in place?"

"Yes."

"People?"

"I have solid workers."

"Good. Get it done."

Elizabeth Haden placed her phone down, walked into her garden and approached her beehive. The bees were quiet, the workers snuggling next to their queen and giving her warmth. Elizabeth was full of wonderment at the duty the lesser bees devoted to their mistress. They knew their place. And everything in the hive was designed this way with precision and purpose. Without the queen, the bees would be directionless. The blood of family was all that mattered.

Even if they didn't understand the queen's agenda.

Elizabeth stood for a while before shivering and reentering her home.

She made a cup of tea and pondered her encounter with the big man who called himself Edward Pope. That wasn't his real name, she was sure. And there was an aura around him that deeply unsettled her, even though there was no way she was going to reveal that to anyone. He wanted to track down her husband. But there was more to his task than that, she knew.

She looked at the vast garden and yard, spotlights in the grass lighting up patches of the
grounds, including the hive. What would happen,
she wondered, if the queen bee ordered the worker
bees to do something unexpected? They'd obey.
All that mattered was what the queen wanted.

NINETEEN

"We've got nothing to go on!" Marsha Gage kicked a stool in the safe house in Virginia, then stood before Pete Duggan, Joe Kopański, and Thyme Painter. "Nothing!"

On the living room table between them were strewn maps, cell phones, spare handgun magazines, and enlarged photos of Cochrane as last seen in the D.C. park.

Painter hobbled up to Gage. "Maybe we should blow this wide open, get every cop on the East Coast involved, circulate Cochrane's sighting throughout the FBI, possibly even get the media on board."

Gage's look was hostile. "You tried that one year ago! It ended in a hostage situation!"

"And you tried it three years ago and it ended with Cochrane putting a gun to your skull!" Painter had no desire to go head-to-head with

Gage, but she was standing her ground. "Regardless, we both need to face facts. We don't have Cochrane's cell phone to trace. Michael Stein is our only lead, but even he doesn't know where Cochrane is. We don't know the specifics of why Cochrane has come out of hiding. We have no cards to play except trying to smother Cochrane with a massive police blanket."

Gage sincerely admired Painter's talents. But Gage was the boss. "When you were a Night Stalker chopper pilot, flying under the radar, would you have liked the cavalry riding into Afghanistan by your side?"

"No."

"Why?"

"I didn't want to be noticed. My missions were top secret and covert."

"The parallels are precisely what we're doing to get Cochrane."

"Or not doing!"

"We have to stay off the radar. Blowing this whole thing up into a nationwide manhunt will likely have one of two outcomes: Cochrane will vanish, or there'll be a massacre."

Painter conceded that Gage was right. "He put a CIA officer out of his misery because Fox was poisoned with polonium by a person unknown. Cochrane was a former CIA-MI6 asset. The chances of Fox and Cochrane encountering each other without an overriding imperative for Cochrane to come out of hiding are nonexistent. Cochrane is on the trail of something. And he'll stay in the open providing we give him enough rope to do so."

"And when the time's right, we hang him with that rope." Sitting on the other side of the room, Kopański put down the sidearm he was cleaning. "You're right, Agent Gage. We have no leads. But we have one advantage."

Gage turned to the big Polish American. "Which is what?"

"Inevitability." Kopański raised his disfigured face. "Cochrane is as good as, maybe even better than, Michael Stein at staying in the shadows. But guys like that inevitably have to step out of the shadows to do their job."

Gage was following his train of thought. "Espionage. Assassinations. Direct action."

"Yeah, and that's when they're most vulnerable."

Hostage Rescue Team leader Pete Duggan joined the conversation. "We think there is a high probability Cochrane is pursuing a lead connected to Fox's death. The endgame for Cochrane will be to track down the person who poisoned Fox."

"That's a hypothesis, Pete. Not fact." Gage resisted the urge to chew on one of her nails. "Cochrane may have just gone to ground, doing nothing."

Painter shook her head. "That doesn't feel right."

Gage asked, "Why?"

Painter placed a hand on Joe's shoulder. "Joe's right about inevitability. Something's been set in

motion. Cochrane is the type of man who won't
stop until he's stopped that motion. He's going
to have to interact with others, good or bad people. And that's where we get lucky. Somebody
somewhere is going to compromise his safety."

"And that's where we step in?"

"We step in when innocent civilians get
frightened. Or whoever poisoned Fox creates a
massive situation and we end it."

Gage turned away from the others in the
room. Quietly, she said, "I've known of Cochrane for three years. And I've been obsessing
about the possibility he's still alive for this last
year. It's a lot of time to get to know a man." She
turned to her team. "There will be no random
inevitability to his capture. Now that Cochrane
was caught on camera, he will suspect that I'm
hunting him. He will also wonder why his face
isn't blasted all over the media. Ergo, he will assume that a small team has been assembled by
me to capture him. Therein is the problem."

"Problem?" asked Duggan.

She addressed Duggan. "What does Cochrane
do best?"

Duggan laughed. "Where do I begin?"

"Fair point, but let me tell you the answer.
He misdirects." Her voice grew louder. "He's on
an operational footing now. Yes, he's the West's
finest killer and was the very best spy, blah blah
blah. That worries me considerably. But what
worries me more is his mind. Unchecked, he
won't make a wrong step now. In fact, he didn't
make a wrong step in the D.C. park. He knew

the risks he was taking when he put Fox out of his misery, but he took them anyway."

"So anything that presents itself as *inevitable*—a chance spotting, random act, anything—will be a calculated act by Cochrane?"

"Yes. He's holding the best poker cards one can have. We can't trust Lady Luck." Gage looked at each team member. They were such fine people: Painter, a war hero and one of the best detectives on the East Coast; Kopański, the other best detective, was an incredible shot with a handgun and emboldened with a soul as deep as the Grand Canyon; Duggan, a hero, second to none, who was the most terrifying sight when he stormed a hostage scene with a Heckler & Koch submachine gun.

Gage picked up a photo of Will Cochrane and brushed a finger over his face. "My husband said men like Cochrane are not to be touched. They're too rare. And we burn if we get too close to them, because they live outside of our understanding. Like Icarus flying near the sun. Icarus got too close." She put the photo down. "I love my husband. But I think his observation is bullshit." She turned to Painter. "When you met Cochrane a year ago, what did you see?"

Painter glanced at Kopański, unsure whether to say what she thought.

Kopański picked up his gun and stood. "Ma'am, Cochrane doesn't look at us, or the room he's in, or the street he's on. I've seen that look in other sociopaths. They think they're better than us. Let's leave it at that."

Gage was agitated. "I wish it was that simple. No leads! I repeat, *no* leads!" She walked up to Duggan. "We need to do something that even Cochrane wouldn't predict."

It was midmorning as Michael Stein parked his car on the gravel driveway that led to the house of one of the most dangerous men from the East. The property was in Virginia, adjacent to a vast glistening lake brimming with trout, no other homes nearby, half the house on stilts over the waterline.

Stein was here uninvited. His visit was a hazardous risk.

He lifted his dog, Mr. Peres, out of the car. The dog was wheezing and his legs were shaking. This was to be expected. Stein's beloved hound was suffering from cancer and arthritis. Stein had resigned himself that he was going to have to say good-bye to his friend very soon. But my goodness, as he walked toward the house, cradling the dog in his arms, he could still feel his pal's heartbeat and desire to be in his arms. More than anything, Stein could sense the dog had surrendered himself totally to Stein's care. That tore Stein apart.

Stein pulled the cord of the doorbell. He lowered Mr. Peres and smoothed a hand over his fur.

A tall man answered the door holding a walking stick with a ram's horn on top.

It was Antaeus—once a Russian spymaster, and the man whose wife and child had been accidentally killed by Cochrane. He was now a defector and archaeologist. The middle-aged man was slender and had a droopy eye and a disfigured face from the bomb.

"We have not seen each other for a year, Mr. Stein." Antaeus's English was perfect, almost no accent. "You're here because dead Cochrane did something in the past that has come back to haunt us. More likely, you're here because you think Cochrane is alive."

Stein nodded. "May I come in? If you permit dogs to enter?"

Antaeus looked at the mutt. "He is old and ill. The weather is inclement. He cannot stay outside." Antaeus gestured for them to enter.

"Is Crystal at school?"

As Antaeus led them along a corridor, he said, "She's on a school field trip to England. She won't be home for thirteen days."

They entered a huge living room strewn with antiquities, ancient charts, handcrafted tables containing flints and other archaeological artifacts, burning oil lamps, Oriental rugs, a library of academic books, paintings, a grand piano, and several sofas and chairs. It would have ordinarily been a place of refinement and indicative of a man of history, though that image was offset by numerous drawings that Crystal had done and stuck to the walls, plus photos of her and Antaeus smiling on fishing trips on the lake. Seemingly, Antaeus wasn't bothered that his precise assembly of furnishings and objects, all reflecting his interests and vast intellect, were made off-kilter by a child's whimsy. He was a very good father.

Antaeus winced as he crouched and grabbed one of his rugs, purchased in Mongolia for $3,000, the cost due to the rarity of the silk. He dragged it next to a woodstove that was ablaze. "Your dog can rest here while we speak. What is his name?"

"Mr. Peres."

"Why did you name him that?"

"Out of affection. My dog has always been peaceful."

"May I?" Antaeus held out his hand for the dog's lead.

Stein gave it to him.

Antaeus gently guided Mr. Peres to the rug, patted it, and smiled as the dog rested his weary limbs in front of the fire. He looked at Stein and held a finger to his lips, before walking out of the room to the exterior wooden balcony on stilts over the lake. A small canopy was above three wooden benches, the decking and lake beyond being hit hard by rain.

Antaeus sat on one of the benches. Stein joined him. Ahead of them, two fly-fishing rods were leaning against the wooden fence that encapsulated the jetty.

Antaeus said, "The American Secret Service still checks up on me now and again, but less frequently than before. I don't believe they are bugging my house. Why would they? It would require motivation to do so and objectives in place. Plus, the resources required for twenty-four/seven intercept would be massive. But I worry about the Russians."

Stein laughed. "You're being paranoid, old man. They know you've given America everything you know."

Antaeus gripped his stick as he kept his eyes on the lake. "Mother Russia knows I've betrayed it in absolute terms for the sake of"—he gestured toward the house—"a daughter. That's not what concerns me. One day, maybe here, maybe somewhere else, the Russians will come for me and end matters. I just pray that doesn't happen until Crystal is in college. Meanwhile, I pay close attention to the possibility that anything that comes out of my mouth inside my home may be relayed to Moscow."

Stein frowned. "The Secret Service could sweep your house for bugs. Plus there's technical equipment—dog whistles, we used to call them in Mossad—that can interfere with bugs even if you can't find them."

Antaeus smiled, his disfigured face making the expression look like that of a gargoyle. "Whether there are Russian bugs in my house or not, long ago I took the view that sometimes it's better for Moscow to hear I'm no threat. I'm buying a few years until Crystal flies the nest. After that, nothing matters." He pointed to the canopy. "I control Moscow by giving them what they don't want to hear: mundanity, everyday life. But out here there *are*, as you call them, dog whistles. They are waterproof and concealed. In the old days the only way to avoid audio interception was speaking to someone via a horn that went from one person's mouth to the other's ear. After that, it was speaking in a bathroom with taps on full. That was less successful. Then it was running a vacuum cleaner amid conversation. Alas, technology caught up and those techniques became obsolete. Now it's dog whistles. Let's see how long that lasts. But for now, on my porch, we're safe."

"*If* your house is bugged."

Antaeus sighed. "Ifs and buts."

Stein looked at the beautiful lake and pictured Antaeus and Crystal on a boat, using the rods to fetch their supper. How times had changed. Years ago, Antaeus answered to no one. He was the most feared spymaster, second to none. "Cochrane is alive."

"Yes."

"How do you know?"

Antaeus's eyes were glistening. "I haven't seen him since the incident on the Brooklyn Bridge. I have no proof of life. But I know Cochrane. He's alive."

Stein clasped his hands and bowed his head. "I've been in the States for a year, trying to find him. I wanted to help, give him resources, that kind of thing. The FBI had me under surveillance. Bunch of amateurs. I could lose them without even thinking. But two nights ago I was grabbed by a small Bureau team. Their leader is a woman called Marsha Gage. She's anything but an amateur. The three others with her were also pros, I'm certain. No doubt this has to do with Cochrane."

"And you've come to me because . . . ?"

Stein looked at Antaeus. The young Israeli wondered how the middle-aged Russian coped with being a single father while at the same time having the possibility of death hanging over his head. "Who are the most brilliant minds in the secret world?"

Antaeus laughed. "I suspect a fanciful analogy will soon come out of your mouth."

Stein remained serious. "Answer."

Antaeus turned to him. "You are one of them. But you are limited by purpose. Fifty percent of your brain has to deal with combat. It quashes your full potential. Still, you are one of four of the finest operatives."

"And the other three?"

"Me."

"I totally concur. Who else?"

"There is a man in the CIA. His name is Hessian Bell. He is very dangerous, but a good man. Never underestimate him. He hates the CIA, yet serves the Agency. He has his own agenda. That agenda is to make the Agency better."

"And the last?" Stein knew the answer.

"Of course, Will Cochrane." Antaeus placed a mottled hand on Stein's shoulder. "We are the four. But only Bell remains employed."

"By an organization he detests."

Antaeus nodded.

"There will be others in the CIA, MI6, DGSE, Mossad, et cetera, who we don't know about and are rising stars," Stein said.

"But we don't know them, so they are of no use."

"What are you thinking?"

"The same thought as you." Antaeus rubbed his leg that got injured in the bomb blast. It always ached when the weather turned cold. "Cochrane needs our help."

"He killed your family."

"By mistake. And three years ago I tried to kill him by design. You of all people know things have changed since then."

He was referring to the help Antaeus and Stein gave Cochrane a year ago when Cochrane was in a desperate state. The help was supplied by the most unlikely of allies because Antaeus and Stein recognized themselves in Cochrane. They were all once lone operators who never really sacrificed their lives for the organizations they served or their countries. They did what they did because they were mavericks who excelled in their work.

Antaeus tapped his staff on the decking. "We became obsolete in the secret world yet daily struggle to have a footprint in the normal world. I try to be an archaeologist but worry about assassination. You load bags of soap in a kibbutz factory, yet remain on many countries' blacklists because of your Mossad days as a hit man. Cochrane is the enigma, because we don't know where he is. But he is the big game prize. So many people want his head above their mantelpiece."

"I'd hoped you might know Cochrane's whereabouts."

"So you can disrupt Gage's hunt?"

"Yes."

"There may be a role for both of us in that

strategy. But not until we know where Cochrane is." Antaeus stood and walked to the fence overlooking the lake. "If, as I believe, Cochrane is alive, he will call for help when it's needed. Like me, Hessian Bell, and you, he's a chess player. But he always moves ahead."

"We're not his pawns! We're better than that!"

"We are. But we're not competing with him. We're helping him. Thus, we become the power chess pieces." He turned. "I was put in checkmate by Cochrane three years ago. It's why I'm here. It was on the back of me being in Russia trying to outplay him. I won battles; he won battles. But he won the war. Why has this current situation arisen? Why has Cochrane been spotted?"

"It will be for a reason. He's working on something that has forced him out of hiding."

"Exactly."

Stein moved to Antaeus's side. "Gage and her team have a huge disadvantage."

"They have no leads to go on."

"So we wait until Cochrane makes his move."

A trout broke the surface of the lake yards away from the jetty.

"The fish are getting agitated." Antaeus turned to Stein. "Are you sure you haven't been followed by Gage's team to my house?"

"Yes."

"Good. I want you to lay low nearby. I don't know for how long."

"I have limited funds and—"

"When we go back inside, I will give you cash,

a mobile phone with my number stored in it, and a sidearm with spare magazines."

"You agree with my idea?"

Antaeus nodded. "If Cochrane puts his head above the parapet, give Gage and her team hell."

The former spies walked into the living room. Stein smoothed his hand over Mr. Peres's fur. "Try not to slow me down, my friend."

"He can stay here."

Stein was surprised. "That's too kind and unnecessary."

"The Bureau grabbed you because you were fleeing with Mr. Peres."

"How did you know that?"

"Deduction." Antaeus walked to the dog and placed two hands over his body. "Crystal loves dogs. It will be a pleasure to have Mr. Peres here." He ran his hands over the full length of the dog's back, an intense expression on his face. "He has arthritis, no doubt."

"And cancer."

"Who told you he had cancer?"

"A surgeon in Tel Aviv."

Antaeus shook his head. "Your dog is predominantly Labrador. Cancer in that breed typically manifests itself as lumps on the skin. Did the vet take a biopsy?"

"No. He said it wasn't worth the effort."

"He wrote your pet off."

"I wanted to get a second opinion in the States. But it was hard because—"

"You needed to stay under the radar. Going to a vet would have required documentation." The dog was sleeping. Antaeus said, "I qualified as a vet before joining the Russian service." Antaeus stroked a finger along Mr. Peres's jaw. "He will die soon, but hopefully not as quickly as you may think. Leave him with me. I will do tests and care for him. When this is over, you'll have quality time with him."

Stein was confused. "Why would you do this for me?"

Antaeus pointed at the dog. "What is the difference between him and us? We help each other when we can."

"What will you do?"

Antaeus moved away from Mr. Peres. "Once the biopsy is done, I will examine the cells. I don't wish to give you false hope, but there is a possibility the tumors under his skin are benign. That said, why is he wheezing and passing blood?"

"You know about the blood?"

"Look at my rug."

There were bloodstains around the dog's groin.

"I'm so sorry."

"Nonsense. It's no one's fault." Antaeus grabbed a bag and gave it to Stein. "Everything you need is in here."

Stein took the bag, his expression amused. "You anticipated the next move?"

"I've anticipated the next several moves. Take the bag, lie low, only use the phone to call me. If it rings, whatever number, it will be me calling you. Go now!"

Howard Kane was in his Pentagon office.

Flail was the only person with him. The ex–

Green Beret said, "There's always been rumors about Haden crossing the line, but on paper he has an impeccable military career. My men are wondering if we should just leave him alone. I may not be like Haden, but I don't want to kick the hornet's nest."

Kane was in a crisp white shirt and pressed pants. He circulated his office while speaking as if he were a lecturer addressing a student. "Nothing differentiates you."

"Everything differentiates Haden from me and men like me!" Flail wondered about grabbing Kane's shirt. "People like you don't get it. I work for a living. But when the day is done I go home and suck a Bud and wish I'd gotten better grades at school so I never had to join the army. Haden's different. You know of Paddy Mayne?"

"Never heard of him."

"Given you're head of spec ops Pentagon, you should make it your business to know of him. World War II, North Africa. A whiz kid British lieutenant called David Stirling comes up with a radical idea to form an unconventional unit called the Special Air Service. He gets permission from high command to form the tiny unit, supported by the Brits' Long Range Desert Group—guys expert in desert navigation and transportation behind enemy lines. The SAS's first mission was a parachute drop. They didn't know what they were doing. Half of them died in the drop, many of them getting killed as their parachutes dragged them across the desert after landing. Catastrophe. But Stirling was adamant they had to succeed in order to maintain the existence of the SAS. In their next missions they destroyed more German planes than the RAF ever did in Africa. They sneaked into air bases, put Lewes bombs on fighter planes, ran as the bombs exploded."

"Your point?!"

"Stirling only recruited brilliant types. And he didn't want anyone who just obeyed orders. He wanted thinkers. The Green Berets, Delta, and Rangers wouldn't be where they're at now were it not for Stirling's ingenuity."

Kane was getting exasperated. "I don't need a history lesson."

"But you do need to know about Paddy Mayne." Flail towered over Kane. "It was very tough for the Brits out there. The SAS lost a lot of men in their small gang. Officers came and went. And then Stirling, now a major, spotted Mayne. Paddy was a rebel in the army, but superb. Well schooled, excellent at sports, and a natural leader. Stirling made Mayne his second-in-command. Thing was, though, one night after an aircraft destroy mission, Mayne and two other men entered the German barracks and shot all the soldiers in cold blood. He wasn't authorized to do so. The Germans were unarmed. It was a slaughter."

Kane was silent.

Flail continued. "Stirling knew Mayne was a sociopath. But he needed him. It was war. Colonel Haden is Paddy Mayne, at least in type. They cross the line but it's tolerated. Don't for one second think I'm like that."

Kane moved away from Flail. "And yet you can chop up a U.S. senator and feed her to pigs."

Flail was silent.

"What happened to Mayne?"

"He died after the war. Crashed his car into a wall."

"An accident?"

"Boredom. He'd turned to drink. He was blind drunk when he died."

Kane folded his arms and leaned against a windowsill, staring at Flail. "Warmongers, sociopaths—call them what you will—need an excuse to kill. I'm fairly certain I'm looking at a sociopath right now."

Flail took a step forward.

Kane held up his hand. "And that's not a problem. You do what you're told. And you serve the higher purpose. What kicks you get out of it are of no consequence to me."

"You know nothing about me!"

Kane was unfazed. "I know you garroted three women in Syria to get a tribal leader to confess to the location of his IEDs." Before Flail could respond, Kane continued. "Like I said, it's of no consequence to me. That is the past and you will answer for your crimes at the gates of heaven. Meanwhile, I need rough men to help innocents sleep peacefully in their beds."

"You're not Winston Churchill."

"And neither are you. But here we are."

Flail backed away. "I can forgive Haden for his war crimes. I can't forgive him for lining his pocket in Berlin."

"A soldier's code of conduct." Kane laughed and then grew quiet. The Pentagon knew Flail and his three former Green Beret colleagues were working for him. Officially they were on the payroll as consultants. But the Pentagon had no idea what they really did for Kane. And Flail and his team had only partial knowledge of what was really happening. Kane alone carried the burden of fully understanding the truth, and it had to remain top secret. "The priority is Will Cochrane."

"The Berlin shooter."

Kane nodded. "You've now met him twice. You know his face. Don't buy that crap that he's a private investigator working for Mrs. Haden. It's far worse than that. He's an ex–special operative and spy. Half American, half Brit."

"SAS *and* MI6?"

"MI6, yes. But no, he wasn't UK SF."

"Foreign Legion, then into GCP?"

"Groupement des Commandos Parachutistes. That was his SF career. Then black ops for the French intelligence services. Cambridge University after his tour ended. MI6 after that. Joint with the CIA in more recent years. The toughest and most intelligent operator we've ever produced."

"Something went wrong?"

"He made too many enemies. Now he's on the run."

Flail was absorbing the information. "Sounds like he's not running away right now."

"Exactly." Kane had never met Cochrane, and

Cochrane didn't know of Kane's role in the Berlin job. But Kane recalled with stark clarity what Unwin Fox had said to him before the mission.

If we activate Cochrane, there will be no going back. He won't take orders from me, you, Haden, anyone. Are you willing to take that risk?

Kane was deep in thought. "We need to neutralize Cochrane before we can get to Haden. So we set a trap."

Flail replied, "A trap?"

"Mobilize your team. You'll need all four of you to take on Cochrane."

"Where and how?"

Kane placed his hand against his chin. "Cochrane's doing a mop-up job. Unwin Fox's house, Elizabeth Haden's house. But I know for a fact the trail runs dry there. He'll have no choice other than to keep Elizabeth Haden under observation. That's where we get him."

Flail laughed. "Dead or interrogated, or both?"

Kane's expression was earnest as he said, "This is no joking matter. Capture Cochrane, find out where Haden is, then kill Cochrane."

TWENTY

Pete Duggan and Marsha Gage unholstered their sidearms and approached the house.

It was night. Kopański and Painter were at the rear of the house, their guns also ready for action.

All of them had so much to lose by this act.

Gage had her ascendancy to the top job in the Bureau in jeopardy. That didn't bother her. Not providing for her husband and two kids did.

Duggan had alimony to pay from a previous marriage and kids from his new lovely marriage to support.

Single father Kopański was saving up to send his injured daughter to a sanctuary in Hawaii.

Painter wanted to help him with that task.

But tonight they were cops. Nothing got in the way of the job.

A fox screeched as Duggan and Gage ap-

proached the house, both silent, knowing they
could be shot on approach if not careful. Duggan was in the lead, his body low, pistol in both
hands. Lights were on inside the house, which
was modest in size and functional. Around them
were trees and a few other properties. Duggan
and Gage crossed the deserted road in front of
the house and reached the front door. Duggan
squatted to one side of the entrance and gestured
to Gage to approach.

Gage knocked three times on the door.

Twenty seconds later, a man responded without opening the door. "Who is it?"

Gage said, "FBI. Open up."

"If you're FBI, put your guns away. I'm a detective with the Virginia PD. I'm armed and
authorized to shoot people I don't like on this
property. If you're not FBI, come in and get a
bullet in your brain."

"We're FBI. We're here to help." Gage glanced
at Duggan before returning her attention to the
door. "We can't put our guns away unless you
can prove you're law enforcement."

"And I can't put my gun away until I can prove
you're FBI!"

Gage asked, "Is this your home, or are you
working here?"

"None of your damn business. Give me your
name and shield ID."

Gage did so and added, "Don't open the door
until you've checked my credentials. Call my ID
into the Bureau."

There was silence for five minutes before the

man said, "Your ID checks out, but that says shit. You could be an impersonator."

"So could you. I want your identity."

The detective told her who he was.

Duggan trained his handgun on the door while Gage called Virginia PD. The department wouldn't verify anything to her, but made a call to the FBI, who in turn called Gage and then the detective.

Gage called out, "You're running a safe house. I didn't know that. You check out and I check out. Our guns are in our holsters." She and Duggan holstered their weapons. "There are two of us out front, two of us in the backyard. Looks like we've stumbled onto something that might interest you. *Please*, let us in. You can keep your gun on us until you see we're no threat."

The door opened. A tall detective had his weapon trained on Gage. At the end of the corridor behind him, a second detective had his pistol pointing toward the backyard window.

"Agent Gage, you'd better be who you say you are. Who's your colleague?"

"Pete Duggan, FBI Hostage Rescue Team." Gage held her hands up. "We had no idea what this place was. We've been working a national case that brought us to this town. We should swap notes."

"Two armed Feds entering the zone," shouted the detective to his partner. "I've got them covered. Stay on point for the rear."

The second detective didn't flinch, maintaining his guard on the yard. Somewhere out there were Kopański and Painter, though it was impossible to see them in the darkness.

The detective in front of Gage and Duggan said to the Feds, "Your credentials check out. But know this: I have a duty to protect this property. You do anything dumb, I can pull my trigger." He kept his sidearm pointed at Gage. "No court in the land will convict me for gunning down two Feds. There's an overriding reason for that. One that I'm not going to share with you."

The detective didn't know that Gage knew all about the safe house that contained Faye Glass and Billy and Tom Koenig. She had the highest security rating on all matters Will Cochrane and had known about the house ever since Cochrane faked his death.

The detective backed away, keeping his gun on the Feds. "Enter. Every move in this house is orchestrated by me. Got it?"

Gage and Duggan nodded.

Duggan estimated he could withdraw his ACP and kill the cop in under a second. But he kept his hands high.

"Can we go to the kitchen? Or somewhere else you think is neutral ground?" Gage walked along the corridor, Duggan by her side.

"Kitchen will do just fine." The detective backed into the room. "I need better proof of identity. Bill, time to take a risk. Get off point and use your cell to get the Bureau to send you photos of Agents Gage and Duggan."

The detective immediately complied, once again using Virginia PD to make the request through official channels. It took ten minutes. The images were e-mailed to Bill's phone. "Checks out. They're one and the same."

The detective holding the gun on the Bureau officers said, "Get your people out of the yard and bring them in here. Do it now!"

Gage called Painter. Twenty seconds later, the former NYPD cops were in the room.

The two Virginia detectives guarding the house stood before Gage's team and lowered their weapons. "You tell us why you're here. Then you leave and forget you were ever here."

Gage walked up to the senior detective. "The Bureau has been working a narco case. I've been in charge. There's a guy down the street who's been pumping around five million dollars of drugs per month into the East Coast. We want to bust him, but only when we've got enough evidence."

"And we're in the middle."

Gage looked around. "Now I can see why."

"I'm sure you can."

"There are other people sleeping here."

"Your assumption, but I'm going to give you a no-comment on that."

Gage understood that the two detectives guarding Glass and the Koenig twins were exceptional. Still, she had to dupe them over. "We've had teams on rotation working this area and others. Surveillance. Intercept. You know the drill. Thing is, though, when you watch someone covertly, sometimes you see other things unconnected to what you're doing."

"Meaning?"

"Meaning there's been a man watching this house for five days. We don't know who he is."

The detective looked urgently at his partner. To Gage, he asked, "You have a photo?"

Gage shook her head. "Only visuals, but at night."

The detective dashed to his attaché case and withdrew a photo. It was of Will Cochrane.

"This man?"

Gage faked confusion. "I've never seen this man before. The person watching your house is around five-eight, probably dark haired, slim build. It's hard to tell because we've only seen your stalker in the dark, but the guy in this photo looks *very* different. Who is he?"

"Classified." The detective put the photo in his pocket. "But answer me this. We're worried about a man who's six feet four inches. Is there any possibility that you've mistaken the stalker's height?"

"None."

The detective turned to his partner. "This can't be random."

"I agree."

"Accomplice? Blast from the past? Revenge? Whatever. Shit. We need to move."

Gage approached him. "I don't need to know the details. A safe house has become unsafe. Take your cares somewhere else. Don't tell me where. No doubt you'll have options."

The detective was as alert as could be. "Takes fifteen minutes for backup! Is the Bureau willing to help Virginia PD?"

Gage nodded.

"Perimeter while we evacuate!" The detective ran into bedrooms. "Out! Out!"

Kopański, Painter, and Duggan guarded entrances, while the detectives woke Glass and the twins.

Bleary-eyed, Faye Glass entered the kitchen. "Who are you?" she asked Gage.

"Help. Essential items only. We have a threat."

Faye left her handbag on a kitchen bench and ran to the twins' room.

Out of sight of everyone, Gage withdrew Glass's cell phone, used it to call Gage's number, then deleted the call from the history log.

Now she had Glass's phone number. And now she hopefully had unsettled Cochrane by moving the twins and their aunt.

Gage and her team protected the perimeter as the detectives ushered the twins and their aunt into two vehicles and vanished. She addressed her team while still in the house. "Cochrane may be watching us now. Maybe not. But either way, pretty soon he's going to know the twins have been moved. When he realizes that, I'm betting he'll call Faye Glass." She held up her phone. "And I have her number. I'm going to trace all calls to the number. Meanwhile, we go back to our house and wait. When Cochrane surfaces, we move on him with speed. Got it?"

Duggan, Painter, and Kopański nodded.

It was close to midnight when the two detectives, Faye Glass, and the twin boys arrived at a new house 216 miles away from the previous safe house. This one was comparable in size with the previous one: four bedrooms, detached, and in the countryside. But it had advantages. The yard was larger. There were spotlights on the grounds and on exterior walls that were triggered by movement. A secure panic room was on the upper floor. Fire extinguishers were in every room. And there were two gun cabinets, locked by electronic code keypads, one on the first floor, the other on the second floor. Both contained semiautomatic rifles and shotguns. Only the detectives had the codes.

The twins were exhausted and confused.

"What about school?" asked Tom as Faye sent them to bed.

Faye responded, "This is only temporary. Think of it as a mini holiday. I'm betting after a few days we'll be going to my house. No more detectives. And you'll be back at school in no time." She faked a smile. "What an adventure we've had. It will be great to see your school pals again."

The detectives were in the yard, checking its perimeter.

It gave Faye a window of opportunity.

She called Will. "We've been moved." She gave him the address and started getting teary. "I can't believe I'm speaking to you. I . . . we all thought you were dead."

Will wondered whether to speak. He made a decision. "Focus on the twins. I can't help right now. But you'll see me soon." He hung up and stared at his phone.

Gage and her team were in the rear of their black SUV. Gage punched the air in jubilation as she removed her headphones, having listened to the call on Faye Glass's phone. "We've got Cochrane's cell phone number! Now we've got our lead!"

TWENTY-ONE

Will removed his cell phone battery and drove through the night halfway across Virginia. Rain was pelting the car, visibility atrocious, and the glare from the occasional oncoming car was near blinding. For the most part, he was in the countryside, woods and open fields the prevailing landscape. So much around him felt familiar from his childhood, growing up in the state. A lifetime later, everything was different. His deployment in wars, assassinations, espionage, and, more recently, being framed for murder made him feel a million miles away from the child who used to giggle when his sister pushed him on a rope swing over their home's adjacent river. He could barely recall his American father, who'd been taken from him when Will was five. But the handful of memories he did have of his dad included seeing him laugh as Will was hurtling over the river, grabbing him when he returned, and giving him a hug. In a suit, his father tried to replicate Will's endeavor, getting on the swing and launching himself across the river. The rope unraveled from the tree it was fixed to, and he crashed into the water, tears of laughter on his face. Will and his sister were giggling so hard they thought their stomachs would burst. When their father strode out of the river, he ruffled Will's head and told him what an idiot dad he had.

Except he wasn't an idiot. Will's father was an expert CIA officer who saved two men in Iran who years later became Will's mentors in Western intelligence. It came at the cost of James Cochrane's life.

What would James think of his son now? It was a thought that Will had carried for his entire adult life. In many ways, they were so alike—compassionate, intelligent, dutiful, with a hunger for the mischievous. But James Cochrane, as heroic as he was, had not been thrown into the cauldron of a life like Will's. No doubt, he'd be looking down from heaven with sadness. His son had been pushed into impossible situations. Will hoped his father didn't think less of him for it.

After two more hours of driving, Will stopped his car and examined Elizabeth Haden's home through binoculars. Rain was abating as the sun rose. But the temperature was still cold enough to freeze a lesser man. Will had to see if she was awake. He scanned the windows from seven until nine A.M. That's when he saw glimpses of her moving within her house. He pulled out a cell phone—not the one whose number he'd given to Faye Glass, but a pay-as-you-go phone. He called Haden's home number.

"Elizabeth, this is Edward Pope."

Elizabeth Haden answered, "How did you know my number?"

From his position overlooking the property within a cluster of trees, Will replied, "It wasn't difficult. I'll explain everything soon. Meanwhile we need to meet. Can I come to your house tomorrow? It's urgent. I have something to tell you about your husband."

"Can't you just tell me on the phone?"

"No. It has to be face-to-face. Your house, preferably. Or another location of your choosing." Will could see her standing stock-still in her living room, her landline against her ear, his binoculars focused on her from three hundred yards away.

She was silent for a moment. "Where are you?"

"New York City. But I can get to you by midday tomorrow if that works for you?"

"Alone?"

"Alone."

"Okay. Midday tomorrow it is. My house. This had better be worth my time."

"It is." Will hung up.

Kane's phone in his Pentagon office rang.

It was Flail calling. "Mrs. Haden's just received a call from a guy requesting to meet her at her home noon tomorrow. I'm certain it was Cochrane—same voice we confronted at Fox's house and outside Haden's house."

Kane thumped a fist against the table. "Damn him!" He composed himself. "Colonel Haden can't be spooked. We have to get him out into the open so we can arrest him. As for Cochrane, do whatever it takes. But no one, repeat *no one*, on your team lays one finger on Elizabeth Haden. Got that?"

"Understood."

"Not even in cross fire. If she even gets a scratch it'll go bad for you."

Flail said, "Me and my colleagues will pose as DEA agents. We've got ID to back that up. But, sir, is Cochrane worth the risk? Surely there must be another way to get to the colonel. Cops? Feds?"

Kane was exasperated. "Colonel Haden is a classified asset who's gone rogue. The president has instructed me to deal with this in-house. When we get Haden in our sights, we capture him. Only then do we hand him over to the Feds. But even then, we'll need an army of security-cleared prosecutors to keep the trial under wraps. Cochrane is disposable. Haden, on the other hand, must be brought to trial. Do I need to fill in the blanks for you, or can I rely on you to make the right judgment call tomorrow?"

"I hear you. We've got this covered."

"Tell Elizabeth Haden to take a vacation until this is over." Kane hung up. He knew who was behind all this. Colonel Haden had to be buried once and for all for what had happened in Berlin.

Senator Charlie Sapper and Unwin Fox had been murdered because of what they knew.

That left only Kane, Cochrane, and Haden.

Kane had to kill Cochrane. It was a nasty task, and Kane took no pleasure in his instructions to Flail. But Kane had to look at the bigger picture. Something was going on. The jigsaw pieces hadn't been fully assembled.

And Kane knew the conspiracy went right up to the White House.

TWENTY-TWO

The White House official code-named Deep Throat received a call.

"Is this line being recorded?" his caller asked.

Deep Throat responded, "Of course."

The person at the end of the line was silent for five seconds before saying, "Mr. C is causing problems."

Deep Throat nodded. "We can't let him get to the truth about Mr. H."

"I know."

Deep Throat slammed down the phone and was deep in thought. If only Cochrane were dead.

A TV channel in the D.C. diner was baying for political blood. Much of the discourse between the reporter and a Capitol Hill adviser had to do with illegal immigration from Mexico, corrupt politicians, and the U.S. Constitution. Some people were watching the channel; many were just tucking into their burgers and fries.

Will walked into the diner. Nearby were a motel and a highway. In his jacket he had his sidearm and spare magazines. He sat opposite Kay Ash.

"Tomorrow we're going to have a problem."

"We?" Ash picked up a pickle and popped it in her mouth. "I don't recall there was a *we* in this." The deep-cover CIA officer eyed Will. "What are you playing at?"

Will didn't directly answer the question. "Have you spoken to Hessian Bell?"

"Yes."

"His response?"

"Leave you alone. Let things play out."

Will replied, "For the sake of anyone watching us, we're a normal couple having a bite to eat. So don't take this the wrong way." He picked up a napkin and dabbed the side of her mouth.

Ash didn't recoil. She was a consummate pro and knew exactly why Will had performed the action. Instead, she smiled and placed her hand on Will's hand. Quietly she asked, "You think we're being watched?"

"Not yet. But we have to be careful."

A waitress came over and asked if he'd like to order. Will replied, "I'll have the same as my girlfriend ordered. No mayo, though. I can't stand the stuff."

When the waitress was gone, Will withdrew his hand and placed his napkin on his lap. "How old are you?"

Ash laughed. "Straight in with that question?"

"Why not?"

Ash looked around. "I don't think anyone's watching us right now. But that means shit if a surveillance team's following you. And if that's the case, you've damn well brought them to my doorstep!"

"No one's following me. Within the last twenty-four hours, I've had two cell phones. One of them is now at the bottom of a lake. The other has its battery removed so it can't be tracked. That's a temporary measure, I hope."

"Temporary?"

Will didn't elaborate. "I wouldn't bring danger to you."

Fully aware that she was now portraying herself as a hissy girlfriend to any diners watching them, she said in a whisper, "Don't patronize me! The biggest threat in this place is you. And yet here I am, sitting and talking to you!"

Will clutched her hands, as if he were a boyfriend trying to make peace. "Danger to you would mean danger to everyone here. I took precautions."

Antisurveillance.

"To get here." He leaned back. "For now, I'm off the radar. Tomorrow I need to be on the radar."

"You could get yourself killed."

"I suspect I will be killed."

The waitress delivered his burger and fries.

Will started eating. "So this could be my last supper."

Kay watched him devour his meal. He looked

like he was famished, barely taking notice of the taste of his food. She wondered how he survived the isolation. In her job as a deep-cover officer, loneliness was the biggest killer. But she always had the release valve of returning to headquarters at the end of an assignment. Cochrane had no release valves available to him. She wasn't aware of the lovebirds Ebb and Flo, whom Cochrane had nurtured. Nor was she aware of the twin boys Billy and Tom, whom Will had desperately wanted to adopt. If she had been, she'd have realized he was like everyone else. He wanted a different path, one with engagement with others. He was not by nature a marauding loner. Life had just made it that way. In his heart, he was a man like his father—someone who wanted to fall into the river from a swing to make his kids laugh, who then returned to the house to get out of his wet clothes and prepared for work while his wife initially chastised him before telling him what a great husband and father he was.

Kay didn't have those facts, but she was extremely astute. She could see in Cochrane's eyes what he yearned for. She said, "I'm thirty-seven."

Will wiped his hands on the same napkin he'd dabbed against Kay's mouth. "And you're . . ."

"Don't analyze me! Hessian Bell accurately ripped me apart within five minutes of my first meeting with him. I know you're able to do the same. It doesn't do anything for me."

"Fair point." Will withdrew cash to pay for their meal. He looked away, seemed lost for a moment, then engaged eye contact with Kay.

Quietly and with an earnest tone, he said, "They trained me too well. The problem with that is they left me with no soul."

Kay hadn't expected him to say that. She touched his hand. "No, they haven't. You're not just some pro killer with the brain of a small planet."

Will asked, "Are you single?"

"Jesus H. Christ! Why not ask me what my bra size is?!"

Will looked away, an intangible expression on his face. Quietly, he said, "I just need to know your circumstances. Whether you have loved ones." He stared at her. "I need your help but can't put you at risk if it will put others at risk."

"But you don't mind putting me at risk!"

"I do. You have a choice."

Kay was quiet for a moment. "I'm single. No kids. My parents are dead. Brother too. So if I go down, the best I can hope for is a few folks from the Agency turning up to my funeral."

Will was motionless. "I'd like to move in with you."

"What?!"

"Not your apartment. Somewhere different."

"Are you crazy?"

Will sighed. "Oh, who knows? But I need somewhere to prepare for what's about to happen. I need new clothes, more ammunition for my sidearm, and above all else I'm getting sick of sleeping in my car. I need a bath. That's all I need from you. Nothing else."

"A bath?" Kay laughed as she drummed her

fingers on the table between them. "There is a place we can go to. But why do I get the feeling you're not telling me everything?"

Dusk around Elizabeth Haden's house brought with it a stillness and the sounds of birds chirping. The air was cool and dry, and frost covered the meadow surrounding her substantial property. She walked into the yard, a flashlight in her hand, to speak to her gardener. He was collecting logs for the house's fireplace—his last chore before clocking off.

"How are the bees?"

Jedd Bartlett looked up, a cluster of sticks in his arms. "They're all good, ma'am. Quiet, as you would expect."

"The queen?"

"She's in the hive. Hibernating or whatever it is they do this time of year. Her workers too. I checked them this morning. No signs they won't make it through the winter. But we'll see."

Bartlett was a forty-seven-year-old veteran from the First Gulf War, having seen active duty as a corporal with the 101st Airborne Division. Fifteen years ago, Elizabeth Haden had found him on a street in Detroit, homeless and strung out on crack cocaine. She'd employed him ever since, his home being a wooden shack at the base of her meadow. Thanks to her, Bartlett had gotten his life on track after the horrors he'd been engaged with in war and after destitution thanks to a government that didn't give a shit about veterans returning from conflict. He owed her his life. With a scant military pension, PTSD that was now just under control, and five days a week of fresh air filling his lungs, he was content to serve out his time here. Haden had told him that she would always employ him and give him shelter, even if she had to bring in a younger man to lighten the burden as he got older.

"Bring the logs in and make a fire. I'll get your wages." Haden returned to the house, Bartlett following her.

Five minutes later, the fire in the living room was under way.

Haden asked, "Do you have time for a coffee before you go?"

It was an unusual request. Bartlett replied, "Yes, ma'am."

"What are you cooking tonight?"

"Beans. Toast."

Haden prepared coffee in the kitchen. She checked her fridge. Inside were two steaks. She brought the coffee back into the living room. "You'd be doing me a favor if you cooked yourself this steak tonight. I've got a spare that I'm cooking for myself this evening. Packaging says they expire tomorrow, so let's make the most of them tonight."

Bartlett gratefully accepted the food. Inside his shack was excellent heating, a single bedroom, a living room with a chair and TV, and a kitchenette where tonight he'd take great joy in frying the steak. The habitat was all he needed. It was a damn sight better than the places he'd slept after being discharged from the army.

Haden handed him an envelope containing his weekly wage. "I have a different job for you tomorrow."

Bartlett laughed but was deferential in demeanor. "Please tell me not the yew trees near my house. Pruning them will have to wait until spring."

Haden sipped her coffee. "Not the yew trees. I have a visitor tomorrow. I'm worried about him."

"Worried for him or about him?"

"About him. He was the man you saw here the other day."

"The big guy. Yeah, there was something about him that was unusual."

Haden said, "He told me he'd be here at midday. I want protection."

Bartlett frowned. "Ma'am, you know I don't deal with that anymore."

"I know. But these are exceptional circumstances. We must protect our estate, yes?"

Bartlett nodded.

"I know you don't have a weapon in your place. I have a gun. Would you check it and the ammunition?"

"A gun?"

"Shotgun. It's only a precaution."

"Ma'am—"

"But you know how to use it." Haden sat in a chair. "I want you to protect me, you, and our property. It's all we have."

This pressed the right buttons with Bartlett. "I've got your back. What do we know about the visitor?"

"He goes by the name of Edward Pope. It's not his real name, I'm sure. He speaks with a pitch-perfect Virginia accent, but in truth he's British. He claims he worked with my husband, possibly the Pentagon or military, but I can't see how an Englishman would have done that." She fell silent.

Bartlett said, "There's more."

Haden nodded. "He wants to find my husband. I told him I hoped he did after—"

"Yes, ma'am. We don't need to talk about that. It was a long time ago."

"He was unfaithful too many times! Long time ago or yesterday?! It's in his blood!"

Bartlett bowed his head. "I'm sorry. I didn't know about it earlier."

Haden placed her coffee to one side. "I don't know why Pope wants to get to the colonel. My guess is he's a private investigator pursuing a paternity suit. But given what my husband did for a living, I can't take risks. This guy Pope could be someone out for revenge. Plus . . ."

"Plus?"

Haden looked directly at Bartlett. "When my husband was in Delta Force, I met some of his men. They had thousand-yard stares. They were charming, but you knew they were killers. This guy Pope seemed far worse."

TWENTY-THREE

Faye Glass left the twins Billy and Tom to sleep in their new bedroom and went into the kitchen to speak to the two detectives who'd protected them for a year. When she was gone, Billy flicked on his bedside light and whispered to Tom, "Are you still awake?"

Tom replied in a whisper: "Yes."

The eleven-year-old boys were highly anxious and confused.

Tom said, "Why were we moved?"

"I overheard Aunt Faye talking to the detectives. They told her a man had been watching our house. They thought he might be dangerous."

"A man? Who?"

"I don't know."

"Uncle Will?"

"He's dead."

Tom gripped his pillow. "Why did he jump off the bridge? He was supposed to look after us."

"How could he? He killed all those people."

"He didn't!"

"I know. But the police think he did. They wanted to shoot him. No way would they let him look after us."

The boys grew silent, each immersed in his own thoughts. Aunt Faye had told them they'd be homeschooled for a few days, until the sighting of the man near their previous safe house had been investigated. It was her intention, she'd told them, to then take the boys to her home in Roanoke. There they'd finally live a normal life, return to their school, have a future. They believed her, just wanting this horrible existence to end. Two years ago their parents had been murdered. Since then, everything had been horrific.

Aunt Faye had tried to shield the boys from what happened a year ago, and she'd reluctantly forbidden them from having smartphones so they couldn't browse the Web. But at school the twins had computer lessons. Secretly, they'd googled Will Cochrane. They'd read what was plastered all over the media.

A year ago he'd woken up in a New York hotel.

There was a dead woman in his room's bathtub.

It was his sister.

He killed six cops.

And the twins' great-uncle and -aunt, Robert and Celia.

Then he took men hostage in a New York restaurant.

And after that, he jumped off the Brooklyn Bridge.

None of it made sense.

Uncle Will was not like that. He'd been the twins' only glimmer of hope in the last two years, changing his life, securing a job as a teaching assistant in their school, buying a house where he and the boys could live, adopting them.

The online papers say he threw it all away due to madness. No mention was made of the twins' names—Aunt Faye had explained to the boys that the media wasn't permitted to reveal their identities. But the websites were permitted to say that Will Cochrane was in the process of adopting children.

Tom said, "Do you remember when Uncle Will used to come visit us when Mom and Dad were alive?"

"Chase us around the yard, pretending to be a zombie or werewolf?"

"I couldn't stop laughing."

"Me too."

They grew silent again.

"Every night I go to sleep wishing he was alive."

"Not dead."

"Not a zombie."

"Zombies aren't dead. They're half dead."

"No, they're back from the dead, but in a different form."

"Half life?"

The boys debated the definition of a zombie.

Billy turned off his light. The bedroom was in complete darkness.

"Auntie Faye once said to me that Uncle Will has the ability to come back to life," Tom whispered. "I didn't believe her. But I liked the idea of it. Maybe he'll come back to life and look after us."

"He won't. He can't."

Will drove fast in the car he'd stolen from an assassin a year ago. Ash was by his side. They were heading to the coast of Virginia—a remote place that Will had never been to before. It was night. They were on a highway, Ash giving Will directions, Will for the most part silent.

But there were moments of conversation.

"I could have driven," said Ash. "I'm trained in offensive and defensive driving, just like you."

"I know."

"But you think you're better than me?"

"No."

"So you think you're the same as me but take priority. That sucks."

Will was unflinching. "This is my car, so I drive it. You're an expert at antisurveillance, and I need you for that. Plus, you're a great shot. If the shit hits the fan, I'm at your mercy."

"How do you know I'm a great shot?"

"You're a deep-cover officer. If you're not a great shot, you're in the wrong job. I'm rolling the dice that you don't have bad judgment about career choices."

"What do you mean, 'if the shit hits the fan'?"

Will gestured to his pants pocket. "My cell phone. It's in two parts. I need you to assemble it."

Ash reached into his pocket, removed the phone, and inserted the battery.

"Turn it on. Leave it switched on for one minute. Then turn it off and remove the battery."

Ash did so. "You've just triggered something?"

"I've just kept interest levels up." Will pulled over on the side of the highway. "You're right. You drive. I need to take point."

When Ash was in the driver's seat, Will swiveled in the front passenger seat and pointed his gun toward the rear window. "Drive. We need to get out of here now!"

They drove for another two hours, barely a word spoken between them except one sentence from Ash. "You've put hounds on us. I don't take kindly to that."

Will kept his gun in position. "I've set things in motion. I'll explain why when it's safe."

Two hundred miles away, Gage barked at Painter, Kopański, and Duggan. "We've got a trace. He's heading east, but the trace is broken. I think he's removed his cell battery."

They were in their tiny house in Virginia. All were fatigued from lack of sleep and frustrated.

Kopański said, "Our two SUVs are ready to go."

He was referring to the fact that he'd supplied their interiors with makeshift beds and latrines, food, and firearms.

The Polish American continued: "I say we go to the spot where the trace picked up Cochrane and wait for another signal."

Gage agreed. "Okay. Girls in vehicle one. Boys in vehicle two."

"Actually, if you don't mind, I'd rather travel with Joe." Painter looked at her former NYPD colleague.

Kopański thought about this. For a long time he'd considered proposing to Thyme Painter. What held him back was his desire to reunite with his estranged daughter. But now, maybe, time was passing too quickly. He was getting old. No woman would match up to Painter. And the chances of his daughter ever forgiving him for dropping her off at a prom where she got raped were fifty-fifty. Years after that event, he knew deep down that he had to think about his future.

He said, "I'm happy with that if our team leader is. We take it in shifts to drive. And if I fart in the car, don't bitch at me."

Painter laughed.

Gage nodded. "No problem. Duggan and I will take vehicle two. Guns prepared at all times. Communications systems tested regularly. We move on Cochrane the moment he activates his cell again."

The Dower House was a six-bedroom property overlooking a dune and the sea. White and rectangular, it had belonged to Kay Ash's brother, before he got dementia in middle age and killed himself in the sea, adjacent to the house. After his death from the fall, the house was passed to Ash. Like his sister, he had hated their parents. The house had no happy memories.

There were no other human constructions surrounding the house. In most respects it was an idyllic location: the beaches, a grass-covered coastal path, and, in the distance, woods where eighteenth-century Quakers once believed shape-shifters lurked. Ash didn't think of the house that way. Long ago, she stopped recognizing the surrounding beauty.

Ash stopped the car. "I don't normally come here this time of year." She explained to Will how it belonged to her. "I get it serviced every six months by a local. He knows we're here and won't bother us until we leave. In any case, he's not due to check on the place for five months."

They got out of the car.

Ash asked, "Do you have a flashlight?"

Will withdrew one from his pocket.

Ash pointed at a broken tile on the ground. "Lift that up. Underneath is the tap for turning on the water. You're not going to get your bath without it."

Two minutes later they were in the house.

It was huge in comparison to Ash's living quarters in D.C. Will immediately sensed sorrow in the house. "Your house was built in 1860 or thereabouts. It has a hint of death."

"It does." Ash picked up two dustpans and brushes from under the kitchen sink. "Dead spiders. There's nothing I can do about them. We need to clear them and their cobwebs."

They set to work, clearing each room of all traces of the arachnids.

Heating on, fire ablaze, and candles tastefully

illuminated in the living room, Cochrane and Ash sat with glasses of calvados on mismatching sofas. Cochrane said, "You don't like coming here."

Ash smiled, though her expression was mournful. "I used to. I'm thinking of selling the place. But . . ."

"Childhood memories. The sound of the waves. The familiar smell of home. Good times."

"You know what that's like?"

"I know similar."

"In my case, they weren't good times."

Will patted the box of groceries they'd picked up en route. "Would you like me to cook us supper?"

Ash was relieved. She was not a good cook, always grabbing stuff on the go. "If you like. Plus, I have no idea why you chose that produce. I wouldn't know what to do with it without going online to find a recipe. But there's no Internet here."

In the kitchen, Will carved pheasant breasts off two birds, pan-fried them with garlic and diced shallots, and added tarragon and cream. He parboiled potatoes, then sautéed them, while at the same time steaming an array of vegetables. The meal complete, he brought it through to the living room and placed the plates on the dining table. "It's not exactly Michelin starred, but it's better than nothing."

"Let's not eat at the table. It's where my brother used to eat. It brings back memories for me. But I can't bring myself to get rid of the table just yet."

"Then we'll sit by the fire and eat on our laps."

They didn't speak as they ate. All that could be heard was the smash of water hitting sand and shale at the base of the massive dune. After washing the plates and cooking utensils, Will rejoined Ash by the fire. She'd topped up his glass with more calvados.

Will said, "That'll be my last drink tonight. Big day tomorrow."

"Who will come for you? The police?"

"I don't think so."

"Worse?"

"Yes."

Ash took a sip of her drink. "So this is the calm before the storm." She studied Will. She couldn't decide if he seemed preoccupied with his thoughts or whether he was otherworldly. "Hessian Bell and I have run aground. It was simple to find Elizabeth Haden's address, but we can't get to any details about your Berlin mission. Unwin Fox took that to his grave."

"I know. And that's why I need to do what I have to tomorrow." He engaged eye contact with her, this time not looking preoccupied. "Why weren't you scared of me when we first met?"

She didn't reply.

"I guess you're used to being up close to danger."

Ash wondered whether to tell him the truth. She made a decision to do so. "When you left the CIA and were later accused of the murders in Virginia, the Agency circulated a paper briefing about you. It said it didn't believe you'd committed the killings because you would never proactively kill innocents. But it gave some details about your career. Just enough. And it concluded two things. First, the consequences of putting you in a corner would be catastrophic for those around you. Second, if you tried to make contact with any member of the Agency, we were to immediately call in SWAT to take you down or, if we were armed, shoot you ourselves." She warmed her hands by the fire. "The Agency was clear that in the history of its existence, there'd never been a killer on its books as effective as you. The problem after you left was that the CIA felt you were an unguided nuclear missile."

Will laughed. "Please tell me they didn't use those words in their circulated briefing."

Ash didn't laugh. "They did. But that's not where it ends. Some of us, I don't know how many, heard rumors about you when you were still in service. We probably were only getting five percent of what you'd done, but it was enough. You were nicknamed the 'American Englishman.' Two years before the circulated briefing, many of us were summoned to the Agency's auditorium. On the stage there was the entire panel of directors, plus CIA lawyers. The head of the Agency spoke for only a few minutes. He said he was aware there were rumors about one of our operatives. He didn't name you, but we all knew he was referring to the American Englishman. The director told us that all talk about you was to stop with immediate effect. He then walked out." She smiled. "Deep-cover officers like you and me know the smell."

"Bullshit?"

"More than that—when one of our own is being stitched up. I knew you weren't a murderer. That's why I wasn't scared when you came to my apartment."

Will rubbed the stubble on his face. "Things were different back then. After I was accused of murder, I vanished and became a bookseller."

"Of what?"

"Rare, out of print, first editions."

Ash was puzzled. There was so much about Cochrane that bewildered her. When they left service, men like Cochrane became guns for hire. They didn't sell books. Then again, she didn't tell him about one snippet of information in the circulated briefing: Cochrane's mind was as powerful as his ability to engage in direct action. The briefing warned never to allow him to talk to you. If he did talk to you, your universe could be turned upside down. It was the most chilling warning in the briefing.

She said, "Never do mind games with me."

The statement didn't surprise Will, but still he hated it. "That's a myth about me. I never do mind games with my friends and allies."

"That reply could be a mind game."

"And therein is the problem. I'm guilty every time I open my mouth. How can I prove that I'm saying the right thing? The truth?" He leaned forward. "Judgment in the counterpart has to take effect."

"And I'm the counterpart?"

"Tonight, yes." Will's smile was genuine. "You know about Antaeus?"

"Bell told me about him."

"Good. So here's my point. People like Hessian Bell, Antaeus, and myself are lionized or demonized. Nothing in between. We're very different people, but that doesn't matter to outsiders. We become myths. The truth, however, is wholly different. We're just normal people."

Ash smirked. "You three are anything but normal."

"Would you give me a shave?"

"What?!"

Will rolled up his sleeve. There was a long scar on the underside of his forearm. "I have nerve damage. For most of the year it's fine. But for some reason, when I'm in the presence of someone I care about, my neurons send electricity down my arm. The scar scatters the electricity in an unproductive way. It can cause my hand to shake. Holding a razor when it's like this is useless."

"And the scar?"

Will shrugged. "A knife fight."

Ash looked at his hand. It was as steady as a rock. She knew he was lying. But she also knew he was after something and her instinct told her to follow his lead. "My brother used a cutthroat razor. It should still be sharp. Will that do you? I taught my brother how to use it."

Will nodded. "A shave first, and when you go to bed I'll take a bath. Sleeping in a car is not all it's cracked up to be."

"'Cracked up to be'?" That phrase tickled Ash. She turned serious. "I have the spare nine-millimeter ammunition you need."

"Thank you."

"I doubt it's armor-piercing."

"As long as it penetrates cloth and bone, that's all I need."

They spoke for a while—Will recounting his joy of salmon fishing in the Scottish Highlands; Ash recounting how she'd waitressed to pay tuition fees for her degree at Harvard. She told him she'd never experienced true love. She didn't know why she revealed this information.

Nor did Will. The black-haired, svelte woman before him was a stunner, yet her eyes were drawn and her midthirties skin had lines. Stress had taken its toll. For too many years, she'd been sent into the heart of darkness.

"Would you shave me now?"

"You want to be like an Islamist or Judaist, purging his soul before martyrdom?"

"I just need a shave."

In the upstairs bathroom, she averted her eyes as he stripped off his shirt. She moistened and lathered his face and moved right up behind his massive frame, staring at his reflection in the bathroom mirror. His huge back was lacerated, yet healed. Holding the razor, she expertly etched it over his stubble. "Is this a test of trust?"

"It's a shave."

The job complete, she ran a bath. "There should be enough hot water until morning. The boiler's temperamental. Don't blame me if it cuts out and cold water comes through."

"That's okay. I've spent a lot of time in cold water. The North Atlantic in winter, for example." He picked up the cutthroat razor, his hand not moving a millimeter. "Forgive me. It wasn't a test about trust. It's just I wanted the pleasure of knowing how it would feel to have you care about me." He smiled at her. "I'm going to take my pants off now. Best you leave."

Ash did so and went to her bedroom. She didn't know how she felt. Shaving Cochrane was like grooming a massive stallion. She hated thinking of it that way. It was demeaning to her sensibilities. She'd strived her entire life to get where she was. No man was her superior. And yet she'd enjoyed dabbing the towel against his jaw after his face was free of stubble. Yes, that was what Cochrane had done. He'd made her an ally. Possibly he'd done a lot more than that.

The sorrowful man had brought her into his inner circle. Ultimately, he wanted her feminine touch.

In two SUVs, Gage and her team were hurtling eastward on Interstate 64 toward the last place they'd pinpointed Cochrane's location. They suspected he was long gone from the location. He was—182 miles away. But they had to try their luck and hope he activated his phone soon.

In Kopański and Painter's SUV, Painter said, "I still think this is a fool's quest. We have no idea where Cochrane will pop up next. And when he does, what chance do we have of getting to him?"

Kopański was driving. "Agent Gage is waiting for Cochrane to make a mistake."

"He doesn't make mistakes."

"She knows that. But there will be one or two mistakes he can't avoid, due to his circumstances. I agree with her on that."

Painter looked at Kopański. "Could you shoot him if it came to it?"

Kopański hesitated. "I've thought about that a lot. We're in the employment of the FBI now. We do what we have to do."

"Could you shoot him?" Painter repeated.

Kopański sighed. "I guess I'd have to. I wouldn't want you or the others in danger."

"And yet, we both think he didn't commit the murders a year ago."

"That's not the point, is it?"

Both SUVs pulled up next to a motel, two hundred yards from where Cochrane last inserted his cell phone battery.

Gage and Duggan entered the motel and showed the receptionist their IDs. Gage revealed a photo of Cochrane. "Is this man staying here?"

The receptionist shook her head. "Never seen him before."

"What guests do you have right now?"

The receptionist told her only three rooms were occupied. "It's a slow time of year." She leafed through her booking ledger. "Young couple in room nineteen. Trucker in twelve. Traveling salesman in room two."

Gage said, "We need to check their rooms."

"They're occupied. They're probably sleeping. Plus, do you have a warrant?"

"We don't need a warrant to search commercial premises. Give me your universal swipe card or keys to access the rooms."

Duggan and Gage searched each room. In room nineteen they found a terrified young couple, startled as their lovemaking was interrupted by two Feds pointing guns at them. In room twelve they were hurled abuse by a thickset trucker who sat up bleary-eyed in bed at the sight of the Bureau operatives. And in room two, the salesman shook when Duggan ran to the bed and pointed his gun at the guest's head. None of the men looked anything like Cochrane.

Gage and Duggan returned to reception.

Gage asked the clerk, "Do you have twin rooms? Single beds? We need to stay here."

"For how long?"

"We don't know. Maybe just tonight. Maybe longer."

"You might not need a warrant to search my property, but you will need cash to stay here!"

Gage handed the receptionist her credit card. "One room for two women. One for two men."

The booking transacted, Gage walked to Kopański and Painter's vehicle. "I've decided to give you beds tonight. Kopański, you're with Duggan.

Painter, you're with me. Us girls have got the tougher night because we'll have the intercept equipment for Cochrane's phone. We take four-hour shifts. One on. One off. And if Cochrane activates his cell, we all mobilize immediately."

TWENTY-FOUR

It was early morning as Will walked along the sea adjacent to Ash's property. Now seeing it in daylight, he could appreciate what a magnificent and rugged home it was. Once, he imagined, it would have belonged to a tobacco tycoon. But now it needed a lot of work. Exterior stone walls required surgery. The slate roof had tiles missing. And inside there was much to be done. As Ash had predicted, the boiler had cut out at some point last night and his bath ran cold. He didn't mind that. But he didn't like the idea that in the future Ash might immerse herself in something so tepid. The sea front, he decided, needed a solid fence. He could make one. The house's walls he could repair. The boiler was beyond his expertise, but he could get a plumber who'd understand what to do. And the flickering ceiling lights in the house were simply a result of bulbs oscillating in their units. Will could repair that too.

Funny how he was imagining fixing up the place. A childish fantasy. Or a desire to live someplace like this. For so long he'd been without roots. He'd had his pad in London—a two-bedroom apartment in Southwark's Edwardian West Square—and had tried to make it a cavern of delights. He'd crammed it with baroque art, antique musical instruments, oil paintings that he'd completed, beautiful furniture, a Garrard record player and vinyl of Segovia and other Spanish greats, and books, so many books. But it was a lonely place. His only solace was his love for his three neighbors on the three floors below him. Dickie Mountjoy was a punctilious former major in the Coldstream Guards. He died of a heart attack just after traveling to New York to give Thyme Painter his assessment that Cochrane wasn't capable of murder. Phoebe was a champagne-swilling art dealer with a heart of gold. All tits and ass, was how retiree Dickie described her. But Dickie loved her, second to none. So did Will. She was like a sister. And David the mortician—flabby, unkempt, always thinking about death and Dixieland jazz and cooking. Together, Will and his neighbors were the most unlikely bunch.

Things had changed. Dickie was gone. David and Phoebe had become an item and moved into a new place in north London. Will's apartment had been seized and investigated by Metropolitan Police officers when he was on the run. West Square was no longer home.

He stopped at the edge of the cliff, looking down at the mangled array of rocks and sand. It must have been so tough for Kay to see her brother down there, his body smashed and bloody, water ebbing and flowing over his carcass as if it were taunting and baiting him.

But this could be a good place, Will decided. Repairs. Construction of a safe perimeter. Sell everything in the house and totally refurbish the interior to be nothing like it was now. And there was a very good school nearby, according to Google.

A fantasy.

He walked into the house. Ash was brewing coffee and frying eggs. She said, "I saw you out there and guessed you'd want something when you returned."

Will stood next to her. He couldn't remember a moment similar to this. Being next to a woman. Her cooking. Her caring.

He said in a quiet voice, "There are twin boys I need you to be aware of. Their names are Billy and Tom Koenig. Their father was Roger Koenig. He was a Navy SEAL before serving alongside me in intelligence. He was my brother. Not in bloodline. Certainly in soul. A braver man I've never met. He's dead. I wanted to look after the twins. Still do. The twins are living in a Virginia safe house with their aunt, Faye Glass, and two Virginia PD detectives. Faye is a good woman. But she has PTSD. She and I know the twins' future doesn't reside with her." He touched Ash's arm.

Alone, Will drove west across Virginia for his rendezvous at Elizabeth Haden's house. His sidearm and spare magazines were by his side. He suspected his journey might be a death run. It didn't matter. This wasn't about Unwin Fox's request to meet him or death. Fox was CIA. That meant he played both sides of the table. It was about Colonel Haden. And ultimately it was about Will's desire to get to the truth about what happened in Berlin.

Will thought he knew what might have happened. Other men would have shrugged it off and laid low, ignoring the need to get closure. Will wasn't cast from that mold. His life now was about making amends, peacefully closing doors behind past escapades, and bringing bastards to the gallows.

His life back in Berlin and beyond was wholly different. Maybe he should just leave Haden alone. Will's life had been a hellish roller coaster—the loneliness, isolation, and constant death. And yet he'd had joy when Kay shaved him. It was a simple thing, maybe. But to him, it meant the world after so long in purgatory. He was human, he knew, and yearned after the same things everyone else yearned after. Specifically, he wanted companionship and fatherhood. A woman, maybe someone like Kay, and the twins. Nothing more complicated than that. And a new life. Liberation from the false accusations. A place to settle down. Somewhere like a renovated Dower House.

But it was a crass fantasy. Today he was driving to a gunfight. In all probability he'd die.

Elizabeth Haden poured herself a glass of lemonade and looked out the kitchen window. Somewhere on the grounds, her gardener Bartlett was hiding with a shotgun. Their code to each other was simple. If the man who called himself Edward Pope posed a threat, she would turn on as many lights as possible. At that point, Bartlett would storm the house and gun down Pope. But first, Bartlett would fire off a couple of rounds in the meadow. He was there, he'd tell police, shooting vermin. Forensics would confirm he was away from the house, just doing his duties on the grounds. He heard screaming, he'd tell the cops. That's when he entered the house and confronted a man assaulting his employer.

No court in Virginia would dispute the veracity of his actions. Mrs. Haden and Jedd Bartlett would walk away without a blemish on their characters.

But it might not come to such drastic action, Mrs. Haden warned Bartlett. They had to see how it played out.

Jason Flail assembled his team one mile away from Haden's house. They were on a farm road, their vehicles parked, each man checking his sidearm, all of them in jeans, hiking boots, and windbreakers. The men wore ski masks that were rolled up to look like innocuous woolen hats. They'd be pulled down when Cochrane showed.

Flail said to his colleagues, "I repeat, the mission: kill Cochrane; kill anyone else who gets in our way; do not lay a hand on Mrs. Haden; get back here; leave."

One of the men asked, "Why do we kill Cochrane and why is Mrs. Haden so damn important?"

Flail answered, "Cochrane is blocking our way to Colonel Haden. Mrs. Haden is our bait. As long as she's alive, there's a chance Colonel Haden might make contact with her."

"And Colonel Haden? Can we kill such a highly decorated officer?"

"He's a thief. Corrupt. Mr. Kane wants him in court to stand trial. I don't know any other details."

"You trust Kane?"

Flail laughed. "I don't trust anyone. But yeah, on this occasion no doubt he's got it right. Haden's a psychopath. Haden and what he did in his last mission are too classified for law enforcement involvement. Kane has no choice—unconventional warfare." He smiled. "And, boys, that's what us Green Berets do best."

The men nodded, clear about their objectives and why they were imperative. They set off on foot. It was eleven A.M.

Will watched Haden's property from the far base of the surrounding meadow. His vehicle was hidden nearby, off-road and with bracken covering

most of it. Using binoculars, he scanned his surroundings. It was one hour until his scheduled
meeting with Elizabeth Haden. But he had to be
patient. Mrs. Haden was too clever to trust him
to turn up by prior appointment and not cause
danger. She'd have taken precautions. Will, on
the other hand, was in no doubt her phone was
being monitored. That's why he'd called her.

But where were the precautions?

He kept scanning the grounds and the windows of the house. Moving positions several times,
he repeated the drill. He was wearing waterproof
pants, boots, and a mountaineering jacket. His
head, however, was exposed.

He was looking for the unusual and the normal. The unusual would include an amateur
bodyguard walking inside the house, past a window. The normal would include a professional
using an established feature in the house or
grounds to remain hidden. But it wasn't an exact science. People were unpredictable, amateurs
and professionals alike.

What would Elizabeth Haden do? he thought.
No doubt she was suspicious of his persona Edward Pope. She'd directly accused Will of being
a killer, based on his demeanor and scars. He'd
given her no credentials to back up his story
about knowing her husband. And his call to her
would have triggered panic.

His call was deliberate.

But she didn't know that.

Worker bees, Will recalled, surrounded the
queen. The queen was Elizabeth Haden. The

workers? Only two that he was aware of: the maid
and the gardener. The maid was too young to be
a threat. But the gardener was older and had a tat-
too on his forearm that was a telltale giveaway that
he was once in the 101st Airborne. During Will's
last visit, he had seen him for only one second. It
had been enough to get the measure of the man:
short, like most paratroopers; midforties, so too
old to have seen recent active service; not making
a wealthy living on the private contractor circuit,
almost certainly because of subsequent personal
problems (drugs, booze; destitution probable);
and Mrs. Haden had saved him—sixteen dollars
an hour working the grounds was preferable to
him compared to the stress of revisits to the shit-
holes on earth.

Yes. He was the worker bee. And a highly
trained one at that. He'd know how to work an
observation post, concealment, weapons. And
he'd have been clean of toxins for some time.
Mrs. Haden would have insisted on that.

But he wouldn't be in the house with a gun.
That would look to cops like premeditated ex-
pectation of assault. So clever Mrs. Haden would
have stage-managed her worker so it looked like
he was coming to rescue a damsel in distress.
He'd have a gun, but he needed an alibi as to why
it was in his hand in a split second when rescuing
his employer. Shooting rats, mice, or rabbits on
the grounds would be the logical alibi. Rifles and
handguns are no good for that, only shotguns.
And that meant the gardener was currently en-
sconced in the grounds with a scattergun. Haden

would have a sign to indicate whether she was in jeopardy when Will arrived. Calling a cell phone would take too long in times of duress. It would have to be something lightning fast, a signal that might be possible if Will was trying to garrote Mrs. Haden. A panic alarm was a possibility, but Haden would have to reach it. No, something more ordinary and accessible. Midday, room lights wouldn't be on. But she stood every chance of reaching one if in flight for her life. That's what the gardener was waiting for.

A light to be turned on after Cochrane arrived, if he caused trouble.

Where was the gardener?

Certainly not far from the house. A sprint for a middle-aged man over fifty yards would take at least five seconds. Then there was house entry, room clearance, getting up close and personal to Will.

There was only one outhouse in that proximity, next to the beehive. Will put away his binoculars, pulled out his handgun, and moved.

Flail and his men walked across open land, avoiding the nearby road. Many times, they'd gone like this to villages in Afghanistan to win hearts and minds, immunize children, speak to the elders about Taliban movements in the area, supply food, arm able-bodied men, and ultimately show the scared village folk that there were people watching their backs. It was what made the Green Berets such a great thinking man's unit. But they were no strangers to use of maximum force. In their time in the unit, Flail and his colleagues had lost count of the number of night- and daytime assaults they'd conducted against scum. Often, it was in small units but with a hellfire of armaments at their disposal. When in service, they used to joke that the Green Berets were like a married couple—there was the tenderness stuff, and there was the total aggression stuff. "Carrot and stick" was how some in special forces wryly adapted the "hearts and minds" mantra.

Today was stick. Flail's team was a hunter-killer force, about to neutralize and mop up shit.

Will ran across Haden's meadow, dodging between trees and avoiding, as much as he could, lines of sight from the house. Speed was of the essence. And surprise. But so much depended on whether his deductions were correct.

Jedd Bartlett aimed his shotgun at the house. He'd done what Mrs. Haden had asked of him and had cleaned her gun and made it ready for use. But this was the first time he'd held a weapon since being in Iraq in the early nineties. Seeing his pals get obliterated in friendly fire by an American fighter plane made him decide warfare was no longer for him. The deaths of encroaching Saddam Hussein loyalists was deemed more important by U.S. military high command than the lives of Bartlett's sixteen-man unit.

There was no going back.

Bartlett's mind was cracked on that day.

When Mrs. Haden saved him from the streets, it was a long road to recovery. Nothing instant. Just him taking each day one at a time. But now he'd found peace with his experiences. His two girls were in college; he secretly visited them without his ex-wife knowing. And he was absolutely clear in his head that he hated goddamn guns.

His hands were shaking as he pointed the shotgun at the house. Firing it was one thing. Hitting a target was another. He doubted he could do either.

Will Cochrane placed the muzzle of his handgun against the back of Bartlett's head. "Nothing silly. I'm not here to hurt you."

Bartlett froze. "Who are you?"

"Edward Pope. The man coming to see Mrs. Haden at noon." Will looked at Bartlett's hands. "Don't be scared."

"I—"

"Yes, I know. We've all been through shit in our past. It makes no sense how some of us can get through it and others can't. We are not enemies."

Bartlett turned to Will. "I just want to keep my job and keep her safe."

"That is going to be achieved." Will crouched beside him and stared at the house. "I'm fairly certain that in a few minutes men will come to the house when they see me enter. They're hostiles. Not law enforcement, though they might be posing as such. They will be coming to kill me, not Mrs. Haden. But you and I both know the risks of innocents getting caught in the cross fire."

"She's scared of you."

"Life sucks. I hate it when people are scared of me." Will smiled sympathetically while keeping his eyes on the house. "I have a sidearm. But if I use it inside it complicates matters. The house becomes a wholly different forensics scene to be investigated. Your story of rescuing your employer will be muddied. It won't be a straight case of intruders versus protectors. My bullets will be in their bodies. That means a third party was present."

Bartlett agreed. "And then I'll be grilled and Mrs. Haden will be grilled. Muddier, yes."

"What were your original protocols?"

"Fire two shots randomly in the grounds. Then kill intruders."

"Would you like to do that?"

"No."

Will patted him on the shoulder. "You've done your time. No need for more of that crap." He turned to Bartlett. "I'll do it."

Bartlett looked uncertain. "I don't know you. How do I know you won't hurt Mrs. Haden?"

"Make a judgment, paratrooper."

Bartlett lowered his head. "I made a judgment in Kuwait in '91. I got it wrong then." He offered no resistance as Will took his shotgun. "I called in an airstrike. I had no idea they'd be happy to rip apart my team to get to enemy forces."

"Presidents and high command suck. We both know that." Will gripped the shotgun. "Is there a loft in the house or another safe place?"

"Yes. A loft."

"That's where I'll put Mrs. Haden. When the shots start, give me two minutes, then call 911. After all, you're pretending to be the shooter. You can't call the cops until it's done."

"Yes, sir."

"Don't call me sir. I was a corporal in the French Foreign Legion." Will didn't elaborate that he held the equivalent rank of colonel in MI6. "It's highly unlikely I'll be successful. But if there are dead bodies, leave them, except mine. Bury my body, throw it in a pond, whatever. Just make sure the cops never find me." Will handed the shotgun back to Barrett. "It's time to go."

Barrett frowned. "I assumed you wanted me back here?"

"We still need those two random shots. Cordite needs to be on your hands and forearms. Forensics will check."

Bartlett understood. He walked out of the hut and fired twice in the air, before reloading the gun and handing it back to Will. "She doesn't believe your name is Edward Pope."

"Nor do I." Will took the gun. He looked around. "Look after Mrs. Haden. I believe she may be confused."

"About what?"

"I have my suspicions, but I can't articulate them at this moment."

Flail and his men heard the shots as they approached the house.

Flail said, "Shotgun. Agreed?"

One of his men nodded. "Groundsman killing wildlife. Or Cochrane has arrived early and blown a hole in Mrs. Haden."

They moved forward, six hundred yards from the house, guns in their hands.

Back in the hut, Bartlett said to Will, "Shouldn't we bring Mrs. Haden in here or get her the hell away from here?"

"We don't know which direction the hostiles are approaching. Correct? You could be walking her into an ambush."

"But—"

"No buts. Remember, the scene must look like a random home invasion. She has to be in the house."

Bartlett asked, "Who are you?"

Somebody that for some reason had an emotional attraction to Kay Ash, thought Will. There was a reason for it. She was like him. He liked her eyes. He doubted she reciprocated the feeling, but he was an eternal optimist that one day he would find love. He said, "I'm a former special operative. Not just the Legion. Other stuff as well. I know what I'm doing." He stood and smiled at Bartlett. "You're doing the right thing. Fresh air, honest work. It beats therapy. But I'm sorry your government let you down." He grabbed the shotgun and entered the rear of the house.

It was 11:58 A.M. when Elizabeth Haden entered her living room, picked up a photo of her husband in uniform when he was in Delta, and smashed it against the mantelpiece. Her eyes were wet as she picked up the broken pieces, put them in a bag, and walked into the kitchen to put them in the trash. That's when she saw the man who called himself Edward Pope. He was leaning against the kitchen sink, her shotgun in one of his hands pointed at the floor.

She shrieked and dropped the bag.

Will went to her. "I mean you no harm. I think men are coming here. They're using you as bait to get to your husband. You need to hide in your loft right now. If you hear shots, stay silent and hidden. I've spoken to your gardener. He's a good man. He will call the cops if there's trouble."

She looked around, panic on her face. "Men? What's going on? I should get out of here!"

"No. I believe the men are professionals, possibly linked to your husband's past. They'll access your property from a three-sixty perimeter. The house is safer than any efforts to run."

"Who the hell are you?!"

"I'm a man who wants to find out the truth about your husband. Show me where you're going to hide. Go now!"

Haden ran upstairs, her mind in utter confusion, tears running down her face.

Will followed her into her attic. It was large and ran the full length of the house. Inside were boxes and floorboards to traverse the rafters. "Go to the back of the attic. I'm going to turn the light off when you're there."

When she was huddled behind a box, she said,

"Edward Pope. I always knew that wasn't your name."

"My real name wouldn't have any relevance to you. But I assure you I'm here to help. Your gardener and I have agreed that if men are killed here, it will have been by his hand. Please stick to that story. It was a home invasion and he was protecting you and your property."

"What have you brought to my doorstep?!"

"If I survive this, I will call you soon. I'll request a meeting—somewhere remote. You'll tell me where that place is and what time. But do not under any circumstances attend that meeting." Will turned off the light. "What I've brought to your house is vengeance."

He walked downstairs and waited, shotgun in his hands.

Flail's team was by the house. Flail gestured to two men to approach from the rear. He said to the man by his side, "Passive entry if she answers. By force if not. We're Drug Enforcement Administration, investigating her gardener, Jedd Bartlett. Got it?"

His colleague nodded.

Flail added, "Bartlett is under suspicion of growing and supplying opiates. That's the story. When Cochrane arrives, he's a suspected dealer."

His colleague moved to the front door of the house and rang the bell.

Will moved to the top of the stairs, crouched, and pointed his shotgun at the base of the stairs.

The doorbell rang again. Will was motionless, his gloved hands gripping the weapon, finger on the trigger. And he had no way of knowing if his hunch was correct that his call to Mrs. Haden had triggered the team he'd encountered observing Haden's house. He wasn't going to take any chances. Mrs. Haden and her husband were all that mattered—one of them was in severe danger; the other was a cold-blooded bastard.

He didn't hear the door open. But he did hear footsteps in the wooden hallway.

From within the garden shed, Jedd Bartlett kept up his observation of the house and the grounds.

He hated violence. But once a paratrooper, always a paratrooper.

No way was he going to let these men ruin Mrs. Haden and her property.

He saw a man walking across the meadow. He was wearing civilian clothes, though he had a pistol in both hands and was moving quickly in the way that Rangers and other special operatives do—feet always flat on the ground so that there was no bounce if they needed to fire a weapon. This guy was ex–U.S. military, Bartlett was in no doubt. He didn't like the look of him—no law enforcement insignia on him, though the man could have been an undercover cop. No, Bartlett decided. This guy was trouble.

His job and life at Mrs. Haden's property meant everything to him. The man who was fifty yards away wasn't going to ruin that. More important, Mrs. Haden only had Edward Pope to protect her. But if there was one armed man assaulting the house, there'd be others.

He called 911, saying the house was being attacked by armed men.

He then sprinted out of the shed, his footfalls silent on the dewy meadow. From behind, he kicked hard into the man's groin, grabbed his throat, and swept his ankles away. The man tumbled to the ground, dragging Bartlett with him. They grappled on the grass, Bartlett repeatedly punching him in the face, the man jabbing him in the torso with his elbow. Bartlett grabbed the man's wrist and twisted it in an attempt to get him to release his handgun. The man elbowed him directly in the face and writhed until he was free of Bartlett's grip.

One of Flail's other men came right up and shot Bartlett twice in the head. He grinned and said to his colleague, "What are you doing? Back to the job."

Both men moved to the house, their guns ready for action.

The footsteps in the hallway were getting louder. Will doubted Mrs. Haden could hear them, but there was a possibility she heard the doorbell moments ago. The last thing he needed was for her to scream. The element of surprise was key.

If the man was hostile and coming after Will, there'd be others. They'd have been waiting for Will to turn up at the front of the house and for Mrs. Haden to let him in. But they'd also be smart. They may have predicted Will was already in the house.

He heard two shots. It could mean only one thing: Bartlett had been killed by men coming from that direction.

He braced himself, stock-still, gun at eye level.

At the base of the stairs, the man came into view, a pistol in his hand. Will recognized him from his encounter at Unwin Fox's burned-out house. The man spotted him and swung his handgun toward him. Will pulled the trigger and blew a hole in the man's gut.

He ran downstairs, reloaded, and looked out the rear windows. Bartlett was fifty yards away, on the meadow, prone and dead it seemed. Two men were approaching the house. Once again, men he'd seen before. Professional operatives. With guns. They'd have heard the shotgun blast. And now they were coming to kill him.

Will sprinted to the conservatory overlooking the backyard. Crouching behind an armchair he aimed his shotgun at the men, waiting for them to enter the house.

Flail was supposed to stay in position at the front of the house, waiting for Cochrane to arrive. Then he'd kill him. He tried to decide if the gunfire he'd heard meant Cochrane was already in the house or whether it belonged to the gardener. It was ten minutes past twelve. Cochrane was overdue. Flail decided Cochrane was already here and the gunfire was his. Flail ran to the front door.

The men in the backyard were drawing ever closer to the house. Will had clear sight of them, but kept most of his body hidden. The sun was in the men's eyes, so Will hoped that meant they wouldn't be able to see through the reflection of the glass. But he wasn't going to take any chances. He fired once, his pellets smashing through the glass but their momentum subsequently diminishing, sufficient to cause only one of the men superficial flesh wounds. Both men split up. Now they were out of view, almost certainly trying to flank him.

He reloaded his weapon and spun around. That's when he saw Flail coming at him, handgun held at eye level. Will pulled the trigger, but Flail dived behind a sofa, the gun blast shredding the top of the furniture. Will stood and walked toward him, pumping one more round into the sofa and reloading again. Flail raised his gun over the barrier and fired three shots blindly. One of them lacerated the exterior of Will's stomach.

In agony, Will retreated to the stairs, grimacing as he ascended to the top. All he could do now was protect Mrs. Haden. He pointed his shotgun down the stairs.

Multiple sirens were encroaching. *Damn*, thought Will. *Bartlett called it in too quickly*. Will didn't blame him. This whole situation was screwed up for Haden, and Bartlett was dead. They didn't know Will or the precise objective he had for being here. The sirens were outside the front of the house. Flail knew he had to get out of here. The front of the house was blocked, so he had to make a run to the rear and escape with his men. To do that, he needed to get past the stairwell that Will was guarding.

He dashed, Will shot, Flail somersaulted and narrowly avoided getting his brains blown out. Out of Will's sight, Flail exited the rear of the house and screamed to his two men on either side of the house, "Abort! Abort!"

His men joined him, and they ran across the meadow and vanished. Their mission had been a failure. One of their colleagues was dead. That still left three of them. They were certain they'd get another opportunity to assassinate Cochrane. And on that occasion, they'd make certain the job was done.

Will moved downstairs, his wound causing him to sweat and grimace. He rested the shotgun against a wall and picked up the dead hostile's handgun. Rapidly, he examined the dead man's clothes. Zero ID. He cursed. At the front of the house, he peered through a window. Four police squad cars were there, men behind them with guns pointed at the house. Will fired pinpoint-accurate shots, decimating one of the car's roof emergency lights, striking another's tires, scraping the hood of the third vehicle, causing an officer to dive for cover, and destroying the engine block of the last vehicle. The vehicles and men were from the local sheriff's department. They weren't trained for this. Through the broken glass of the window he'd fired through, he shouted at them in a false American accent: "I got a woman hostage. If you want her alive, you let me go."

A cop shouted back, "SWAT's on its way. Give yourself up now."

"I'm not going to hurt her. Just let me be."

"Put down your weapon and walk out the door!"

"Me and my buddies ain't going to do that. You're going to have to wait. The woman will be fine. But if you come in here, there'll be trouble."

"How many of you are there?"

Will responded, "Four. We only came here for cash and jewelry. We didn't expect there was a man with a shotgun. Things got nasty."

"Then you'd better turn yourself in."

Will deliberately hesitated for five seconds, before saying, "Let me talk to my brothers. Personally, I don't want a shoot-out. But I've got to get their vote. You okay with that?"

"Take your time."

Will limped to the back of the house, dropped the pistol next to the dead ex–Green Beret, and picked up the shotgun. He knew Flail and his two men had long gone. He looked at his stomach. Blood was oozing through his jacket. *Shit!* The last thing he needed was his blood on the crime scene. He grabbed a fistful of paper towels from the kitchen and shoved it over his wound, under the jacket. Entering the rear meadow, it took every ounce of strength for him to walk. He dropped the shotgun next to Bartlett and carried on walking.

Under other circumstances, he would have taken a moment to pay his respects. No doubt Bartlett broke cover and assaulted one of the intruders. And he'd done so unarmed. His bravery cost him his life.

Three miles later, Will reached his car. He was in agony as he squeezed himself into the driver's seat. *Don't pass out, drive, focus,* he told himself.

He drove to Kay Ash's sea residence. Along the way, he called Ash's cell phone from a public pay phone. "Things didn't go well. I need you to call Hessian. He needs to meet us at your place. He also needs to call the person I told you about—the Russian. I'm injured. I need help."

From his White House office, Deep Throat made a call. "There has been an assault on Mrs. H's residence. One assaulter dead. One employee of Mrs. H's dead. I'm not happy about that. Are you?"

The person at the end of the phone replied, "No. Things are drawing too close."

"And yet you are complicit. Kill Mr. C. Is that clear?"

The person answered, "Yes."

Uniformed police, detectives, and forensics swamped Elizabeth Haden's home. Haden was questioned by the detectives repeatedly and stuck to her story: unknown men assaulted her house—no doubt they were criminals; her trusty gardener shot one of the men and chased three others into the grounds, but they returned fire and killed him. The detectives told her that she'd need to make a formal statement but for now they needed to examine the crime scene.

While they were going about their examination of her home and surroundings, Haden went to her room and made a call. "What the hell is going on? I could have been killed!"

Silence on the end of the line.

She added, "Cops are here. I pretended to be scared when the man came. He told me he'd call me soon to arrange a fake meeting."

Howard Kane replied, "You and I agreed, we have to use a sledgehammer to get to your husband. I couldn't tell you about my men coming. I worry about Cochrane's capabilities. You had to be surprised about the assault."

"So what should I say when Cochrane calls again?"

"Don't use his name on the phone! Just play along. We'll take care of things."

"And my husband? How are you going to take care of that?"

"It's like we talked about. People won't thank us when this is done, because they won't know what's been done. But at least we've made our world a better place."

"If we succeed. No more surprises." She hung up and walked downstairs.

The lead detective approached her. "Ma'am, we're pretty much done here. Forensics has a good picture of what happened. Your gardener attacked at least one man. But in total we think there were five armed men in and around your property."

"Mr. Bartlett was such a good man."

"Are you going to be okay here or can you go somewhere until the mess is cleaned up?"

"I . . ." Haden looked at the yard. "The worker bees will be unsettled. I need to attend to them. I'll stay."

"The bees?"

"In my hive." Haden watched forensics bag up Bartlett's body and put it on a stretcher. She turned and saw Kane's man being removed. Cochrane had barged in here and caused this mess.

Like Kane, she wanted this to end.

TWENTY-FIVE

Four hours later, Will pulled up to the front door of Ash's property in Virginia. Shaking with pain, he struggled to get out of the vehicle and collapsed on the gravel driveway. Kay opened the door, held her hand to her mouth, and ran to him.

"Help!" she screamed.

Hessian Bell bolted out of the house. Both helped Will get to his feet and supported him as he limped inside. They placed him in a chair. Urgently, Kay ripped off his shirt.

She said, "Gunshot wound. One inch deep, twelve inches long. The bullet exited. Lots of blood loss. Will, describe the symptoms!"

Between gritted teeth, he said, "I'm not lightheaded. Pain excruciating. Possibility of infection. Check for shrapnel and cloth. No hospital or doctor."

Bell shouted, "What medicines have you got?"

Ash kept her eyes on the wound. "Wicker basket on top of my fridge. They won't be enough."

Bell returned with the basket and a glass of water. He gave Will four aspirin and the water and handed Ash disinfectant, Q-tips, and gauze. "Patch him up. I need to make a call."

"No doctors!" shouted Will.

Six minutes later, Bell returned to the room. "Help is on its way." He sat in front of Will. Will's wound was cleaned and covered. He remained shirtless. "Color has come back to your cheeks. The painkillers are working but are temporary. The wound needs stitches."

"I know."

"Neither Ash nor I are qualified to administer that procedure. I'm hazarding a guess that the bullet went through a nerve. That's why you're in so much pain."

Will didn't care about the pain. What he cared about was getting mobile. "It's nice to meet you again, Mr. Bell." He patted his wound. "This is an inconvenience."

"It's a scratch." Bell smiled. "A big one, though."

"I'd love a cup of tea."

Bell stood.

"Not you. I'd like Miss Ash to make it for me."

Bell nodded. "Interesting."

Will replied, "Yes."

Ash went to the kitchen to make the tea. She knew why he'd wanted her to make the tea. It was the same reason he'd wanted her to shave him. He wanted her. The thought made her feel unusual and special. Her entire life she'd been lacking love. Even her dear brother couldn't articulate his emotions due to his medical condition. Often, he didn't know who she was. And adult love was remiss in her bizarre choice of career. She went undercover in the misguided belief it would give her something she didn't have in normal life. The tactic hadn't worked. When Will confronted her in her D.C. apartment, he was the first person ever to make her truly unsettled, just by his presence. Now she was making him a cup of tea.

In the living room, Bell said to Will, "I need you to remain lucid."

"I'm always lucid."

"I suspect so, but your body is in shock."

"I got shot by a random bullet."

"Life is full of ups and downs."

Will laughed, then winced. "So true." His expression serious, he said, "Is he going to come here?"

"He said he would. He's en route now. He should arrive any moment."

"Be very careful with him."

"We must all be careful, should we not?" Bell clasped his hands together. "You know what I now do for a living?"

"You misdirect and teach the Agency."

"I hadn't thought of it like that, but yes, you're right."

"But you do other stuff as well. You run a private foreign army."

"Ash told you that. My army is street urchins and dispossessed adults. It's hardly an army."

"And yet you are the most successful CIA officer that has ever served."

"You might give me some competition." Bell studied the huge man in front of him and tilted his head toward the kitchen. "She is a good person, lost perhaps."

"I know."

"Maybe she won't want you."

"That's been the theme of my life."

"Kay needs a way out. You and I can give her that," Bell said.

The doorbell rang as Kay brought Will his tea. Bell braced himself. "To your stations! Let's see what mood he's in. I will get the door."

Will and Kay withdrew their firearms and placed them on their laps. Will glanced at her, just briefly, but enough to show his concern.

Antaeus walked in, the dog Mr. Peres on a lead. The former Russian spymaster looked around the room. "Hessian Bell, I came up against you many times. And you, lady, I don't know, but I can tell you're a deep-cover officer with the CIA. Mr. Cochrane, you continue to cause us all problems. Put your guns away. They won't be needed tonight." He said nothing as he withdrew a tobacco tin. "You've disinfected the wound?"

Ash nodded.

"Used tweezers to remove any debris?"

"Yes."

Cochrane grabbed Antaeus's forearm as the Russian removed items from the tin and slid thread through a needle. "What do you know about treating injuries?"

"I was a vet before joining the KGB. Shut up, keep your tongue away from your teeth, and bear the pain."

He stitched Will's wound.

The pain was excruciating but Will made no sound.

After disinfecting the surgery, Antaeus said, "I'm expecting a guest."

Bell said, "That wasn't part of the deal!"

"There was no deal. You asked me to come here. I did." Antaeus looked at Ash. "What's your name?"

"Don't answer that!" exclaimed Bell.

"I could find out in one minute." Antaeus kept his eyes on Ash.

"Kay Ash. I'm CIA. For now."

Wind blustered into the house as Michael Stein entered. The tall Israeli assassin laughed as he looked at Will's stitches. "I never took you to be someone who couldn't dodge a bullet."

Will didn't move. "Random shots are always the worst."

"Ah."

Stein patted his dog and addressed Antaeus. "I came as quickly as you asked. How is Mr. Peres?"

Antaeus replied, "I've removed benign tumors. He will live longer." He turned his attention to Will. "But who knows for how long?"

Bell surveyed the room. The intelligence within it was palpable. "Who are you?" he asked Stein.

Stein told him.

"It's okay," said Will. "He's with me."

Stein said to Will, "You don't seem surprised I'm here."

Will shifted in his seat, trying to get comfortable. "Recently I was spotted on camera. I knew the sighting would be reported to Agent Marsha Gage at the FBI. I'd made it my business to know that you'd been in the States for a year, trying to establish if I was dead. After the sighting, I watched your apartment in New York. I saw you getting captured by Gage and three others."

"I wasn't captured! I surrendered."

"Because of your dog." Will stroked Mr. Peres. "I knew that you'd deduce you were snatched because there'd been a development about me. As a result, I thought it highly probable that you'd seek guidance from Antaeus. So, when I asked Hessian Bell and Antaeus to come here because I was injured, I believed there was a good chance Antaeus would ask you to also come." Will smiled. "Mr. Bell and Antaeus are getting old. They're not men of action. You are."

Stein crouched before Will and said quietly, "You saved my life two years ago. Do you want me to take out the bastards who did this to you? I will."

Will didn't answer the question. He sipped his tea and addressed everyone in the room. "Three years ago I was tasked by a CIA officer called Unwin Fox to kill a terror financier called Otto Raeder. In the rural surroundings of Berlin, I shot him from distance. Raeder was being tailed by a man called Colonel Haden. I'd never met

Haden, still haven't. But on that day we had audio communications with each other. Haden's role was to confirm I had the right target and to make the shot. I did so, then exited the area, as per protocols. Recently, Fox contacted me. He was poisoned by persons unknown. Before he died, he told me that two others were involved in the Berlin job. I'm trying to find out who they are."

Antaeus asked, "Why?"

"Because they might lead me to the truth. The last thing Fox said to me was that Haden vanished immediately after the Berlin mission. I want to get to Haden."

The room was silent for a moment. Bell broke the silence. "How much money was the financier carrying?"

"Five million dollars. He was traveling to give the cash to a terror cell in Munich."

Bell and Antaeus exchanged glances.

Antaeus said, "We are dealing with theft. You took the shot. Haden was first on the scene after the killing. He took the money and vanished."

"The problem is that Fox had his suspicions about Haden." Will put his clothes back on. "Fox is dead. Haden is a ghost who I can't get to. But I have one lead. Four men have been watching Haden's wife's house. I'm certain they don't work for Haden."

"They work for someone else involved in the Berlin mission," said Bell.

"Yes."

"That person is also trying to get to the truth.

If you can establish who that person is, you might get closer to Haden."

Will tried to stand but failed. Slumping back into his chair, he muttered, "I need to get fit fast." He said, "I'm missing facts. I need the armed team to come after me again. They're monitoring Mrs. Haden's phone. That's how I'll get them close to me. A call to her. But I have a separate issue."

"Agent Gage." Antaeus pulled out a cheroot and lit it, not bothering to ask Kay if he was allowed to smoke. "She will be frustrated she can't find you."

"*Partly* frustrated. I made a call to someone else. I'm not going to tell you who. I knew that Gage was monitoring that person's calls. Gage now has my cell phone number. She'll be tracking me. The problem she has is she can only do so when I insert the cell's battery." He smiled.

Bell asked, "Why did you give Gage your number?"

"A tactic." It was Kay Ash who was speaking. "Why did Will want you all here?" She addressed Bell: "You could deliver Antaeus." She looked at Antaeus: "You could deliver Stein." And finally Stein: "And the reason you needed to be here is because Will has plans for you, though they may not be what you expect."

God, Ash is smart, thought Will. "Will you help?"

Stein nodded.

"Good. Miss Ash and Mr. Stein, would you mind helping me up and taking me to the kitchen?

I need to see if there's anything in the cupboards that might allow me to rustle up a meal."

After they were gone, Antaeus and Bell sat side by side on the sofa.

Antaeus said, "You thwarted me in Vienna."

"And you thwarted me in Tanzania."

"Different days."

"They were indeed."

Bell looked at Antaeus's cigar. "Ottoman tobacco. The best in the world. You are a man of refinement."

"Or a pretentious fool." Antaeus chuckled before turning serious. "You know what Mr. Cochrane is planning?"

"Yes."

"As do I. But he will need help. Stein won't be enough."

"I agree. There will need to be another nudge, something else that can support the evidence that suggests Mr. Cochrane is innocent."

Bell nodded. "I will plant the truth."

"You know the truth about the murders?"

"Not all of it. But before I leave I will speak to Cochrane and get him to tell me everything."

"And then it's smoke and mirrors?"

Bell replied, "Not on this occasion. It will be as it happened."

Antaeus agreed. "I'm sorry about the loss of your wife."

"Yours too. And yet here we are helping the man who killed your wife."

Antaeus crushed the tip of his cigar, sending

embers to the floor. He used his foot to extinguish any traces of burning. "Mr. Cochrane is not cooking. He is briefing Stein and Ash. He doesn't want two vulnerable men, as we are—one still in the Agency, the other under scrutiny by the U.S. Secret Service—to be party to what he's saying. Miss Ash is right—I am here purely because I delivered Stein."

"With me it's different. Will's taking Ash and Stein into battle. But he won't do so if you and I object."

"Yes. And do we object?"

"No."

"Even if it gets them killed."

Bell bowed his head. "Too many people die."

Antaeus stared at nothing and quietly said, "They do." He smiled. "You and I have been lauded as spymasters. Now, we are just tired men who've seen too much. But there is one last gasp. Stein wants to help Mr. Cochrane. It would be wrong of me to hold Stein back. And you mustn't hold Ash back. We are like their tutors."

Bell looked up. "I'm betting you and I both wish we were younger and could do this ourselves."

Antaeus nodded. He picked up his coat. "Let's just make sure they get out of this alive."

TWENTY-SIX

The following morning at six A.M., a bleary-eyed Agent Gage hammered on her adjacent motel room door. Inside, she could hear fast footfalls. Duggan answered the door, wearing only boxer shorts. She said, "We need to move. Cochrane's activated his cell. He's heading west across Virginia."

Within ten minutes, Gage, Duggan, Painter, and Kopański were in their two SUVs, hurtling west on a freeway. All of them were in communication via earpieces.

Duggan asked Gage, "Current location?"

Gage checked her telephone intercept. "He's on Route 460. Eighty-seven miles ahead of us."

Painter asked, "Why's he activated his phone? I don't like this. Feels like he's drawing us into a trap."

"I agree that's one option. The other is he's

got no choice other than to activate his cell. He has to maintain open lines of communication with someone." Gage checked her watch. "Either way, we've got to make up ground." She called the chief of Virginia PD. "This is Agent Marsha Gage of the FBI. I have two Bureau SUVs heading west across your state." She gave him the plate numbers. "We're in unmarked vehicles and are going to have to break speed limits and probably a heap of other laws. Can you alert your officers and sheriff's departments to leave us alone?"

"What are you doing in *my* state, Agent Gage?"

"We're pursuing an international assassin. I can't say anything more than that."

"You need our help?"

"No thanks, sir. It would spook him. He'd go to ground."

Kopański accelerated hard as Duggan's vehicle in front picked up pace. "Cochrane has made his first calculated mistake," Kopański growled to Painter, who was by his side. "It was always about inevitability. He's in a situation we don't understand. But one thing's for sure, he's leading us right to him."

Alone now, Ash walked along the coastline outside her property, watching the sea swirl as if it were moody and petulant. The sky above was gray and carried a fine rain. Wearing jodhpurs, Wellington boots, and a fleece, she looked like a dog walker. Except there was no dog. Antaeus had taken Mr. Peres back to his home; Bell was now at CIA headquarters; Stein was gone, running errands; and meanwhile Cochrane was enacting his plan.

She understood why she liked Cochrane. He hadn't needed to come out of cover to pursue Haden. Most people would have just laid low, saving their skins. But he did what was right because his friend Unwin Fox had been killed. She knew Cochrane trusted her. That meant a huge amount. Trust was a wafer-thin concept in her life and vocation. To have someone believe in her was a surprise.

But there was more to it than that. She just plain liked him.

The realization made her smile.

Cochrane's wound had been expertly treated by Antaeus, but still she worried about him being on the move. He should be resting for a day or so.

Four hours later, while pursuing Cochrane on the road in an increasingly rural landscape, Gage spoke to her Bureau technical team back at headquarters. Kopański and Painter were on her tail. The technical team didn't know why they had been asked to triangulate Cochrane's cell phone. Nor did they know whom Gage was pursuing. She frowned as she listened to the Bureau technician talking to her. She said, "You sure about this? My equipment says he's stationary within twenty miles of where I am."

"Your equipment is less sophisticated than ours," replied the technician. "We can pinpoint him to within ten yards. You can pinpoint him to within twenty miles." He told her what he knew.

Her quarry was at the bottom of a lane fifteen miles outside of the city of Roanoke.

"Jesus fucking Christ!" Gage punched the dashboard.

"What is it?" asked Duggan, who was driving.

"Cochrane's gone to the scene of the first murders he's alleged to have committed."

A scene at the base of a mile-long lane that led to a ramshackle house. One year ago, Cochrane allegedly shot two uniformed cops in cold blood there. They were protecting the twins Billy and Tom and their great-aunt and -uncle. The cops' instructions were clear: shoot Cochrane on sight if he tried to make his way up the lane.

Perceived wisdom was that instead he shot them. Now it seemed he was just waiting at the scene, doing something.

Duggan said, "I don't like this. Despite the rain, visibility's okay. But Cochrane's luring us in."

"I agree." Gage relayed this latest update to Kopański and Painter. "We don't know what's going on. Be very careful."

The Bureau technician monitoring Cochrane's whereabouts called Gage again. "His phone's off. I've lost track of him."

Gage and her team were one minute away from the road. "Phone me the moment his cell is back on. The next person you'll speak to is Agent Painter. You have complete authority to tell her everything you know. Got it?"

The technician replied in the affirmative.

Gage tossed aside her own substandard tracking device. "Damn heap of shit." She drummed fingers on the dashboard. "Something's playing out. Why would Cochrane go to his crime scene?"

"Ghoulish? He wants titillation for what he did a year ago." Duggan put hazard lights on and pulled the car over on the shoulder. The hazards were a signal to Kopański and Painter's SUV. They pulled in behind him.

Gage kept drumming her fingers, both vehicles stationary and without engines on. "No. Cochrane is doing something completely different." She turned to Duggan. "But that doesn't mean we hesitate to gun him down." She jumped out of the car and ran to Painter's vehicle. Thrusting her cell phone in Painter's hand, she said, "This is our lifeline. If it rings it will be a technician from the J. Edgar building. He can spot Cochrane better than my mobile device. You have complete authority to talk to him and relay anything he says"—she pointed at her earpiece—"to me and the rest of the team."

Kopański was out of the vehicle, Duggan by his side. Gage said to the men, "Three hundred yards on foot. Hopefully then it's showtime."

All three agents moved along the main road on foot, Duggan holding a Heckler & Koch submachine gun, Gage and Kopański gripping their sidearms.

Taking point, Duggan muttered, "You sure we shouldn't bring in HRT or SWAT?"

Behind him, Gage replied, "You scared, Pete?"

"Not a goddamn chance."

"I thought not."

In expert formation, they reached the bottom of the farm lane where Cochrane's signal had last been detected. This was where Cochrane had approached a stationary police squad car and shot two cops a year ago. Trees ran the entire length on either side of the road up to the valley. The road at its base was quiet, a tributary. No cars passed Gage's team.

Gage said, "He's not here."

Duggan swung his gun left and right. "Careful, though. He could be in the trees."

"Waiting to take us out." Kopański covered the arcs that Duggan couldn't—Kopański's Webley pistol capable of taking a man down from a hundred yards. At least in his hands.

Painter spoke in all their earpieces. "His phone is still disengaged."

"Let's go up the road." Duggan pointed his weapon that way.

"Not yet!" Gage walked into the former crime scene, once cordoned off with police tape and containing two dead cops on the ground. She spent two minutes scouring the area. Then she spotted a sheet of paper, laminated to protect it from the rain. On it was written:

A Russian man called Viktor Zhukov shot the police officers here.

Gage grabbed the note and stuffed it in her jacket. "Up the lane. Fast!"

The trio ascended the steep mile-long road,

guns at the ready. In their earpieces, they heard
Painter say, "Cochrane's activated his phone
again. He's at the house you're heading to."

Gage and her team started running. For Duggan the task was a breeze. Gage and Kopański
struggled but maintained pace, their chests heav-
ing as they sucked in air, their lungs feeling raw
from the exertion. But their minds were focused
and their gun hands steady. Getting to Cochrane
was all that mattered.

They reached the top of the lane. The large
house before them was now occupied by a family who'd bought it at a price way below what it
would normally have cost. They knew it once
belonged to Robert and Celia Grange, great-
uncle and -aunt to Tom and Billy Koenig. They
also knew that a year ago two detectives protecting the place were gunned down here, that Robert and Celia met the same fate, and that Tom
Koenig was kidnapped from his bedroom. But
times were hard for the couple now living here.
The wife was heavily pregnant with triplets. The
husband didn't earn much. Yet they needed the
space to raise a family. What happened here a
year ago, they'd both agreed, was history. Their
future as a family was all that mattered.

"Take it steady," said Gage as they reached the
front of the house.

The team was walking now, catching their
breath.

"Kopański, what's the setup here?" Gage approached the door.

Kopański told her about the man and woman

who now lived here. "No vehicle parked out front. They only have one car. Husband's at work is my guess."

"Wife?"

"She doesn't work. Maternity leave."

Gage rang the doorbell.

In her earpiece, Painter said, "He's turned off his cell."

Gage heard bolts being unlocked. A woman partially opened the door, a security chain still in place. "Yes?"

"Ma'am, we're FBI." She showed the woman her badge. "We have reason to believe a man may have entered your property."

Urgently, the woman opened the door fully. "It's not possible. We keep every window and door bolted."

"Is your husband home?"

"He's at work, not due home until seven."

Gage said, "We don't have a warrant to enter. And I need to make it clear that the only way we could force entry without a warrant is if we believed you were culpable of a crime or in danger." She looked at the heavily pregnant woman's stomach and smiled. "We need to make sure you're safe."

"Come in. Be careful with your guns around me."

"Go to the living room. Stay there."

This time Kopański took lead. Shooting criminals in urban environments was what he excelled at. More important, Kopański was a cop; Duggan wasn't. Duggan was brilliant at split-second executions. So was Kopański. But the Polish American also knew when not to shoot.

All three of them moved through the house, room by room. On the first floor they entered a bedroom. Kopański said, "The first detective was shot outside the house. The second detective was killed in here. Both were shots to the back of the head. It was cowardly."

"That's not Cochrane's style." Gage nodded her head toward the stairwell.

They ascended the stairs.

From his office at CIA headquarters, Hessian Bell called Antaeus. "I've decided what our nudge should be—not a media exposé, rather an intelligence report."

"Excellent idea. But it must be sourced. And that's why you're calling."

"The profile of the source must be right."

"Russian. Died in the last twelve months after the murders. Ex–special operations," Antaeus said. "I can find such a person. Let me make a suggestion—this was someone who died in the last two weeks. It was a deathbed confession to you."

"And I was running him as my agent. Perfect."

"You'll need an audit trail. Previous contact with the asset. Create a history."

"Give me a name and I'll craft that trail." Bell hung up.

It felt odd that the former Russian spymaster was helping him. But then again, it wasn't so strange. Antaeus, Bell, Ash, Cochrane, and Stein were a ragtag bunch. But they shared one thing in common: they were expert spies who wanted to help one another.

Crouching on one knee, Kopański pointed his handgun down the thirty-yard-long second-floor hallway. He was guarding the route in case Cochrane sprung out from one of the rooms at the end. They suspected his location was the bedroom at the end on the left. It was where Tom Koenig was kidnapped a year ago. But there were other rooms to clear first. To the left and right of Kopański, Gage and Duggan stormed other bedrooms, closets, a study, and a laundry room. All were empty. That just left the final bedroom and a bathroom at the far end of the hallway. Gage stood to one side of the bathroom, her handgun pointing vertically. Duggan was on the left-hand side of the hallway. Kopański was motionless, twenty yards behind him. Both men had their weapons trained on the bathroom door. Gage looked at them and raised three fingers, two, then one. She kicked the door open, her gun at eye level.

The room was empty.

That left just Tom and Billy's former bedroom.

Duggan took point as Kopański ran to back him up. Duggan said to him, "You know how to do this?"

"Screw you." Kopański was an expert at room entry. He placed one hand firmly on Duggan's shoulder, standing directly behind him. The action was required because Kopański was his second pair of eyes. If Cochrane was in the room but Duggan was covering the wrong arc, Kopański would swivel Duggan to face the right direction. It was also vital for speed and momentum. The man behind pushes his colleague fast to ensure the job is done in seconds.

They readied.

Gage nodded.

The men entered.

The room was empty.

It was a nursery, decked out with three cribs, murals on the wall, and children's artifacts everywhere. This was where the wife's triplets would sleep after birth. Sleep alarms were in place, presumably linked to the master bedroom directly opposite. It looked so unlike the horror scene a year ago when Uncle Robert had been gunned down in his pajamas outside the interceding bathroom, and Aunt Celia had heroically tried to protect Tom Koenig before her death.

Gage entered.

She looked at a teddy bear pinned to the wall, adjacent to which was a note. She barked, "Kopański, Duggan: check every door and window in the house. Cochrane's not here, but he was and somehow he got out before we arrived. When you're done, bring the woman to this room."

While the men went about their duties, she kept her eyes on the bear and the note next to it. But she didn't touch either item.

Kopański and Duggan returned ten minutes

later, Duggan escorting the owner of the house, Kopański with his gun in both hands.

Kopański whispered in Gage's ear, "Dead bolts on every exit. All on the interior. No way he could have gotten in or out unless he was Harry Houdini."

Gage said to the pregnant mom, "What's this?" She pointed at the bear and note on the wall.

The mom looked terrified. "I've never seen either. They don't belong here."

"A teddy bear belongs here! This is a kids' room!"

"No! No!" The woman started weeping. She patted her tummy. "My triplets are not allowed anything that can choke them. They have to be over two before they can have toys like that." She went to remove the bear.

"Don't!" said Gage.

The expectant mom said, "It's the arms. They're too thin. Newborns can gag on them. That's what I've been advised."

Gage believed her that the bear didn't belong here. "A man got in here, left this, and exited before we arrived. There is no way in or out of this house. The only explanation is you let him in."

"No, no!"

"A big guy. Cropped hair. You know him?"

The woman was distraught. "I don't know what you're talking about." Tears were running down her face. "My husband left for work at eight A.M. this morning. I haven't seen anyone since, apart from you."

Gage darted a look at Kopański. He nodded,

agreeing with Gage that the woman was telling the truth.

He said, "Pete, do you mind taking this lady downstairs and making her a cup of her choice? Tea, coffee, whatever she wants. Ma'am, I'm sorry if we caused you any distress. We just had to be sure." The woman and Duggan gone, Kopański stood next to Gage, looking at the bear. "You must feel like shit."

"Yeah."

"Don't envy you. But what you said was needed." He pointed at the note. "Do we get forensics in?"

"No time for that."

"I agree." Kopański pulled down the note and held it in front of him and Gage.

I gave Tom and Billy Koenig identical toy bears. Inside were recording devices. On the back is a drawstring. Pull it once to record. Pull it twice to play back. This is Tom's bear. Pull it twice to listen to the voice of the man who killed everyone, Viktor Zhukov. He kidnapped Tom in this room after murdering Celia. Make no mistake, I will admit to what I did and refute false allegations. I didn't kill any cops. I didn't kill any civilians. But I did kill Zhukov and his eight-person team. I did so to rescue Tom.

Gage gripped the bear. She pulled twice on the string. A lisping Russian man's voice came out of the speaker: "I know you're under the bed. It's going to hurt if I have to drag you out." She

lifted the small toy bear to her nose and turned to
Kopański. "You know Zhukov was killed alongside his colleagues. You and Painter examined
the crime scene. And when Cochrane rescued
Tom Koenig and handed him to you, he made
no effort to deny what he'd done to Zhukov. He
spoke the truth."

Quietly, Kopański said, "Painter and I believe
that to be the truth. The problem we had when
we were investigating the crimes is that the evidence against Cochrane was so overwhelming.
We had to do our job."

Gage was deep in thought. "All we have is a
recording of a man's voice and Cochrane's allegations of innocence. I'm willing to go out on a
limb for Cochrane, but only if I have more than
this." She frowned. "This doesn't make sense. He
made a call to Faye Glass. He realized her phone
was being monitored. Therefore he deliberately
gave us his cell phone number. He only activates
it when he wants to be tracked. He deliberately
brought us here. Yet he knows that what he's
given us doesn't change things."

"It has changed one thing."

"What?"

"It's put doubt in your mind."

"That was already there." Gage spoke quietly.
"I've spent the last year trying to establish if Cochrane was alive. I wanted to talk to him, reopen
his case, and see if there was a way I could prove
his innocence." She shook her head. "We're missing something. Why has he come here?"

Kopański looked out the window. Cochrane

was long gone, he was in no doubt. "He knows we're hunting him. He doesn't want to be caught. At the same time he wants something from us."

"What?"

Kopański turned to face Gage. "When he came out of the shadows to meet Unwin Fox, there must have been an overriding reason for him to do so. He's onto something and needs to be at liberty to pursue that something. He wants distance between us and him. This is a false trail. He wants us to be where he's not. That's my hunch."

Gage nodded. "That sounds like Cochrane. But that means . . ."

"He was never here."

"So who was?"

In tandem, they both said, "Michael Stein."

TWENTY-SEVEN

Five hours later, Stein stopped his car outside Ash's coastal residence. He knocked on the front door. When Ash answered, he asked, "How is he?"

"He's getting better. Job done?"

"Job done."

They entered the living room. Will was there, only in boxer shorts, doing push-ups. He stopped when he saw Stein and got to his feet.

"Should you be doing that?" asked Stein.

Will patted the white pad that covered his wound. "The stitches Antaeus used are stronger than skin. There's no bleeding. The pain's still there. The danger is my body will try to compensate for that and the muscle area around the wound goes dormant. Other parts of my body will pick up the slack. But they're not supposed to do what the muscles around my wound do. So

I could get temporary back and leg problems. The trick to avoid that is to make the whole body hurt. Then there's no compensation." He wiped himself free of sweat with a towel.

Ash tried to avoid looking at his muscular, scarred torso but failed. To Stein, she said, "He's been doing this continually for the last six hours. Push-ups, jogging, chin-ups on a beam in my barn, lots of other stuff. I told him not to."

"But I didn't listen." Cochrane smiled. "How did it go?"

Stein told him everything went to plan. He'd activated Will's cell phone, drawn Gage's team to the place near Roanoke, planted the things Will had given him, and then vanished.

Will dressed. "Excellent. A rhetorical question— you know what Gage and her team will think?"

Stein answered, "Subterfuge. You want them to know you're hundreds of miles away from Roanoke. It doesn't matter if they realize that because they're back to square one."

"Fifty percent correct. They know they've lost my scent. But also there's another big thing in play. They will have taken stock of the notes and evidence you planted. I need my innocence proven. Hessian Bell and Antaeus are complementing what you've done."

"How?"

Will walked up to him. "My friend, will you go back to Israel?"

The question had been plaguing Stein. "Antaeus has given Mr. Peres a new lease on life, thanks to his clever skills. But really, it's a stay of execution. I can't put Mr. Peres on a plane again. He won't survive."

Will looked at the dashingly handsome Israeli. "Why do you have no woman in your life?"

Stein pointed at Ash. "We could all ask ourselves that question."

"We're damaged goods," said Ash. "You'll stay in America until Mr. Peres passes?"

"Yes."

Ash smiled, though she looked sad. "Then when this is over, I'd like you to come to dinner. I have a best female friend. She is very smart and not suckered in by charm or beauty. You'd like her. Meanwhile, I'd like you to help Mr. Cochrane get fit and gun-ready. Practice. Drills. Get this pain in the ass in shape."

She watched Stein lash ropes to boulders on the escarpment outside her home and get Cochrane to scale the mighty drop. Just like her grandfather had done on a ridge in Shanklin, Isle of Wight, Britain, when he was a U.S. Ranger about to be deployed to Normandy in World War II. Up and down the ridge he'd gone, training instructors barking orders at him. Exhausting work. And all for nothing. He was shot dead within twenty seconds of disembarking his landing craft at Omaha Beach. Cochrane didn't need the training. He was so strong and honed with skills that it amused her. But he was right. He needed to trick his body. Making it exhausted was key. After that he'd rest.

And how did she feel? She knew Cochrane's plan and she knew she'd be integral to it. She picked up her sidearm and walked to the barn where Cochrane had done chin-ups. Empty gin bottles were there, the contents drunk by her mother. The gin sucked the life out of her. That's why Kay couldn't get rid of the bottles. Her ma was an abuser; it riled her father. She would hit him, he'd hit back, and then they'd turn on Kay and her brother. For years after her mother's death from liver cancer, she'd reasoned that the bad parts of her mother were in the empty bottles, sucked out by the booze.

She lined seven bottles up against the back of the barn, took fifteen paces back, and used her pistol to blast all the bottles into smithereens within five seconds.

There. Finally the bad part of her mother was dead. Ash hoped she and her long-deceased volatile husband were watching from heaven. Maybe now they'd be at peace.

Stein left in the evening to collect his dog from Antaeus's house. He didn't know if he'd ever return to Kay's house, or indeed if he'd ever see Will Cochrane again. His role in helping Will was played out. He'd asked Will if he could help him bring matters to a close. An extra gunhand, he'd told him, could be useful. But Will had declined the offer.

"One of us has to survive," he'd declared to Stein. "One day you can tell people about our adventures."

But before he drove away, Ash knocked on his car window. He lowered it.

"Will you be all right?"

Stein smiled. "I can't remember a time when I've ever felt certain of that."

Rain was falling on Ash, standing with her arms folded, shivering because she was wearing nothing more than jeans and a T-shirt. "You and Will are so alike."

"We know that." He stared ahead, his expression now neutral. "Will has a lot of enemies. If he survives what's to come, look after him."

"I . . ."

"I will also keep an eye on him. He's playing a high-risk game and he knows it. If in the off chance he clears his name, people will come after him."

"Not here they won't."

The comment touched Stein's heart. "You've known him a long time?"

"Only for a few days."

"Yet when people like us meet each other, it's as if we have a lifetime of history together."

Ash nodded.

"Good luck, Miss Ash. You have my number. Give me a call if you ever want to set me up on the blind date you mentioned." He gunned the car and drove off.

"I hate it here!" Billy Koenig was crimson faced and yelling at his aunt.

"It's not that bad," said an exasperated Faye Glass.

"There's nothing to do!"

They were in the twins' bedroom in their new

safe house. Tom Koenig joined in. "No Internet. The TV is crap—"

"Language!" exclaimed Faye. She breathed deeply. "I know you've been through a lot. More than most children. This is only temporary."

"But then what?" Tom was crying. "We go back to the other horrible safe house? We go to your house?"

"I'm hoping it's my house," said Faye soothingly.

"But we know you think it's difficult to look after us." Billy was rocking on his bed. "After Mom was murdered and everything."

Faye sat next to him. "I'm trying my best."

Billy hugged her. "Me and Tom know that. Our counselor told us that you haven't had the space to properly grieve. We don't exactly know what that means. But we know your hands shake when you cook us dinner. And sometimes we hear you crying."

"Maybe I just need a vacation." It was Faye's attempt at a joke, but instead it produced tears. The boys had their moments of naughtiness, but not as often as they should. For the most part they were not like other kids their age. They were quiet, withdrawn, scared, and confused. The biggest problem was she felt she was merely their caretaker—not a parent, not a role model, and certainly not an expert in raising kids.

She prayed that Cochrane would call her, clear his name, and adopt the twins. It was a foolish fantasy. For that reason, for now she couldn't tell Billy and Tom that he was alive.

Will stoked the fire as Kay descended from her bedroom, wearing a sweater and pajama bottoms, her hair wet from the shower. She sat on the floor by the fire and began untangling her hair with a comb.

Will sat on the floor opposite her.

She said, "I still don't fully understand why you didn't ask Michael to help with this last part."

Will watched the glow from the fire caress her face. It made her beauty shine through. "I'm a fugitive with nothing to lose. You have Hessian Bell covering your back. Stein is different. He has liberty and a future."

"But he's alone with no one to support him."

"Precisely. He can't be sucked into everything I'm doing. I knew he was the perfect person to infiltrate the house and plant evidence. But getting him involved in a shoot-out would have been too much. He's turned his back on that life and I'm not going to do anything to corrupt that evolution."

Kay stopped brushing her hair. "And what about you? When will this chaos end for you?"

Will stood and looked away. Quietly, he said, "Chaos? I hadn't thought of it that way. But yes, that's been my life."

She went to him and wrapped her arms around his huge torso. The act wasn't premeditated. It just felt right. "You're not the man they say you are."

Will couldn't remember the last time a woman had put her arms around him. It felt so good. More than that, it was feeling Kay's body warmth and protection that made him feel special.

They stayed like this.

Will touched her hair. "I don't know much about this stuff, but I like the way you cut your hair. It shows your face."

She squeezed tighter. "I'm not going to sleep with you. We're both in a heightened state. As a result, our emotions are flawed."

"Because we might die tomorrow."

"Feelings run high and wild in these circumstances. What time will you make the call?"

"Seven A.M. Mrs. Haden gets up early to tend to her bees and other matters. She'll take the call. You'll be with me, if you want. But only from distance."

Kay released her grip on him. "Don't try that crap on me! From distance?!"

Will lowered his head. "I've told myself a foolish story. It involves this house, me repairing it, and you and two eleven-year-old boys. And it involves my freedom." He looked at her. "I can't risk your life."

"It's a nice story." It was one that resonated with Kay. "But to make it work, I have to be up close and personal when it goes down tomorrow."

Will put his face inches from Kay's face. He whispered, "You'd do that for me?"

"I'd do it for me," she whispered back.

Their faces moved closer.

* * *

Kane called Flail. "What have we got?"

"I've still got two able-bodied men is what I've got."

"Equipped and armed?"

"Leave that to me. We're ready when he shows his head."

"And Haden?"

"Mrs. or mister?"

Kane answered, "Both."

"We assume the colonel is circling. Maybe he's in cahoots with his wife. They conspired to get the money. That's my bet. We're watching her house day and night. I'd know a lot more if you'd been straight with me from the outset."

"I couldn't. And I still can't. If we bag this, it will be the trial of the century."

"You're risking a lot."

"Yeah, my career and everything. But here's the thing. What would you do if your commanding officer became a piece of scum?"

Flail hesitated before saying, "I'd shoot that dog in the head."

TWENTY-EIGHT

At five A.M., Will knocked on Kay's bedroom door. She answered wearing nothing more than her panties and an undershirt. He said, "I'm cooking bacon and eggs. After that, it's time to hit the road."

Two minutes later she was downstairs, ready and dressed. In the kitchen, she said, "I'd prefer a smoothie."

As Will was flipping bacon, he replied, "Your choice. But today I'd recommend something more filling."

They ate their bacon, eggs, and toast in silence, neither of them acknowledging that last night they had embraced in front of the fire. That was a memory for an altogether different time. Today was a day to kill people.

Thirty minutes later, they were on the road, heading west. They stopped in the town of Windsor and Will called Mrs. Haden from a pay phone. "Can we meet? Twelve o'clock today. Somewhere private."

Elizabeth Haden knew the call was the one Will had warned her about. She said, "The George Washington and Jefferson National Forests. Do you have GPS?"

"Yes."

"The forest is huge. Program in this grid reference." She gave him the exact location within the Virginia forest. "I'll be there alone. I presume this is about my husband. Will he be there?"

"I don't know. Be very careful."

"Someone may be listening to this call."

"If so, that someone may help us get to the main objective."

"My—"

"That's all to be said!"

Will and Kay drove across Virginia.

He said to her, "Would you do me the honor of allowing me to take you on a date?"

She laughed.

"I'm sorry."

Kay tried to control her laughter. "Don't be. It's just, under the circumstances, your question is absurd."

"I know. Forget I asked it."

"Please don't forget you asked it." She was no longer laughing. "Two minutes in."

"Two minutes in." Will pulled the car onto a deserted country road. "Guns concealed. Only out when necessary." They got out of the vehicle and walked into the George Washington and Jefferson National Forests. They were two hours ahead of their intended meeting with Mrs. Haden.

Flail's colleague was watching Elizabeth Haden's house. He called Flail. "She's still in there. Not moving. Something's odd."

"Break cover. She's of no use to us now. Convene with us at the forest. It'll take you three hours to get to us."

"Why's she not moving?"

"Two options: she got scared or she's sent her husband to wipe Cochrane and us out. We can deal with Colonel Haden. Cochrane is the major problem. Make sure you're fully alert."

Will and Kay walked through the vast forest. They stopped when they were close to the rendezvous point.

Will said, "I'm not patronizing you when I ask the following questions. I'd ask the same questions of a man under my command. Will your handgun malfunction?"

"No. I've cleaned every millimeter. It's pristine. The workings are oiled and smooth."

"The magazine and spare magazines?"

"Springs checked. Cartridges perfect. Three spare mags in the same condition."

Will looked around. "Where will they come at us from?"

"Unpredictable."

"Good." Will took out his handgun. "They want me dead. They don't know who you are. If this goes tits up, get to Hessian Bell or Antaeus. If I'm dead, don't play the hero. I want Haden brought to justice. That will be your next objective."

They didn't speak after the exchange. Instead they moved farther into the forest, their handguns at the ready. Will signaled to Kay. She moved. He moved. They were near a clearing—a large open area of dewy grassland that was surrounded by trees. They waited.

The man who'd been watching Mrs. Haden's house pulled up adjacent to the forest and Flail and his other ex–Green Beret colleague. He got out of his vehicle and approached the two men.

Flail said, "Tactical time." He pointed at the trunk of his car. Flail's asset opened the trunk and donned coveralls from within, plus other equipment. Now he looked like Flail and the other team member—full-on spec ops who were about to engage in combat. They had headgear, radio mics, assault rifles, spare magazines, emergency medicines in case they were injured, and military knives, and were wearing combat boots and head-to-toe fire-resistant Nomex gear. In previous comparable situations, they'd sometimes carry Tasers. Not today.

Today was a shoot-to-kill day.

The three men moved into the forest.

Kay watched the clearing from behind a tree, her pistol in two hands. She repeatedly looked over her shoulder, knowing there was every possibility men would strike from behind. Her job, however, was to monitor the clearing. If men came there, she'd shoot them without warning. That was the drill. No empathy. No conscience. No second-guessing why they were there so long as they were armed.

But one of them had to be kept alive. That was Will's instruction.

Flail's team dispersed.

One of Flail's team members whispered into his throat mic, "I've got a female tango. Stationary near the clearing. Behind a tree. I don't think she knows what she's doing."

Will Cochrane knew exactly what she was doing. It was one of the bravest things he'd ever witnessed, her significant bravery being that she knew she'd be spotted and probably killed. It was a risk she had decided was necessary. Will had disagreed. He'd told her that he couldn't guarantee her safety.

Flail's colleague moved silently to her, no smile on his face, but certainly inside he felt good. This would be easy. She had her back to him and was no match for the ex-commando. But Flail had said that gunshots weren't permitted until Cochrane was spotted. The former special forces operative slung his rifle against his chest and pulled out his knife.

The woman was only fifteen yards away. He decided she didn't have a clue what was going on. He approached her, ready to shove the knife in her kidneys.

But as he got to within five yards of her, a hand grabbed his throat and held him upright. The hand then adjusted position to his jaw. A second hand grabbed the other side of the jaw. It started twisting his neck. The power was immense. The man's legs started kicking and he lashed out with his arms. It was to no avail.

Will twisted the neck like unscrewing a wine cork. When the man's neck snapped, he dropped the dead body to the ground. Kay turned and nodded at Will. The tactic had paid off. She moved position.

Flail's last remaining team member circumvented the clearing from the other direction, unaware his colleague was dead. His assault rifle was at eye level; he was walking slowly and silently. For him, this was a walk in the park. He'd conducted so many missions like this in Afghanistan, Iraq, Pakistan, and deniable operations in other parts of Asia and the Middle East. He was searching for an observation point. When Cochrane turned up in the clearing, he'd shoot him without being seen. It was an assassination job. They'd remove Cochrane's body thereafter and feed him to Flail's pigs. The ex–Green Beret reached an oak tree and clambered up. Squatting on a branch, he pointed his gun at the clearing. Now he had to wait until noon. But if Colonel Haden turned up first, it was a priority to capture him and take him to local law enforcement. Flail would kill Cochrane while that task was under way.

Flail and his men were under no illusions that Kane's orders were brutal. They didn't care. They weren't Green Berets anymore. They were men who needed cash. And they knew that Kane's unconventional methods dovetailed perfectly with their training. Unconventional was what it was about. Kane had to bring Haden to justice and put him on the stand.

The ex-commando whispered in his throat mic, "I've got clear sight. If Haden or Cochrane arrive, I've got them."

Flail replied, "Good. When you shoot, I'll go in and make sure the job's done." By putting bullets in the back of Cochrane's head and ensuring Colonel Haden was in plastic cuffs. *If* Haden arrived.

The man in the tree was motionless, just staring through the sights of his rifle, his breathing calm and shallow.

This was a perfect trap.

The bullet to the back of his head sent him spiraling to the ground. Kay put another bullet in his brain to ensure he was dead. Was it premeditated murder or self-defense? Right now she didn't know or care. Will had told her there'd be one more man. That person was the team's boss, and he'd be the hardest person to deal with. But she didn't have sight of Will, nor did she know if the other man was here.

Will watched Flail run fast after he'd heard the gunshots. Will had known that Flail was the person who would finish the job and that gunshots would be the trigger. If shots were fired, it meant to Flail that Cochrane was dead. If Haden was there also, it meant he was incapacitated. It would be so easy to kill Flail. The guy was so focused on reaching the clearing, oblivious to Will's presence behind him and out of sight. But Will needed Flail alive.

He tucked his sidearm under his belt and followed Flail.

Flail reached the clearing, looked around, then sprinted. He crouched by his dead colleague whom Ash had shot. "Break radio silence!" he said to his other colleague in his throat mic. "One man down. Where are you?"

He heard nothing in return.

"Where are you?! Cochrane or Haden's here."

Still nothing.

Will grabbed him from behind and tossed him to the ground. He placed a foot on Flail's throat, but Flail wrenched his ankle aside, twisted it, and upended Will. Flail got onto his knees; his rifle was on the ground out of reach. He pulled out his sidearm a split second before Will booted him in the face and leaped to his feet. Will grabbed Flail's wrist, flicked it back into an excruciating hold, and used his other hand to smash Flail's pistol out of his hand. Now on the ground, Flail moaned. Will stamped on Flail's chest.

"Enough!" Will tossed Flail's sidearm to one side. "Enough!"

Flail lay there, looking at Cochrane. "Go ahead and shoot me!"

"Not yet." Will called out to Kay. "Far side of the clearing. I have him."

Within twenty seconds, Kay was by Will's side, her gun trained on Flail.

"Get up!"

Flail did as Will ordered.

"Lose the combat knife and communications set."

Flail looked venomous as he tossed both aside.

Will said, "You have two choices. The first is I kill you; the second is we talk and you clear up this mess. *Completely* clear it up. No bodies. No DNA. Understand?"

This was the first time Flail had ever been beaten in combat. The defeat stung badly. But he recognized he'd been bettered. "Go fuck yourself."

"Wrong answer." Will turned to Kay. "Kill him."

She stepped one pace forward, her handgun aimed at Flail's head.

"Okay, okay. Stop!" Flail could see that Kay wouldn't hesitate to drop him. He looked at Will. "What do you want?"

Will turned to him. "The truth. If you don't give it to me, I'll punch your nose cartilage into your brain. Choose your next words wisely."

"That's easy for you to say when you've got a woman pointing a gun at me!"

Calmly, Will said to Kay, "Lower your weapon."

She did so, predicting what would happen next.

Will pounced on Flail, put Flail's arm in a

lock, thumped his boot into Flail's gut, and used his right leg to lift Flail's body and toss him away. He said to Kay, "You can raise your firearm now."

Writhing on the ground in agony, the ex–Green Beret spat out blood. "My team's orders were to kill you and arrest Colonel Haden."

"You know Haden?"

"Never met him. But I know what he looks like."

"You know me?"

"Only that you're ex–spec ops. You were getting in the way of our takedown of Haden."

"Do you want to live?"

Flail grimaced as he got to his feet. No bones were broken. No doubt that was deliberate on Cochrane's part. But Flail felt like he'd just done twelve rounds with a heavyweight boxer. "I've nothing to hide. My team was legitimately employed."

"By whom?"

Flail said nothing.

Will grabbed him by the throat. "Best you speak."

In Flail's career, he'd never encountered anyone like this. He wasn't scared. But he knew he stood no chance against Cochrane. And now Will loosened his grip. "I'm an ex–Green Beret. So were my three colleagues. They worked alongside me in numerous theaters of war, and yet you two killed them in a blink of an eye. We've been working off the radar."

Will squeezed Flail's throat again. "For who?"

Flail choked as he said, "Kane. Howard Kane."

"Don't know him." Will glanced at Kay, who nodded. "But my friend does." He looked back at Flail. "He wants Haden?"

"Yes."

"Why?"

"Because of something that happened in Berlin three years ago. Me and my men removed Raeder's body. Haden was supposed to be there. So was the cash. But all we found was Raeder."

Will released him and asked, "Why do you think Haden wasn't there?"

Flail rubbed his throat. "We think Haden stole Raeder's cash and vanished. That was Mr. Kane's assessment."

Will asked Kay, "What do you think?"

"He's telling the truth."

"Agreed." To Flail, Will said, "I suspect you've done some serious dirty work. But I also suspect you don't know all the details of what's going on. If I ever see you again *anywhere*—on the same street as me, same subway, same city—I'll snap your neck. Understood?"

Flail nodded.

"And if you have any contact with Kane from here on out, I'll come after you."

Flail got to his feet. "Kane is trying to do the right thing."

"That may be, but zero contact!"

The former Green Beret said, "You can't be certain I won't contact Kane. And you can't monitor me to check."

"Try your luck at that." Will asked Kay, "Who's Kane?"

"Pentagon staffer. Big shot. Runs the department that liaises with U.S. SF. He's a civilian."

Will said to Flail, "There's your problem. You have the skills to communicate from deniable phones and then vanish. Kane doesn't. When I meet with Kane, I will know if you've been in contact with him. And if you have, I'll hunt you down." He picked up Flail's rifle and pistol. "The police don't need to know we were here today. Are you happy with that?"

"Yes."

"You have transportation?"

"A car."

"Take the bodies far away from here and—"

"I know what to do."

Will smiled, though his look was menacing. "I'm sure you do. Get it done." He walked, Kay following him, though she kept her gun trained on Flail until they were out of sight.

TWENTY-NINE

Four hours later, Kay was standing outside the Pentagon. She called Hessian Bell. "I need you to call Howard Kane at the Pentagon. The call must be from an official Agency line, so he knows it's legitimate. We need to urgently flush him out. Perhaps tell him to get his ass straight over to Langley."

"I know what to say." Bell hung up and called Kane. "Mr. Kane, this is Hessian Bell. I'm a director at the CIA. Would you like to call me back so you can check my credentials?"

Kane replied, "That won't be necessary. I have the Agency on speed dial. I know you're calling from the CIA."

"Good. We have a major problem. I can't go into it, even on a secure line such as this. What I can say is that it concerns a colonel. I'm in the dark on this and need your help to fill in the gaps. Can we meet in the next hour?"

Kane's heart was racing as he replied, "Sure."

The Agency was the last institution Kane needed meddling with his plan. He didn't know Bell but knew of him. He was dangerous and way too smart. But he was also significantly powerful. Kane had no choice other than to meet him and find out what he wanted. Plus, if he had fresh intel on Haden, that would prove very useful. Kane hadn't heard from Flail or his men, but that was normal. The protocol was that they'd always go dark after a hit job for at least twenty-four hours. No calls, nothing. That meant Cochrane was dead and they were lying low.

He exited the vast Pentagon building and entered the parking lot. He didn't know Kay Ash was following him on foot. Even if he'd turned around to see if he was being trailed, he wouldn't have spotted her. It was only when he reached his car that she broke cover and sprinted. Will had been watching her the whole time. Her role was to identify Kane.

Will didn't hesitate. He ran to her side, grabbed Kane, and said in his ear, "Get in your car and drive."

"What the . . . ?" Kane was no match for Cochrane as the Pentagon highflier was bundled into his car by the former special operative.

Kay and Will sat in the back.

Will said to Kane, "We're armed. You'd do well to follow our instructions to the letter."

As they approached the security post where all

drivers of exiting vehicles had to show their ID, Will said, "We're undercover CIA officers. We can't show ID. You have the authority to escort us off the premises. We have an urgent matter. Any dispute of that should be directed to Hessian Bell at the CIA. But if we're delayed, there will be hell to pay. Got it?"

Kane nodded. At the security post, the excuse wasn't needed. All Kane had to do was flash his ID. The tighter security was inside the Pentagon building.

They drove out of the complex.

"Where are we going?" asked Kane.

"Your home. I presume it's not far."

Fifteen minutes later, they entered Kane's apartment. In the living room Kane took a seat, fuming. Will and Kay sat in chairs opposite him.

"What is this about?" said Kane. His demeanor was calm, though internally his mind was racing.

"You know what this is about," replied Will. He pointed at Kay. "You know who this woman is?"

"Yes."

"How do you know her?"

"She works for the CIA. Our paths have crossed. Her name is Kay Ash."

With a smile on his face, Will looked at Kay. "Oh dear, he knows your name." His expression was deadly serious as he returned his attention to Kane. "And you know who I am?"

Kane smirked. "I do. Will Cochrane."

"Superb. Now we have introductions out of the way." Will placed his fingertips together. "Three years ago I was hired to assassinate a man called

Otto Raeder in Berlin. Unwin Fox brought me in for the job. Colonel Haden was also involved, though I never met him. I killed Raeder. The mission was a success. Or so it seemed. But Fox was recently killed after his house was torched. I met Fox before he died. He told me something was wrong with Berlin. Logically, others had to be involved in a mission of that magnitude. I've been trying to find out who."

Kane looked confused.

"You were one of them!" Will said.

Kane looked back and forth at Kay and Will. "It was a black op job. There's nothing wrong with that."

"Who else?!"

"Senator Charlie Sapper." Kane was utterly composed. "You're making a big mistake."

Will wasn't flummoxed by the comment. "You had four men protecting you. They were good, but not good enough. Where is Sapper?"

"I don't know. She's vanished. Just like Haden."

"Really?" said Will. "You tried to kill me."

"My men—"

"That option failed."

Kane ran a finger along the cuff of his immaculate white shirt. "I was just trying to get to the truth. To Haden."

"By killing me?"

Kane was silent.

Will said to Kay, "Leave the apartment. Wait for me at your place."

She frowned. "Why?"

"Just do it." He didn't want to say in front of

Kane that she couldn't incriminate herself by being privy to what Will was going to say next. She had already broken laws, but Flail could cover that up by disposing of the man she'd murdered. But things were about to get worse. Will placed his hand on hers. "Trust me on this. Public transport only. I'll reimburse you the costs."

She left feeling resentful and bewildered.

Will peered at Kane. "I've been doing this kind of stuff all my adult life. In MI6 we call it 'using our antennae.' In the CIA and FBI, they call it 'following a hunch.' But basically it's the same thing—an extremely rapid combination of deducing evidence, reading people, and using imagination." His fingertips were back together. "This is what I think happened. Unwin Fox sourced the intelligence about Otto Raeder. It was legitimate intelligence, though Fox was worried that it would be wrongly actioned, most certainly handed over to the Germans. Raeder could escape or be acquitted in a trial. So Fox took the intel to a bunch of powerful bastards—you, Colonel Haden, Senator Sapper. Still, just because you're bastards didn't make the job wrong. The problem was there was one bastard worse than the others."

"Haden."

"It's nice to think of it that way, isn't it?" Will's voice was calm. "Yes, Haden was a nasty piece of work, but he did his job in earnest. No subterfuge. No duplicity. He followed the target and gave me the green light to take the shot. What I had to go on was the license plate of Raeder's car.

That plate number was given to me by Fox. But it was you who gave Fox the plate number."

Kane was trying to hide his fear. "So what? We were all pooling intel. Haden had been tailing Raeder for days. He got the plate number and relayed it to me. I relayed it to Fox. Fox relayed it to you."

"And Sapper's involvement?"

"She was our protection. If things went wrong, she'd tell the Senate the truth about how the hit came about. Fast-moving situation. Heroic Americans and a Brit. Instant terror plot. Et cetera."

"She was a stooge and a corrupt one at that." Will shook his head.

"I—"

"You got your men to torch Fox's house so you could flush him out. When that didn't work, you got your men to kill Fox."

Kane was silent. He knew what Will was saying was true.

Will continued. "I don't think Sapper was involved in what actually happened. But I suspect she believed Haden had committed a crime. Instead of doing something about it, she decided to cover her political ass and keep silent. She's dead, isn't she?"

Kane lifted his head. "Yes. Haden stole Raeder's cash and vanished. We had to keep quiet. All that mattered was that Raeder was dead."

"That's one option. Here's another one: You gave Fox and me the wrong license plate number. I shot Colonel Haden—a man I'd never met before and in any case he was heavily disguised. You did so because you wanted Haden's job. Probably you have significant aspirations beyond that post. But he was in the way. When Fox presented you with the intel about Raeder, you spotted an opportunity. You got Haden to tail Raeder and got me to kill Haden." Will was motionless.

Kane tried to smile but failed.

"Haden has been dead for three years," Will said.

Kane was motionless.

"Your assets cleared his body from the car after I shot him. Maybe they didn't know what Haden looked like. But if they did, it would have been impossible to identify his body. My sniper rifle obliterated most of his head. They disposed of the body. But why did you kill Sapper and Fox? There was no need to for three years. And then something recently triggered an escalation." Will leaned in close. "I reckon you got new intelligence that Raeder had been spotted again. You couldn't have that intel released to your team because then they'd know that Raeder hadn't been killed in Berlin. Fox in particular would suspect the wrong man was killed. He'd further suspect you were behind everything."

Kane felt sucker punched.

Will held Kane's chin. "After the recent sighting of Raeder you panicked. Your solution was to eradicate all traces of all matters Berlin. Because the Berlin mission against Raeder was off the grid, it didn't matter that others knew Raeder was still at large. But it damn well mattered that Sapper and Fox were taken out of the equation.

They were the only ones who'd blow the whistle if they discovered Raeder was alive."

Kane held his head in his hands.

"You poisoned my friend Unwin Fox."

"Not me."

"One of your men." Will stood. "I believe there might be two things you're not telling me."

Kane felt like he was tumbling down a ravine. "I've told you everything."

"No, you haven't." Will spoke to him for one minute.

Kane knew there was now no way out of this situation. "I had you kill Haden because I wanted his job and more. I killed Fox and Sapper. I tried to kill you. But you're right—I was told to do this."

Will pulled out his handgun. "You've been on borrowed time for a while, haven't you?"

Kane rubbed his face vigorously. "Fuck you!"

"You shouldn't have done it."

"You want me to beg?"

Will pointed his gun at Kane. "Do you think you'd survive prison?"

Kane laughed. "Of course. I'd thrive. It would be my fiefdom."

"I thought you'd say something like that." Will pulled the trigger and blasted open Kane's head.

THIRTY

Will pulled up in Kane's car outside Elizabeth Haden's house. He knocked on her door. When the svelte and elegantly dressed woman opened the door, he said, "I've just killed Howard Kane."

She tried to shut the door, but Will kicked it open and entered. Grabbing her hair, he dragged her into the living room and dumped her on the floor.

"Get up. You're no threat to me."

Haden complied, her eyeliner smudged.

"Queen bee." Will prodded her on the forehead. "That's who you are."

"What are you talking about?" Haden's voice was trembling, her fear genuine and absolute.

Will grabbed her jaw. "You get your workers to do everything for you. You dicked over Howard Kane, telling him you loved him, telling him you wanted to marry him, telling him your husband was a cheating bastard. At the same time you were grooming Kane. You and someone in the White House. Even Kane didn't know his identity, though he spoke to him on the phone. But the deal was you help get Kane into power. If you could do that, you'd get something in return. I don't know what. Maybe cash, maybe the affections of the White House man, maybe Kane himself." Will forced her onto a sofa and stood over her. "What was it?"

"This is absurd!"

"What was it?" he repeated.

She said nothing.

"You're not getting out of this room unless you tell me the truth!"

"Fuck you!"

"I'm going to help you if you wish. You did nothing wrong apart from wanting your husband dead. Kane did all the action. Talk now or I'm your enemy!"

She rubbed her jaw and sighed. "Kane was a pawn. I told him what to do. Kill my husband. Kill Unwin Fox. Kill you when you started interfering. I was to be Kane's First Lady."

"First Lady?"

Haden bunched her knees up under her chest, her arms wrapped around her legs. "Kane was perfect. His views were . . . extreme. That's what I wanted. And that's what my White House friend wanted. Somebody who could take office in five or ten years' time and bring back American values. We've been screwed over for so long. But Kane needed a clear way to the top. My husband was blocking that. Kane had other plans and could become a hero."

"American values are based on compassion and rule of law, not your principles."

"It doesn't matter now." Her eyes were imploring when she said, "Can I have a cigarette?"

"You don't smoke."

"I do in times of stress."

"And you are stressed now?"

She smiled but looked sad. "No, actually I'm calm. But I'd still like a smoke. How do you know I don't smoke?"

Will was impatient. "No smell of tobacco in the house; no stains on your fingers; your teeth; you're not the type—I could go on."

"I only smoke once a month. I have a pack in my rear pocket. Can I pull it out?"

Will whipped out his handgun and pointed it at her. "Slowly."

She reached behind her back. "I knew it was you when your car arrived. It gave me a few seconds to get my cigarettes." She pulled out a handgun and held it to her head.

"No!"

Mrs. Haden smiled. "We make mistakes in life. Mine was the quest for power. Don't worry—this gun means you no harm." She looked beautiful and forlorn as she asked, "What is your real name?"

Will answered with his true name.

"That's a pretty name. Are you descended from Thomas Cochrane, the famous British admiral who used a false American flag to capture a Spanish frigate twice the size of his boat?"

"Probably." Cochrane was breathing fast. "Don't do anything silly. There's a way out of this."

In her laconic Southern accent, Mrs. Haden replied, "No, Mr. Cochrane. Sometimes in life we meet a roadblock."

"Don't!"

Elizabeth Haden put a bullet in her brain and slumped to the floor.

As Will was driving away from Haden's home, he stopped Kane's car on a deserted country lane and walked to a pay phone. He called Kay and told her what had happened. "Are you at home?"

"Yes. Coastal residence."

"Stay there."

"Will, this is—"

"Shit, I know. Listen to me, Kay. I have to let them get me. This has been going on too long."

There was twenty seconds of silence on her end of the phone.

Kay said, "Don't hurt them." She sounded tearful.

Will said with sorrow in his voice, "It's okay. I'll find a way to get back to you."

"You want that? Do you really want that?"

"Yes." Will ended the call. He got back into the car and drove.

In his mind there was no way back to Kay. And even if he got there, what did she represent? Did he like her? Love her? Was it just the house that appealed to him? Was it merely a way out, Kay not being the central feature of that emotion? No. It wasn't a muddled emotion. He wanted a future with Kay. The trouble was he was facing death or life imprisonment.

He called Faye Glass. "This will end soon. I didn't do what they say I did. Always remember that I wished to care for the twins. Tell them when they're older what kind of man I was. Please."

He ended the call and continued driving.

Gage shouted, "We've got him! Drive!"

Gage, Kopański, Duggan, and Painter mobilized their two SUVs. They were eighty miles from Cochrane.

Painter said, "His cell phone is still on. Why's he not turned it off?" She was looking at the tracking device in her hand.

"I've no idea." Gage was speaking into her throat mic, her communications linked exclusively to her team.

In the car behind her, Kopański and Painter kept pace.

Painter touched Kopański's hand. "Joe, if Cochrane kills us today, know that . . ." A tear ran down her cheek. "Know that . . ."

"I know." He squeezed her hand. "The feeling's mutual. I've felt like that for years. Let's make sure we don't die."

"And then we can talk about things?"

Kopański looked at her, a smile on his face, his heart at peace for the first time he could remember. "It would be my honor."

Whether they died today, at last these two

battle-hardened cops had spoken the unspoken truth. They were meant to be together. Not just as police partners. Way, way more than that. It was a mighty good place to be, even if it was just for a few hours.

Will kept his cell phone on as he sat in a café in Washington, D.C.

He sipped black coffee, marveling at the taste and wondering when he'd next have a chance for a fine beverage. The café was almost empty; he was in a booth. His hands touched the table and he felt it was the last time he'd ever experience anything like this. But he had to go through with this. Enough was enough.

"Heap of crap!" Gage tossed her tracking device to one side. "He can't be static and have his cell on!" She called the FBI technician who had more sophisticated technology to track Cochrane. "What?! Are you sure?!" She ended the call and spoke to Duggan. "He's in a café. 1052 Thomas Jefferson Street Northwest. And he ain't moving."

"He's deposited his cell there and is a million miles away from that place."

"That's my guess, but we have to be sure."

Duggan said, "Kopański and I will go in. But we need a sledgehammer to back us up."

"Pete . . ."

"No, Agent Gage. I'm an expert. So is Kopański. But this is Cochrane we're dealing with."

They were on the outskirts of D.C.

Reluctantly, Gage said, "Okay. Get your friends mobilized."

Will finished the remains of his coffee and placed cash on the table. But he stayed where he was, waiting for fifty-eight minutes.

The Critical Incident Response Group van pulled up at the head of Thomas Jefferson Street. Inside were fourteen FBI Hostage Rescue Team operatives. All of them were under Duggan's command. They weren't permitted to exit just yet. Duggan had to tell them when. They were in full antiterror gear and armed to the teeth. There were some antiterror units in other parts of the world that were as good as HRT. But none was better. HRT waited, clutching their assault weapons.

Duggan's and Kopański's SUVs stopped at the head of Thomas Jefferson Street. The HRT van was visible. Duggan and Kopański got out and walked down the street, Duggan holding his submachine gun, Kopański his sidearm. FBI badges hung from chains around their necks.

They entered the café and yelled at everyone, staff included, to get out. One person remained.

Will Cochrane.

He was calm, his hands still on the table.

Duggan radioed to HRT. "Now! Now! Now!"

HRT streamed out of the vehicle, sprinting down the street, onlookers shrieking at the sight of the soldiers.

Duggan and Kopański approached Will.

"Gentlemen, would you like to take a seat?" Will smiled.

The two FBI agents remained standing, their guns pointing at him.

"You're under arrest," said Kopański.

"Of course I am." Will's smile remained. "Pete, Joe—take a seat. I'm unarmed."

"Bullshit."

Will's smile vanished. "Most of my friends and former colleagues are dead. That just leaves a small number of people who I'd take a bullet for. You are two of them. And you know why." He looked out the window. HRT wasn't visible yet. He said to Pete, "Tell HRT to give us a moment. It would be very kind if you would."

Duggan and Kopański exchanged glances. Duggan got on the radio. "Hold position. If you don't hear from me in ten minutes, enter and incapacitate."

They sat opposite Will, their guns still trained on him.

"I'd offer you a coffee but"—he nodded toward the bar—"you've ushered the staff away."

"What are you doing?" asked Duggan.

"Waiting to be taken to jail." Will mopped his brow with a napkin. He sighed as he looked at them. "Either of you could be sitting where I am. Has that occurred to you?"

Both nodded.

"Circumstance is a bitch, isn't it?" Will laughed. "I'm tired of circumstance." His face was serious as he said, "Joe, I'd like you to be the arresting officer. After all, you pursued me relentlessly a year ago. You deserve the accolade of apprehending me." He looked at Duggan. "Pete, I want you to lead me away. Back in the day, when we were in that gunfight in D.C. nearly three years ago, you did an incredibly brave thing. Probably you saved my life." He held his arms out. "I have no tricks, no weapons, no desire to kill you."

The law enforcement officers stood. Kopański placed cuffs on Will, while Duggan kept his submachine gun trained on Will.

Duggan said, "We're going to take you outside now. There are a lot of HRT men in position. I know you could take us and them on. Don't. There are civilians around."

They walked him up the center of the street, each end now barricaded by local law enforcement. Onlookers whooped and cheered, believing Will must have been a major felon. None of them knew who he really was. If they knew his history, they'd have screamed their support for him.

He was placed in the HRT van and driven to a D.C. police precinct.

THIRTY-ONE

One month later, Will was guided into a D.C. court. He was in an orange jumpsuit and had ankle and wrist shackles attached. A judge was sitting at the head of the court. Only three other civilians were in the room. They were sitting in the front left seats. Will was marshaled to the front right seats by his two guards.

The judge addressed Will. "This is a closed court session. No cameras. No lawyers for the prosecution and defense. You have no rights. You are not under oath. Do you understand?"

Will nodded.

"Aside from your guards and me, who else is in this room?"

Will looked left. "Agent Marsha Gage of the Federal Bureau of Investigation. The attorney general. The other man I don't know." Will looked at Hessian Bell.

Hessian Bell looked back, his expression neutral.

The judge asked, "Are you sure you don't know the other man?"

Will lied. "Yes."

"He works for the CIA. I can't name him. He has provided me with a confidential document. In order for me to view the document as authentic, I need to be convinced the document isn't the result of a conspiracy between you and the gentleman standing to your left."

Angrily, Will said, "You presumably know my background. I had two controllers when I worked for the CIA and MI6. They were both murdered. I was top secret. Very few others knew about my existence. I don't know this man."

"Very few others? Yes." The judge picked up two other documents. "I have letters. They were sent to me via the attorney general and are dated yesterday. One is from the prime minister of Great Britain. The other is from the previous president of the United States of America. They both say pretty much the same thing: you are a killer, not a murderer. Personally, and from a legal standpoint, I struggle to differentiate between the two definitions."

"I did what my governments told me to do."

"And yet you did more than that."

Will was silent.

"The letters go on to say that no man on this planet has sacrificed as much as you to protect us. Would you concur?"

"How would I know? I don't know everyone on our planet."

"No flippancy, Mr. Cochrane!" The judge put on reading glasses and surveyed Hessian Bell's document. "This intelligence report is sourced to a dead Russian. He claimed to the CIA man to your left that he was party to the killings in Virginia a year ago. He gives a very detailed account of what happened. You were framed for the murder of your sister in New York. Your boot prints were copied so their prints could be planted at the scene in Roanoke where police officers and the Granges were murdered. And the police and media were manipulated into believing you were responsible for gunning down two police officers in Lynchburg. It is quite a story." He removed his glasses and stared at Will.

"It's the truth."

"Yet I'm led to believe you have something to confess."

"Yes. A year ago I killed a Russian man called Viktor Zhukov and his team. They did the murders and they kidnapped a boy called Tom Koenig."

"How did that make you feel?"

"Elated and in tatters. I rescued a boy; I'd lost a sister."

The judge picked up Bell's report and tossed it to one side. "The timing of this is curious. Too curious. Allegedly, it's a dead man's confession. But I wonder."

The courtroom was silent.

The judge placed his glasses back on. "Agent Gage has also produced some evidence that casts doubt about your purported crimes. Two of the most powerful people in the West have endorsed you. The CIA has explained exactly why you are innocent of your alleged crimes. But it is for me to look you in the eye and decide who you really are."

Will said nothing.

Agent Gage held her breath.

Hessian Bell was motionless.

"Take off his shackles"—the judge removed his spectacles—"and allow Mr. Cochrane to approach the bench."

Will stood before him.

In a loud voice, the judge said, "Mr. Cochrane, it is beholden to me to advise you that a charge of arrest can be overturned by the law courts if the charge is deemed to be incorrect. Do you understand?"

Will nodded.

"All charges against you are overturned."

The attorney general blurted out, "But what about the other killings?! Zhukov and his team? Probably others we don't know about?"

"They were sponsored by the American and British states." The judge held up the letters from the two leaders. "That's what they're saying. I have no power to overrule that. Nor do you, Attorney General." He looked at Will. "You are a free man. You will be given an American passport. You have no criminal record."

"Like a gladiator made a free man of Rome?"

The judge smiled. "There is a lot more about you that I haven't raised in this court but was privy to thanks to the CIA. You do not deserve to be in chains. Your record of achievements is beyond remarkable." The judge stood and held out his hand.

Will shook it. "I'll remember this. I always remember people who help me. Call me if you ever need my help."

"Court closed. Good day all." The judge turned and left.

Along with Will, only Gage and Bell were left in the room. He went to them and shook their hands.

"Did you get to the truth?" asked Bell.

Will didn't respond, acutely aware that the judge may have been lying and that cameras were on him.

Bell understood. He adjusted his question. "Are all matters now closed?"

"Not all."

Bell held out his hand. "*Bon chance*, Mr. Cochrane."

Will pulled him close and whispered in his ear. "Kane was groomed by someone in the White House. That person wanted Kane to be president. I don't know who the White House person is. Endgame: get Kane in power. I can't identify and get to that person. But maybe you can weave your magic and in time identify who it is. Meanwhile, there is something more immediate you can do for me." He explained what he needed, stepped back, and then turned and shook hands with Gage. "I didn't give you a gunfight." He smiled.

"I didn't want one with you. None of us did." She was relieved that things had turned out this way, but she still worried about Will. "You've done your time."

Will looked around the courtroom. "Trouble will always come for me. Take care, Mrs. Gage."

He left.

It was three months before Will had the opportunity to track down Kay Ash. In the interim, she'd been away on a CIA assignment. He'd been busy getting his life back together. Now he was Will Cochrane again. The Justice Department had given him a passport in his name. He'd been to see lawyers. He'd visited Faye Glass. And thanks to Hessian Bell he'd resecured the teaching assistant post at Billy and Tom's school. He'd live in Virginia, his adoption of the boys legalized. They and Faye were over the moon with delight. Faye had helped him decorate the three-bedroom house near the boys' school. The boys had separate bedrooms, and Will had converted the attic to have an en suite bathroom for them, accessed by spiral staircases from their rooms. And the master bedroom contained a bed and nothing else. That didn't matter. What mattered was the constant smile on the boys' faces. They had a father again, one as good as their dead father. They'd see their pals again. No more detectives and safe houses. A proper home.

Faye lived only five miles away, on the outskirts of Roanoke. She came over often and helped Will. He thought of her like she was his sister. Once, he told her that. She liked that idea. Parenting was not for her. Family was.

Today, Will knocked on the door of Kay's coastal house.

She answered.

"I missed you."

She hugged him, tears running down her face. "I heard what happened. Why didn't you come sooner?"

Will rubbed her back. "You were away. I was doing stuff. Want to go for a walk?"

Hand in hand, they walked over the coastal footpath adjacent to the top of the dunes. Light was fading but features were still discernible. Kay was in a sweater, fleece, and jeans. Will was similarly dressed. The waves below were crashing against sand, shingle, and rock. They hiked their way over moorland, within which was a tiny route, carved out by human feet.

Will said, "This is where your brother used to walk."

"And me sometimes."

"But the groove belongs mostly to your brother."

"How did you know?"

"He was lost. He'd want to walk to make sense of it all." He spotted a large stone, two feet wide, smooth as marble. "That's an unusual feature."

Kay said nothing.

"Your brother loved the sea."

She looked out over the huge dune. "He killed himself here."

Will followed her gaze. He touched the stone. "You planted this in memory of him." He smoothed a hand over it. "You polished it free of blemishes. Due to its size, it must have once been a boulder."

Kay placed a hand on his shoulder. "Should I have shot that man in the forest?"

Will gently caressed her fingers with his. "Should you and I have done so much over our careers? Did you want the stone in the water?"

"I did. I didn't have the strength."

"With your permission, would you like me to take it down there?"

She looked at the steep incline below. "What would you do? Just throw it down there?"

Will lifted the boulder and secured it in one arm and armpit. Kay watched him. He had no fear, no uncertainty, as he descended using only one arm. When he reached the beach, he lugged the stone to the water's edge and looked up. She nodded. He hurled the stone into the sea and climbed back up. Breathing fast, he sat next to her. "Now your brother is at peace."

She placed a hand on his thigh. "How did you manage that?"

"Obstinate willpower." He took her hand. "Who am I?"

Her eyes were watery as she answered, "Not the person I thought."

Will looked at the ocean taunting the beach and nodded. "Not the person everyone thought." He looked at her. "All I've wanted is love. Death has instead been my option."

"For a while?"

"Since I was seventeen."

Kay rested her head against him. "Twenty-eight years? No one can survive that."

"Apparently you're wrong." Will stared at the ever-darkening sea. "I've seen and done things you wouldn't believe. Time stands still when I think about those moments. My friends are dead. My employers are dead. I tried to rescue them. I failed. People say I'm the great Will Cochrane. But actually, I'm a failure."

Kay hugged him, emotional and tearful. "No, you're not. You're everything we've ever needed."

Will smiled, but it was wistful. He smoothed his hand against hers. "I did what I had to do. You did what you had to do. So did Antaeus, Stein, and Bell. Does it make a difference?"

"Yes, it does. You've saved thousands of lives!"

"But I haven't saved my own life."

Kay rubbed his arm. "No man, or woman, has done what you've done. Hold on to that!" She pointed at her brother's house. "It's up for sale. I've finally decided to let go. Any notion of you and the twins moving in here is nuts. The coastal path is too dangerous."

Will closed his eyes. "That makes sense."

Kay pulled him closer to her. "You've been through too much." She stroked his hair, holding him, her tears dropping onto his head. "Too much." She kissed his head, just where her tears had dropped. "What are you going to do?"

Will held her. "I have adopted the twins. I have a house. I have a teaching job. All will kick into place in two weeks."

Kay kept holding his hand. "Do you think some help might be good?"

Will nodded.

She kissed him fully on the lips and murmured, "I can help."

"You'd move in?"

She nodded.

"The Agency?"

"Gone."

"Are you sure you want to do this?"

Kay said quietly, "I've been waiting for a moment in my life. I'd always known when it would arrive. You understand?"

"Yes."

She ran a finger over Will's lips. "Then that's settled."

Flail watched his boars in the mud scrum of his farm pen. They were full from the decomposing bodies of his comrades killed by Cochrane and Ash. Soon, he'd slaughter them and sell their flesh to burger joints. It was a living. He had no employer now. Kane was dead. The Pentagon was not an option now. He smiled as he tossed human flesh to the pigs. Cochrane had ruined him. That wouldn't go unpunished.

Kopański felt normal in a suit and tie, but uncomfortable in the circumstances. He was in an Italian bistro, waiting for his date, feeling nervous. He'd ordered a starter and a nice bottle of red wine. But his palms were sweaty. He was anxious. And he was hoping to make a life-affirming change to his career.

Thyme Painter walked in, her prosthetic limb hurting her. She sat opposite him. "Hello, Joe."

Joe smiled. "Bad day?"

She rubbed her limb. "Bad day."

He straightened the knot on his tie, even though it was unnecessary. They spoke for thirty minutes, before Joe said, "I'm going to quit the Bureau. I've got a bit of a pension. I'm thinking of a vacation in New Zealand. Would be great if someone came with me."

"Quitting the force?"

"Yeah."

Painter said, "You want this?"

"I do."

She placed her hand over his. "I'll come with you to New Zealand. I'd love to."

"It would mean resigning from the Bureau."

"So what?"

They stared at each other.

Kopański gently rubbed his huge hand against her face. "A different life."

Painter nodded and said in a hushed tone, "A different life."

During their vacation, they got married on a beach. When back in the States, Joe took a job as a janitor at the school that Billy and Tom Koenig attended. He was significantly overqualified for the job. But he reasoned the boys and Will needed looking after. Thyme returned to flying helicopters, running civilian aviation courses. None of her clients knew she was once a special forces Night Stalker pilot. It made her smile when men looked at her in the driver's seat with an expression that suggested, "Are you sure you should be doing this?"

They lived near Will and Kay and visited Will's house many times. Faye was also sometimes in attendance. Faye was right. This was family.

During the following months, Joe was able to meet his adult daughter several times. He found a good therapist and persuaded his daughter to attend therapy. The therapist insisted that Joe attend the sessions with his daughter. It worked. Their joint grief was released. Joe and his beautiful girl were back on track as father and daughter. They saw each other often. It meant the world to Joe to have his daughter back and Thyme Painter as his wife.

Kay and Will held hands as they watched Billy and Tom Koenig jump on a trampoline outside the modest house that Will had procured near the boys' school. He turned to her. "I have never had a moment like this in my life."

She placed a finger on his lips. "Hush now. You have a new adventure ahead of you. Parenthood."

Faye turned up with a glass bowl stuffed with shepherd's pie. Will kissed her on the cheek. "Will you stay for supper? Kay and I aren't going out."

Faye laughed. "Miss Ash will hate me if I continue to come over with meals. This is my last run. After that, it's down to you two."

Will held her. "Thank you for everything you've done."

"The boys are in the best hands." Faye's eyes were imploring as she said, "People will come after you. Do you understand?"

"I do." Will hugged her. "When they do, I'll kill them. The boys will be safe."

She stepped back but still held Will. She looked at Kay. "No man is better than this man. You understand?!"

"I do, ma'am," Kay choked out.

"They broke the mold. They broke the frickin' mold with this man." Faye kissed Will on the cheek. "Peace now. Peace."

She walked to her car.

Kay walked to Will while marveling at the boys jumping on the trampoline. "I don't know why I'm here, but it makes me happy."

Will hugged her. Later they had dinner and made love. This was their home now.

Will had the most perfect woman's arm around him as they lay in bed. Kay whispered to him, "What was this all about?"

Will embraced her, loving the feel of her skin against his. What a magnificent woman she was. He looked at her. "It was about chess. Antaeus, Bell, and I knew that."

Kay smiled. "And you got checkmate."

Will didn't smile. "No. There are two moves to play out yet. One of them is to identify and neutralize the senior White House politician who groomed Kane and Elizabeth Haden. I can't do anything about that. Bell is our best hope to solve that riddle. But it could take him months, maybe years. But the other chess move is something I can make. Bell called me earlier today. I'm going to be gone for a few days. Can you hold the fort?"

Kay rolled over to look him squarely in the eyes. "Gone where?"

He hesitated.

"Will, where are you going?"

He brushed his hand against her hair. "This will be the last secret I ever keep from you."

They kissed. Kay whispered, "Come home safe. I love you."

"I love you too."

THIRTY-TWO

William entered the lobby of the five-star Schlosshotel Grünewald. It was located on the outskirts of Berlin, near a large nature reserve. Redesigned by Karl Lagerfeld in the 1990s, the restored 1914 villa had fifty-four rooms and twelve suites, a swimming pool, a golf course, tennis courts, and two restaurants. The hotel was a favorite venue for the rich and famous who wanted absolute luxury and discretion.

Will bypassed the front desk and headed down a corridor, rooms on either side of him. Wearing an immaculate suit and overcoat, he looked the part of a wealthy guest of the establishment. He withdrew his cell phone and texted Hessian Bell.

Still in location?

Bell immediately replied.

Yes. Good luck.

Will knocked on the door of one of the suites. In flawless German, he said, "Mr. Müller, sir. Hotel security."

There was no response.

"Mr. Müller, we have received a call from the police. They asked whether you were staying here. I told them we never reveal details of our guests. What are your instructions?"

The door opened an inch, the lock preventing it from fully opening. A man was there. "The police?"

"Yes, sir. Is there a problem?"

The man looked confused. "There must be some kind of mix-up. I have no quarrel with the police."

Will looked serious. "Our priority is always our guests. I can legitimately tell the police that you are not staying here if you leave now. Get somewhere safe until this blows over. They are coming for you now."

"Somewhere safe?"

"I can help you. Trust me, things like this have happened before in our hotel. We can get you relocated in five minutes. I will give you a courtesy limousine. I have a very trusted hotel I can recommend. Then leave me to speak to the police. I'll give them nothing. Get an attorney to find out what's going on. Only answer your cell if it's your lawyer."

Müller opened the door fully. "I have so many things to pack."

"We can do this." Will entered the suite. "I don't want the bellboys to be involved, so let's do this together. Empty suitcases on the bed. We move fast."

Müller grabbed expensive clothes from the wardrobe and crushed them into his case. "This is crazy!"

Will entered the marble bathroom, ripped down the shower curtain, withdrew a silenced pistol, and wrapped the curtain around his hand and the gun. He reentered the main suite and pointed the gun at the man.

He shot Otto Raeder twice in the head.

One day later, Will was back at his home in Virginia. Kay hadn't asked him where he'd been, but she knew he'd been tying up loose ends. And she could tell by the look in his eyes that it had involved death. She made him coffee while the twins played outside. Within ten minutes of Will being home, his expression completely softened. He smiled as he swigged the brew. There was a look in his eyes that said he was at peace. That look made Ash's heart pump faster with joy.

"This is all I've wanted," he said as he finished his drink.

"Peace and love?"

"Peace and love. Will you help hold this future together?"

"I'll never leave you and the boys." Ash ran her fingers through the big man's hair. "It's time to hand over the baton. You've done enough. Our future together is all that matters. You'll make an excellent teacher at the boys' school. But never tell the pupils who you really are. Some things are better left unsaid."

Will walked into the yard alone. He looked to the sky and involuntarily dropped to his knees. His beloved Kay was right—he'd done this too long, with too many deaths, too much isolation, no time for himself, no time for love, no chance of redemption.

Now, finally, he was where he wanted to be.

As he continued looking at the sky, he said, "I don't believe in you. But if you do exist, thank you, God. Thank you." Tears ran down his cheeks. "By the way, why did it take you so long to give me this?"

He wiped his tears from his face and looked back at the house. Kay was in the kitchen, watching him, a warm smile on her face. She knew what was happening. She was going through it as well.

For both of them, it was a massive step into the realm of humanity. And it was a damn fine place to be.

Will got to his feet and went to the twins. The eleven-year-old boys squealed with delight as they ran around the yard, chased by Will. The former special operative had his arms outstretched and was pretending to be a lumbering zombie. The boys were laughing so much they thought their tummies would burst. Later, Will cooked for them and told

them that he and Kay were engaged. Kay had
held his hand as he explained to the twins what
that meant.

The twins smiled. For the first time in years,
they felt like they were in heaven.

Will Cochrane was a hero of the finest pedigree.
But beneath that hallowed accolade, there were
layers of disagreement.

Some people thought he was a murderer.

Others, a killing machine.

Most thought he was the smartest man one
could ever encounter.

All who knew him agreed on one thing: there
was no other man you'd want by your side if the
shit hit the fan.

Will wasn't a devil. He was an angel. And he
walked on the earth, roaring like a lion who de-
voured every devil in his wake.

He was British.

American.

A spy.

A soldier.

A parent.

A lover to a brilliant woman.

He was Will Cochrane.

Nothing more, nothing less.

From his office in the White House, Deep Throat
made a call. "Kane is dead. Elizabeth Haden is
dead. Sapper is dead. Fox is dead. Colonel Haden
is dead. With Kane's departure, you are next in

line to the throne. Kane failed. You won't. I will ensure that. Do you understand?"

"Yes."

"Don't fail me." Deep Throat added, "There is a man called Will Cochrane. He could spoil matters. Get experts. Track him down. Kill him and anyone around him. Show no mercy."

ACKNOWLEDGMENTS

With thanks to my two brilliant mentors, David Highfill and Luigi Bonomi, and their second-to-none teams at William Morrow/HarperCollins Publishers and LBA Literary Agency, respectively.